By the same author

FOUL SHOT

HARDBALL

Doug Hornig

CHARLES SCRIBNER'S SONS
New York

Copyright © 1985 Doug Hornig

Library of Congress Cataloging in Publication Data

Hornig, Doug.
    Hardball.

    I. Title.
PS3558.O68785H3   1985   813'.54   85-11835
ISBN 0-684-18440-0

Published simultaneously in Canada by
Collier Macmillan Canada, Inc.
Copyright under the Berne Convention.

1 3 5 7 9 11 13 15 17 19   H/C   20 18 16 14 12 10 8 6 4 2

Printed in the United States of America.

For Jenny,
without whose support I might never have begun

1

PATRICIA RYAN AND I WERE IN BED.

"You know," I said, "I've been thinking. How long have we been, uh . . . dating now?"

" 'Dating,' " she laughed. "Now there's an expression you rarely hear anymore."

"Going steady?"

"Worse. Isn't that what they do in junior high?"

"I don't think they even do it there these days. Words tend to disappear from the language when what they stand for becomes obsolete, you know. And what's steady in modern life? Where's the rock on which to build? The only ones out there are the ones you founder on. If there're no constants, then you could hardly 'go steady,' eh? Who'd know that better than the kids? They probably 'go awry' or something like that."

"Loren, you have a terrible sense of humor."

I bowed slightly. It was as close to a compliment as I ever got for my penetrating insights.

"Plus you have a rather gloomy philosophy of life."

"I can't help it. It goes with the job."

"And what job would that be?"

She had a point. I'd made a modest living for a number of years as the only licensed private investigator in Charlottesville, Virginia. But after a particularly ugly case my taste for the work had soured. I'd gone through the motions for a while. Then, when I'd come into a little money, I'd taken an extended vacation. I hadn't worked for three months now. But in conversation I still often reacted like a man who knew what his job was.

"I don't know," I said. "Maybe it wasn't the P.I. business. Maybe that's the *real* me. Maybe without you I'd be wallowing in the pit of existential despair."

"I'm not flattered," she said.

"Ah, but you burn with a gemlike flame, nevertheless."

"Stuff it."

That was Patricia. She definitely does not believe in sweet nothings as a form of courtship. But I don't mind. A lot of that is just people's attempts to keep a relationship in the infantile stage. Given the choice, I prefer an adult. Someone with an equal quality of mind, independence, and the kind of inner toughness that is not merely a stupid imitation of the worst of male macho. Someone you can make a date with and know that she'll be there. Someone so passionate in bed that the question of an outside affair never arises simply because you've got no excess sexual energy. Miraculously, Patricia is all of those things. So she's not quite as romantic as I might like. Okay. That seems a small price to pay in order to get the rest of the package.

"Why'd you ask me how long we've been 'dating' anyway?" she asked.

"Well, how long *has* it been?"

"I don't know. . . . Yes, of course I do. Eight months or so."

"Right. And isn't it amazing that we still spend so much time in bed?"

She smiled. The green eyes. God, the green eyes.

I was reaching out to tongue one of my favorite parts of her when the phone rang.

"Are you home?" I said.

2

"No way," she said, sliding her arms around my neck and breathing into my ear. I'd follow her anywhere.

There were some squeaking noises from the living room. The phone stopped ringing. After a moment, there was a knock on the bedroom door.

"Are you two decent?" Patrick yelled. Patricia's kid brother. He's lived with her since an auto accident confined him to a wheelchair.

Patrick and Patricia. Two Irish drunks for parents, no doubt. Couldn't think of more than one name between them before they got back into the whiskey.

"Does Nancy Reagan pee in the shower?" I yelled back.

"It's for you, clown."

"No respect," I said to Patricia. "These young people just have no respect for the wisdom of years. Should I answer it?"

Patricia shrugged and looked bored. "Maybe it's good news or money. I could always arrange to be here when you get back."

"Okay."

I pulled on my pants and went into the living room.

"Hope I didn't interrupt anything," Patrick said with a studied innocence.

Smartass kid. He looks a lot like his sister. Same green eyes, ruddy skin, dash of freckles, long auburn hair. A fresh seemingly naive face that somehow suggests the razor-sharp intelligence lurking inside. Yeah, but he's still a smartass kid.

I answered the phone.

"Swift. It's Rid."

A familiar gruff voice, but one I hadn't heard since we'd both testified at a murder trial several months earlier. Ridley Campbell, Albemarle County Sheriff. A tough cookie, but a man with whom I am on not unfriendly terms. On the other hand, when he called it invariably meant trouble. For me.

"Sheriff," I said. "Long time. How'd you know to call me here?"

"You think I don't know who your girlfriends are?"

"Girlfriend. Is. Womanfriend, for perfect accuracy."

"Yeah, yeah. Okay. Look, I need to see you. We need to . . . talk."

Now one thing the sheriff had never shown the slightest interest in was my sparkling conversational style.

"Well, sure," I said. "Your office?"

"No," he said a little too quickly. Then he paused. "No, that wouldn't be . . . convenient. Meet me at McIntire Park. You know those picnic tables on the east side of the softball fields?"

"Yeah."

"There."

Curiouser and curiouser.

"What time?" I said.

"Make it two."

"I'll be there."

"Good. And, uh, thanks."

He hung up.

Thanks? Thanks for what? I didn't like the sound of this. For one thing, it had the unmistakable tone of trouble, and I was officially out of the P.I. trade. And for another, the trouble was on its way in the form of the county sheriff, who was acting suspiciously like *he* was in trouble. Nothing good could come of it all.

Still, when a man like Ridley Campell said, "Jump," the only thing you asked was, "How high?"

I must have been staring stupidly at the phone because Patrick said, "What's up, Swift?"

"Oh. Nothing," I mumbled. "Nothing. I hope."

I went back into the bedroom.

"Still here," Patricia said brightly. Then, "What's the matter, Loren? Who was it?"

"Ridley Campbell," I said, sitting on the edge of the bed.

"And what does our sheriff want with you?"

I shrugged. "He wants to . . . talk."

"It wouldn't be a job, would it?"

"Could be."

"Loren, I don't think this is a good thing for you to be getting into at this particular time."

"You're probably right. But what could I say?"

"How about, 'Thanks, but no thanks'?"

"To Ridley Campbell? Not if I ever want to work in this town—" Well, now I'd gone and said it. Or almost. There was one of those deadly meaningful pauses.

"That's what it comes down to, doesn't it?" Patricia said, finally.

"You'd really rather I gave up the game for good, wouldn't you?"

"Loren," she sighed, "Why can't we get this straight between us? I don't want to control you. The only thing I want is for you to do what *you* want to do. I'm not your wife, damn it!"

She sure wasn't. Years earlier, I'd married a domineering woman who tried to direct my working life. Now I'm just a half-remembered face in someone's fading memory. At best. I suppose an important part of me was still clinging to the belief that all women are like that.

"I know you feel that way," I said. "I guess I have a problem trusting what I already know."

"Trust it."

"I'll try."

"Good."

"But you'd also rather I found another line of work, wouldn't you?"

"God, you're impossible," she cried as she jumped me and began beating on my chest.

An hour later, when I left her house, we had laughed and played and talked of inconsequential things. But it was still there in the air. Ridley Campbell's phone call. It lay over us like a small cloud of sulphur dioxide.

On my way out to McIntire Park, I tried to figure just what in the hell I was doing.

I'd lived in central Virginia for five years, having fled Boston for sunnier weather and to establish some distance from my ex-wife Marilyn. I chose to settle in Charlottesville for a number of reasons. It's a town of nice size, not chokingly large or incestuously small, and it's in the Sun Belt, sort of. I had some familiarity with the area from my college days, such as they were: a semester-long party, after which I was not invited to return to the University of Virginia. Perhaps most important, when I arrived, there were no other private investigators in town. I wasn't in the mood for competition.

Over the years, I'd made my niche. Legwork for lawyers, the occasional runaway, divorce cases, whatever I could get. As an exciting lifestyle, it normally ranks right up there with chicken sexer. But it pays the bills most of the time. And then, you never know. In twenty-four hours your whole life can get pounded senseless. That's one of the job's dangers. One of its attractions, too, or none of us would ever be drawn to it.

Trouble is, it's not the sort of work that tends to get you engaged with life. You spend your hours on the outside, looking in at what's going on in other people's lives. You're not really involved in the outcome of a particular case. In fact, you can't afford involvement if you hope to survive in the business. If you did put your feelings on the line every time you went out on a job, you'd be talking to yourself inside of a week, and in two you'd be doing it in the privacy of a padded room. In a way, it's a lot like it was during the war. There you didn't dare make friends. Your fellow soldiers got themselves killed or got rotated home, went over the hill or simply disappeared. If it mattered to you, you had to live with more grief than you could bear.

You don't choose to go to war, of course. Most folks don't, anyway. But you do choose your profession, at least to some extent. And when it's one that serves to isolate you from other people, rather than bringing you closer to them, then there are some predictable results.

You can end up in a very low place.

I know, because I've been there. It's where I was at the beginning of last winter. Down, and almost out.

Suddenly I was thirty-three years old. If I'd been Mozart, I'd have only had two years to live; if I'd been Jesus, they would've been bricking me into the cave. Being Swift, and less than a genius or a god, my problem was more mundane. Every part of my life up to then looked better to me than the

6

one I was living through. It seemed like none of the dreams of my youth would ever materialize. That sounds corny but, to borrow a phrase, there it is. I felt I'd hit the long slide. The one between the day when anything is possible and the day when nothing good will ever happen again.

Then I met Patricia. That's the good news. The bad news is that I met her during a case that left a trail of bodies across central Virginia such as I hadn't seen since the war. Before the case was over, I'd had to confront one of the most painful facts of life: that innocent people sometimes die in ugly and undeserved ways.

Patricia had been there to help me through the aftershocks of the experience, but I'd still become turned off to my job. I dropped out of the business. And I'd stayed away from it, subsisting on some guilt money one of the principals in the case had sent me. I vegetated.

Now, for the first time in nearly eight months, my old devil was coming out of hibernation. Curiosity. The one thing that keeps us coming back for more no matter how much sand gets kicked in our faces. I found myself asking again the only question that matters: what happens next?

I pulled into the parking lot at McIntire Park and Sheriff Campbell was there, over at one of the picnic tables. As promised.

Rid's a big guy. Looks a little like Jack Lambert, the Pittsburgh Steeler linebacker. He goes maybe six-two and two thirty, none of it flab. That gives him four inches and nearly sixty pounds on the likes of me. I wouldn't want to fight him. But then, who would? A few have tried. He's taken on men a lot bigger than himself and the last thing they called for before they passed out was their mama.

He's tough, and not just physically. Yet he's no one-dimensional cartoon Southern hick cop, either. He has a mind of high-quality carbon steel. He has a sense of responsibility to the people that's tempered by a finely developed feel for which laws are in need of most vigorous enforcement. (He prefers putting away rapists and child abusers to harassing those who smoke pot or bet on the World Series.) And he's honest. Among elected law enforcement officials, that's pretty rare. Sort of like finding a working single mother of eight in the President's Commission on Hunger in America.

One other thing about Ridley Campbell. Most cops you're likely to meet in the South favor those mirrored aviator sunglasses that they think look so cool. Not Rid. He never wears shades of any kind. He *wants* people to see his eyes. Especially people who might be contemplating giving him some grief. He can stop you dead with a stare, and he knows it. No point in defusing one of your best weapons.

So the first thing I noticed as I approached the picnic table was that the sheriff had sunglasses on. The mirrored kind.

"Rid," I said, chuckling a little. "First time we ever met I can't look you in the eye."

He didn't say anything. He just reached up and slowly peeled off the mirrors.

I stopped chuckling. Campbell looked like hell. The black of the pupils was intact, but all around there were signs of trouble. Dark gray pouches. Skinny lines of red crisscrossing the whites. Bad.

"Jesus, Rid," I said. "You look like you need a good week's sleep."

He nodded, putting the shades back on. "I do," he said.

And then I was overwhelmed by the urge to get out of there. Just turn my back and move. Go. Anywhere at all. The sensation was so powerful that my legs began shaking. In another few seconds I wouldn't be able to stay upright. I sat on the edge of the picnic table to keep from falling.

During the years I've been a P.I., I've learned to trust my instincts. Now they were telling me clearly that I didn't want any part of whatever was wrong with Ridley Campbell. In my rational mind, I knew that my instincts were probably dead on. I also knew that in some intangible way it was already too late. If I could help the guy out, I would. At that moment, I was about as capable of turning my back as Richard Nixon is of telling the truth.

"You call me out here to talk about it?" I asked.

"Yeah."

"I'm not licensed to prescribe sleeping pills," I said.

That got a small smile and seemed to loosen him up a bit. "Swift, I got myself a little trouble here," he said.

"A little?"

"Well, maybe more than a little."

"Tell me something I don't know."

He weighed what he was going to say next. When it came, it was nothing. "Somebody's after my job, Swift."

I let out a big breath that I hadn't known I was holding in. "Of course they are," I said. "It *is* an election year, you know. But hell, Rid, the people of Albemarle County ain't gonna turn you out. You're as good a sheriff as the county's had. They're aware of that. Actually, you're the *only* one a lot of 'em have ever known."

He shook his head. "Anyone can get run out of office. Anytime people vote."

This was crazy. Ridley was popular. He'd successfully stood for reelection more than once and been returned by a landslide. It was old stuff to him. Not the sort of thing I'd expect him to lose sleep over.

"Who's going to beat you, whatsisname?"

"Lester Beavans."

"Right. Brother Les. A good ole boy if ever I saw one."

And you couldn't miss seeing him. The smiling, jowly face beamed at you from every other telephone pole, it seemed like.

"Brother Les," Campbell said. "Tell me, Swift, you ever know a political disputation to heat up this early?" That was pure Ridley. He liked to drop phrases like "political disputation" from time to time, just to make sure you weren't tuning him out.

"I don't know. I haven't exactly immersed myself in your politics since I moved here."

"Okay, I'll tell you then. Campaigns around here don't run on for years like they do for president. Which is fine, the way I see it. Don't nobody have the money, is the main reason.

Usually, the heavy politicking starts Labor Day. Two months later and it's all over. But you take Les Beavans, he's already spent I don't know how much. And it's what month?"

"First of August."

"You noticed. Did you also notice when his face started showing up around here?"

"No. I've been, ah, a mite out of sorts this . . . year."

"So I hear. Well, let me fill you in. Lester's been campaigning, and hard, since June."

That did sound odd.

"He must really want it," I said. "What's he do for money?"

"Apparently nothing. Campaigning for sheriff would appear to be his full-time job."

"He independently wealthy?"

"Not that I know of. Local boy. Comes from the hills up in northwest Albemarle. Worked at this and that. Went to Florida for a few years, I don't know why. Then he turned up back here last summer and suddenly he's running for sheriff. You figure it."

"Somebody's backing him."

"Good detective work, Swift."

"You know who?"

"Nope. I've tried like hell to find out and I can't."

"With all your pull?"

"With all my pull. Don't look so consternated, boy. My influence has its limitations. Besides which, this job don't exactly give me a pile of free time to go running after such things. Which brings us to the point."

"And the point is?"

"The point is: I want you to find out where the money's coming from."

"Aw, come on Rid. I'm retired."

"I want you should unretire."

"Why me? Look, it's a nothing job. Use one of your deputies. They wouldn't mind moonlighting."

"I can't."

Campbell had that grim look again.

"Tell me why," I said.

He spoke slowly, as if testing each word before saying it. "First off, I don't know about the ethics of the situation. Using someone in the department to investigate a political opponent. It might be legit, but I wouldn't feel right doing it, and if Lester found out there'd be hell to pay. And second, damn it, you're better than anyone else in town right now."

"Well, I never thought I'd see the day when you said that. But thanks."

He waved it off. "Let's don't play mutual admiration society. I know my staff's limitations and I know what you can do. I also know I can trust that it'll be done quietly."

I nodded. Naturally, I was pleased at the professional recognition I was getting here, but I didn't let on. "I imagine there's a third reason coming, isn't there?" I said.

"Yeah. I don't know exactly how to put this, Swift, and it's very, very far off the record, you understand?"

"I understand."

"Okay, I feel like somebody's . . . *gotten* to some of the people around me."

"I'm not sure I follow you."

"It's hard to explain," he said. "Maybe some guys wouldn't of even noticed anything. I can't be positive myself, but you know how you're with people in some nasty situations, you get to know them over the years. You get a *feel* for who they are. There's a kind of feeling that you share, that you're a part of something that functions smoothly and efficiently, that you can *rely* on anyone around you, no matter how tough it gets. You know?"

"I guess so. It was like that in Nam, once in a while."

"Right. Well, something's happened to my team. That feeling is gone. I can't tell you how I know it is, but I do. The trust, the respect, it's not like before. Morale is bad. And I just can't put my finger on the cause. The only thing I can think is that someone has gotten to a few key people and turned them against me. I don't know if it's with money or what. But something's going on. It's like an effort's being made to convince me that I'm not cutting it as a leader any more."

I could see Ridley caving in to a feeling like that. Physically, he'd face the toughest guy in town without batting an eye. But something out of sight, slowly undermining his confidence in himself, that'd get to him.

"You think Beavans is behind it?" I asked.

"Could be. If someone's trying to buy the sheriff's spot, it wouldn't hurt to screw up the department before election time. Be even better if I dropped out of the race. You get what I'm driving at?"

I nodded and we sat in silence for a minute.

"I don't come cheap," I said with a straight face.

"I can pay."

I laughed. "Ridley, last December I was halfway to losing either my license or my freedom. Neither of which happened, because you covered my butt for me. So if there's one thing in this miserable world that's true, it's that I owe you a very large one."

"You don't owe me, Swift. If you'd of broke the law, you'd be in the can. I don't do special favors."

"I know you don't. Okay, let's put it this way. You do things like you do because you're the person you are. Much to my benefit. I'm the person I am. And that person says that this one's on the house. Done?"

"Nope." And that, I knew, was that.

"You're a hardass, Campbell," I said.

"Man does a job, he deserves compensation."

"All right," I sighed, "consider me employed." There was no point in fighting him. Besides, my bank balance was on the precarious side. I've never been good with money. Someone says "IRA" and I still think of Dublin.

"Now," I went on, "here's my first deduction. I've heard a story about some guy spending a wad of money to get himself elected sheriff. This same guy may or may not be sowing seeds of discontent in the incumbent sheriff's department. This is causing the incumbent some worry about his job security. So far, so good. Only thing is, the incumbent happens to be you, Rid. And I know you. You're as tough as they make them. Now your situation may be bad, and I can see you getting a little bent about the threat to your leadership, but none of that explains the man I see here. This guy is a stranger. Which means you've left something out. If you want me to work for you, you've got to level with me, Rid."

"I didn't leave it out," he muttered. "I was going to get to it."

"Let's have it, then."

He sighed. That in itself amazed me.

"It's a couple of things," he said. "Three weeks back my wife got food poisoning at Guillermo's. Not bad enough to put her into the hospital. But bad enough to make for a pretty miserable night."

"What does that mean?"

"Well, I might not of thought much of it. But we both ate the same thing."

"Oh."

"And far as I been able to determine, didn't nobody else get sick there that night."

"You think—"

"Swift, I don't know what to think. I only know what's happened. The other thing is, last Sunday my boy was walking home from the store. Nobody else on the street. Some car came fast around the corner, ran up on the sidewalk and damn near hit him. He dove out of the way. Missed him by maybe a foot, then took off before he could get a good look at the plate.

"That's two things in three weeks. In my business, I don't believe much in coincidence."

And there it was. The real reason that Campbell looked like last week's potato salad. Rid might be a hard old bastard, but when it came to his family you could mash him with a feather.

"Me neither," I said.

"You think somebody's trying to tell me something?"

"Christ, I don't know," I said. "If they are, these guys are playing hardball, Rid."

"My feelings exactly. I couldn't stand anything happening to my family, Swift. I really couldn't. It's beginning to get to me. But you see how my hands are tied. There's the political ethics of the situation. Then there's the fact that ain't no one broken any laws I can point to. All I've got is a bunch of things that only add up to something bad if they're linked together. And they may be totally unrelated. I may be getting a little nuts in my old age. On the other hand, if they *are* out to get me, I want to lay hands on the sonsofbitches." His fists clenched reflexively as he said it. Then he relaxed. "You know I wouldn't ask you to do this if I had another choice," he said.

"I know."

"And you know if it gets nasty, I'll be there."

"Yeah, I guess I know that."

"Well?"

"I'll see what I can do," I said.

There wasn't any more to do after that. People like me and Ridley Campbell, we don't need to shake hands or wish each other well or crap like that. When we've said our piece, we just walk away from it.

And that's what we did.

It was a bright, pleasant late summer afternoon, mercifully free of the oppressive humidity that plagues central Virginia during the hot months. It was also Sunday. There wouldn't be much I could do to help Ridley Campbell until the work week began, so I drove over to the Rivanna River and set down to think for a while.

Foremost in my mind was the question of my "retirement." Over the past several months I'd considered a number of options that might be open to me. Mid-life career evaluation, I think they call it these days. I realized that if I was going to undertake a radical change of jobs, I'd need retraining. And even then it would be tough, with unemployment figures as high as they were.

What to do?

There were a couple of vocational training centers in Charlottesville. They'd teach you the rudiments of carpentry, bricklaying, plumbing, etc. Maybe enough to catch on as an apprentice somewhere at minimum wage. (No unions hereabouts.) On the plus side, those kinds of skills would always be in demand. Then there's the minus side. I don't like working outdoors in the winter, for one thing. For another, I'm a little too ornery to make anyone a good apprentice at my age. It just didn't look like a good bet for me.

Patricia suggested real estate. That wasn't a bad idea. I could get my license in a couple of months. The market was good. The local companies were always looking for new people. And I'd be more or less my own boss, the way I like it. But then, I've never been a terrific salesperson. I've got this nagging little streak of integrity in me that I'd have to stamp out to be able to sell anything. I'm not sure I'd want to part with it. There have been times when it was all that kept me going. I put real estate salesman on hold.

Then Patrick, Patricia's brother, tried to get me interested in computers. There, as he put it, is where the money is. He's probably right. And learning to program is easy, he assured me. Maybe so. But in the end what it comes down to is sitting in front of a cathode ray tube for hours at a stretch. That to me ranks right up there with being forced to sit through the collected films of Andy Warhol. (You remember them: eight hours of a guy sleeping, twelve hours of the Empire State Building, so on.) Hell, I don't even like TV. If it wasn't for sports, I wouldn't watch it at all, and I've never felt the need to own one. How could I deal with depending on a computer terminal to pay the rent?

The only other thing that had occurred to me was writing. Outside of preparing investigation reports, I hadn't done any in years. But I'd worked on the staff of my high school paper and had enjoyed the experience. I felt that I was good at expressing myself. In addition, newspaper work is a field where a college degree isn't an absolute must. And it wouldn't hurt that I had a good friend at the local daily. He'd probably let me do a few stories on spec, to see if I was up to it. I'd been on the verge of pursuing this option when Campbell "hired" me.

The Rivanna, depleted by drought, flowed on by. It doesn't

rate very high in the scenic river department, but it's the one we're stuck with. And just the sight of moving water seems to strike some chord inside a person.

It calmed me to where I could ponder the Ridley Campbell problem in the light of my own flounderings.

Okay, so maybe I wasn't destined to become a famous journalist. Maybe I was back in the detective business again. Just maybe. I'd wanted to run from it, and I hadn't been able to. It had come looking for me. And then there was this: I simply couldn't deny that itch, that urge to unravel a mystery. If there was one.

For better or worse, I had a job to do. I had to try to connect a series of events that might have no connection. Which is what I'm good at, and what I most like to do. At least, I always thought I did. This would be the chance to find out. If I turned in a good effort, and took satisfaction in it, then I was a real P.I. and no point in pretending otherwise. If it didn't work out, so what? They'd hold my Pulitzer.

2

My landlady, Mrs. Detweiler, was in the front yard, taking some late afternoon sun, reading the Sunday paper.

I live in the Belmont section of Charlottesville, over on the east side. It's not one of the town's more fashionable addresses. But it's quiet, well away from the thousands of children who attend the University of Virginia. And the price is right. My neighbors are a solid, working-class bunch. Quick to throw a punch on Saturday night, but first to help you out when you're in a jam. I'd rather have to depend on one of them than any Saabful of pointy-headed intellectual types from over at the U.

I parked Clementine, my battered '72 orange VW, on the street, and walked over to say hello to my landlady. She's a crusty old woman, somewhere in her early eighties. You have to speak a little above normal with Mrs. Detweiler, but otherwise she's as spry as I am. She occupies the top story of a pre–World War II frame house. My apartment's in the basement, around back.

"Mrs. D," I said. "How—"

"Reaganomics!" she fumed, slapping the front section of the

paper on the ground. "Bah! Tell me, young Swift, do people your age actually believe this claptrap?"

"Well, I don't know. They say he's brought inflation under control."

"Nonsense! The only reason inflation's down is because the Arabs haven't been able to jack the price of oil for a couple of years. He can't take credit for that."

"But you can bet that he will."

"Ex-*actly*. And look at this, will you? U.S. Steel closing another slew of plants. Thousands of people out of work. It's not right."

"The company says they're not profitable."

"Lord help us. You know, there's only one thing wrong with the economy of this country, Swift: the workers do not control the means of production."

Did I forget to say that Mrs. Detweiler is a socialist? Well, she is. One of those old-timey ones who was involved in the life-or-death labor struggles of the thirties. She has many a tale to tell of those days, but she doesn't live in them. She's very much a person of the present, clinging stubbornly to her dream right down into the dismal, self-centered eighties.

I have a great deal of respect for her.

"Do you suppose," she went on, "that if the workers owned U.S. Steel, that you'd see all these shutdowns? Hell no, you wouldn't. It's the damn capitalist greed. Those fat cats can't make their ten million a year out of forty plants, so they arrange to make it out of thirty-five instead. And in the meantime, you got another five thousand people on welfare. Now where's the sense in that, I ask you?"

I shrugged. "There isn't any," I said.

"You're damn right there isn't! Lord, I never thought I'd get to be this old and not see any change in the system. The workers ought to just *take* those factories, run them themselves. They'd stay open then, I guarantee you."

"In addition to which," I said, "anything's better than welfare."

She grinned. "Weirton Steel," she said. "Now you watch them if you really want to see something."

I'd read about Weirton, the first employee buy-out of a major steel producer.

"Yeah, they'll be interesting to watch," I agreed.

"There you go, young man. I believe there may be hope for you yet."

"Don't count on it. Socialism's fine in theory, but it doesn't seem to work so well in real life."

"That's because no one's ever tried it proper. If you just substitute one blasted bureaucracy for another, you can't call it socialism."

"I know, Mrs. D. But there's also that one other thing. I don't think my kind of lifestyle would be tolerated in a socialist state. I value my independence too much to be a good communard."

"You'd find something better!"

I laughed. "Perhaps so. I'll remember that when I'm rotting in some gulag for counterrevolutionaries."

"Ach, I was wrong. You *are* hopeless, Swift. Always the ego, always. To you it is such an important thing."

"Sometimes it's all I've had."

"No . . . no. It is nothing. Someday you will appreciate this. There is so much that is more critical. Try to live for something bigger. You will end up liking yourself more."

"That would be nice."

"Yes. How do they say, 'Try it, you'll *like* it!' "

"Actually, what I'd most like right now is to get out of the heat and into a cold shower and a little Jameson on the rocks. Is that too capitalist a thought?"

"Sure, sure. But . . . ah, forget it. It's the waste of an old woman's good breath. Have you seen this rag?"

"No, not yet. I rarely bother."

"Probably best that you don't. Here, take it. It hurts my poor eyes."

"And I'll bet you don't mean eyestrain."

She handed me the Sunday *Press*.

"And I don't mean eyestrain," she said. "Go on, take your shower."

I took the paper and gave her a little peck on the cheek.

"Aggh," she muttered, making a face. "Hopeless. The man is hopeless."

I stood under the shower for a long time, pretending that it was the cool summer rain we'd been denied so far by the drought.

Then I poured myself some Jameson on the rocks. If you're going to drink whiskey, I figure it makes sense to go to the people with the experience. That'd be the Irish. And if you're going Irish, it might as well be from John Jameson & Son of Bow Street, Dublin.

I sipped the whiskey and thought again about what I was doing from a detective's point of view. Just to see if the deductive process was still functioning.

The question was: Was Ridley Campbell right? Was someone trying very hard to shove him out of his job? Had the attempt at persuasion gone considerably north of friendly? And if so, why?

Make it a working assumption that something's going on. Something that can't be simply chalked up to the usual workings of the political process. Assume that the opposition has decided to play a dedicated game of hardball.

If that's so, certain conclusions follow. The most obvious is that there is something to be gained from the defeat of Ridley Campbell in the race for county sheriff. Except for psychos, people don't mindlessly do things on the fringe of, or beyond, the law. They do them for a reason. Personal gain, usually. Nine times out of ten that gain can be measured in terms of either money or power. In a state as traditionally corrupt as Virginia, the two are often one.

On the surface, the person who had the most to gain if Campbell got the boot was Lester Beavans. He'd be the new sheriff. And he was campaigning as if it was what he'd wanted all his life.

Maybe it was. But according to Ridley, the guy had no visible income. Unless he'd made his fortune down in Florida.

In which case you'd have to wonder what he was doing running for Albemarle County sheriff instead of lying in the sun on Key Biscayne.

The more logical explanation was that Brother Les had a backer, and a big one. Again, logic would suggest that the unidentified money man was not in this because he and Lester were old army buddies, or some such. He or she could safely be presumed to have a stake in the outcome. A substantial stake.

Two things to do, then. First, find out as much as possible about Lester Beavans. Second, learn the identity of his cash source. If possible, do both at once.

How? I chuckled. In light of the options I'd been considering for my life, the answer was simplicity itself.

I called Jonesy.

Jonesy is my man at our local newspaper, the Charlottesville *Daily Press* (or the *Depressor*, as it's more familiarly known). It's not as good a paper as it should be, considering that it has the resources of a university community to draw on. But I suppose it's average as small city dailies go, and, actually, I doubt if there are *any* really fine newspapers these days. Most of them seem to be interchangeable subsidiaries of some communications conglomerate or other. And am I wrong, or has the quality of writing dropped considerably in the past fifteen years or so? Maybe the critics of our school system have a point.

Happily, Jonesy is an exception to the curse of mediocrity that seems to plague the *Depressors* and the rest of them. Of course, he's only staying on in Charlottesville until the *Washington Post* begins to show some interest in his résumé. So he says. He and I drink a lot of beer together during the University of Virginia's basketball season. I buy a lot of those beers. Plus I give him exclusives whenever I get mixed up in something newsworthy. In return, Jonesy lets me tap into his knowledge of the local scene and what goes on behind it.

On a hot Sunday afternoon in August, I figured Jonesy just might be at home watching the Orioles. I was right.

"Swift," he said. "I hope this is important. Boddicker's got a no-hitter going."

"Oh yeah," I said, "the foosh baller. Or is it the nosh baller? My grandmother could hit him if he wasn't keeping the Vaseline company in business."

"You're a cynic, you know that, Swift?"

"That's what they always say when the truth hurts them, Jonesy."

"Oh, God. Jesus H. Christ and both his parents."

"What?"

"Winfield just hit one into Baltimore harbor. Man on, on an error. We're down two-zip. The way Guidry's going, I doubt we'll get 'em back." He sighed.

"C'mon Jonesy, Guidry never could go nine."

"Hey, you're right. And besides, it's only August; come September, we leave the Yanks in the dust. So what can I do you out of, Big Time?"

"The usual. Your beer money."

"Careful what you're saying. I only drink Moosehead now. If I want to make the *Post*, I've got to start cultivating the image."

"Sure. Buy yourself a Volvo while you're at it. Join Common Cause. Start hanging out in fern bars."

"Very funny. Too bad you're not literate as well."

"Don't need to be in my line. I can't imagine it's a prerequisite at the *Press*, either."

He laughed. "Okay, okay," he said. "What do you need?"

"How much will a case of Moosehead buy about Lester Beavans?"

"Ah, the would-be sheriff. It'd get you a lot if there was a lot to be got."

"Not much, eh?"

"Nope. Certainly not more than a six pack's worth."

"What off the top of your head?"

"Lester Beavans," he said. "Known to most everyone as Les. Local boy. A redneck from up around Nortonsville somewhere. In his early thirties. Bit of a hell-raiser when he was younger.

Drinking, brawls, car chases with the cops, that kind of thing. Knocked up a girl named Connie Shifflett, married her, divorced her. One kid. Bitch of an auto mechanic from what I understand. Earned a decent living off it and pretty much stayed out of serious trouble after his teenage years. Never remarried. No one would ever have invited him to a debutante ball, but in his own circles he seems extremely well-liked. All the good ole boys see him as one of their own and would love to have him sheriff. That's a pretty formidable voting bloc out in the county.

"Five years ago he dropped out of sight for a while. Told people he'd had enough one winter and that he was heading south. Gossip is that he washed up in Florida. Then nothing until last summer, when he showed up back in Albemarle County, apparently with enough money that he didn't have to work for a while. Come spring, he announced for sheriff and the last month and a half he's been campaigning like hell for the job."

"You think he's got a shot at it?"

"Yeah, maybe. Stranger things have happened. He can play himself up as the real native son. Campbell was born and raised in Carolina, you know. Didn't move to Albemarle until high school. And all other things being equal, the local boy usually wins elections around here. Plus Les's going after the transplant vote by favoring conversion to a county police department. Plus he's spending more money.

"Of course, he may have started *too* early. You got to be careful not to peak prematurely in this game. The public is a fickle beast. It bores easily."

"But he's got no qualifications," I said.

"You don't need any. I could run if I really wanted to. That's the way they set up elective cop jobs, back when there wasn't any such thing as 'police science.' "

"What about Campbell? Isn't he still pretty popular?"

"Among some," Jonesy said. "But a lot of those good ole boys think he's too tough a cop. Beavans is more their type, a guy they wouldn't be uneasy drinking with because he's the law, you know what I mean? And we got a slew of newcomers in the county who don't know the one from the other. They might just vote the issues. Never can tell.

"Anyway, what do you want the dope on Lester Beavans for? You on a case?"

"Nah."

"C'mon Swift, I thought you was retired."

"I am."

Jonesy paused, then continued. "Reason I asked," he said. "You get too deep into local politics, you could find that these boys play the game a mite rough."

"You have any idea who 'these boys' might be?"

"You mean behind Beavans?"

"The very ones."

"Actually, I don't. The official word is that Les is financing the campaign himself. Somehow I doubt that. But I'm not assigned to the story, so far be it from me to try to prove otherwise."

"The auto repair business must be awfully lucrative down in Florida."

"Could be. All those Rollses and whatnot."

"Okay. How much more does the case of Moosehead buy?" I asked.

"You ain't used it up yet. But truth to tell, Swift, I don't know what more I can get for you. It ain't big news. The guy who's covering the story is a real plodder, and he's only got it very part-time at this point. Beyond that, I don't know. I'll see what I can dig up."

"You want to know what I'm up to, don't you?" I asked.

Jonesy was a friend. He wouldn't bug me for something I didn't want to tell him. But his curiosity would be killing him.

"It's your business," he said. I could see him down the phone line, shrugging his shoulders, pretending disinterest.

"Well," I said, "I've decided I need a career change, Jones."

"Give me a beer for every time I've heard that one."

"No, I'm serious. I think I'd like to do some newspaper writing." .

"Oh, for Christ's sake. Yank my leg and you'll get a handful of splinters, Swift."

"It's not a joke. I've got just a little inside information. My source says that the Beavans campaign might not quite be on the up-and-up. That a story?"

"Who's your source?"

"Sorry."

He sighed. "The man is learning," he said. "Okay, you want something from me, right?"

"I want to know if it's a story."

"Of *course* it could be. Depends on what you've got. What else you want?"

"I need to talk to people. Beavans for starters. I want to tell them I'm working on a feature for the *Press*. Can I use your name?"

He thought about it.

"You can use my name," he said finally. "But here's the ground rules. I've asked you to work up a story on spec. If anyone calls me, I'll cover for you. If they go over my head, management will have never heard of you. In that case, you're just another free-lancer and I never talked specifics with you."

"Fair enough," I said. "My guess is, they won't even bother to call. Offer them some free publicity and chances are they'll fall all over themselves to be accommodating."

"Chances are."

"Thanks, Jonesy."

"Thanks for nothing. I don't know what you're doing, and I'd rather keep it that way. Just don't screw me over, is all I ask. In the meantime, I'll see what else I can find out. You still got the answering service?"

Come to mention it, I hadn't even thought about my former answering service.

"As of tomorrow I do," I said. "How's Boddicker making it?"

"Don't ask. They've gone to Tippy."

"Good. The Yankees can't hit lefties."

"You wish. Don't forget the beer now."

"I won't."

"I'd say it's only a six-pack at this moment, but I'd like it before next weekend. The Tigers are in for three and they're hot."

"I'll try to catch one with you," I said. "Even though it isn't roundball."

"Done. Watch yourself, Swift," he said, and hung up.

Watch myself? My experience said it was a whole lot better to keep your eye on what the *other* guy was doing.

I finished the Jameson, then got down to business.

If I was going out on a job, I needed to see that the tools of my trade were in good working order. In my business, that means my guns. I have two of them. One is a Walther PPK automatic. Good German craftsmanship. Accurate. About as reliable as an automatic gets. I keep it locked away in my desk drawer, unloaded, with the shells locked away separately. The other gun is a .38 calibre Colt Police Positive revolver. It's loaded and taped to the back of the sofa, which is shoved up close to the windowless north wall of my apartment. The arrangement will probably never do me much good, but at least I know it's there and an intruder wouldn't. Under the right circumstances, that could conceivably save my life.

I got out both guns, checked and cleaned them, and put them back. Normally, I don't carry one. The times when you really need it are far too few to counterbalance the potential for misuse. The guns are there for when I *know* I'm going to need some help, and I'm licensed to conceal them on my person.

When I'd finished, I poured another Jameson and fixed myself a light supper. In the summertime, I don't like to eat much. A small salad will usually do it for me.

Afterward, I sat down with the Sunday *Depressor* Mrs. Detweiler had given me.

In general, I tend to read the sections of the Sunday paper in the following sequence: Sports, National/International News, Editorial. And lately I'd begun scanning the Want Ads in a halfhearted way. After that, my interest drops off a lot. I poke around, looking for anything that might catch my eye. If nothing does, I quit.

So it was a while before I got around to Local News. It's a section that I've been known to pass up entirely. But I had no plans for the evening, and who could say, I might have come across some vital information about Lester Beavans.

I didn't.

But what was there was quite a surprise.

"Well, gag me with a spoon," I said to the four walls.

The lower part of the Local News section of the Sunday *Press* is an ongoing ditty called "Blue Ridge Bios." Catchy, eh? It features a profile of some person living in the Charlottes-ville/Albemarle County area. How the powers that be choose the subject is a mystery to me. But as a rule, it's someone outside the mainstream of area news, someone whose name you wouldn't expect to find in the paper otherwise. Very small town stuff. And more than a little cornball. Occasionally, however, it can be nice.

Like today.

There, looking up at me with a typically mischievous smile, was the befreckled face of Patrick Ryan.

The story began, "For many people, an automobile accident which deprived them of the use of their legs would be an embittering end to life as they knew it. For Patrick Ryan of Charlottesville, it was the beginning of a new one. A three-letter athlete at the city high school, this engaging young man was the blameless victim of a late-night drunk driver the summer after his senior year." And so on. Some stuff about his long convalescence. Learning to adjust to life sitting down. How he resumed an active sports life. Chair skiing. The founding of the Charlottesville Redbirds, a wheelchair basket-ball team. And a lengthy discussion of his current vocation, computer programming.

Patrick had originally taken up programming because it's a field in which being chair-confined is no handicap (a word he detests, by the way, except as it applies to his golf game). He invested some of the insurance money he got from the accident in an elaborate microcomputer setup and began teaching him-self. To no one's surprise who knew him, the learning came easily. Somewhat to his own surprise, he discovered that he also loved it. He became what is known as a "hacker"—someone who can spend hour after hour in front of a screen, talking to the machine. Hackers are invariably young, rarely bother with college, and often know more about their computers than the people who designed them. They are the leading edge of the high tech revolution currently going on in this country. A lot of the time they're hired by the computer companies that have proliferated around Boston and the San Francisco Bay. Or else they start their own companies. They're in a field in which there are a lot of very young millionaires.

So far, Patrick hadn't shown any inclination to leave Charlottesville for Silicon Valley. He was content with the stimulation he derived from his own labors and his association with a number of other locals who had founded a loose hacker network. He and his friends set themselves hideously complex problems and then solved them. They sold custom-designed software to area businesses. In their spare time, they played elaborate games over the phone lines. To keep the mind nimble, Patrick said.

In addition to doing something he enjoyed, Patrick was earning a good living from this stuff. The *Press* article tabbed him as one of the three or four most knowledgeable micro-computer people in town. (No small accomplishment when you share that town with a major university and all the Ph.D.s in its computer science department.) It went on to say that Patrick had been wooed by every hardware or software vendor in sight, but had turned them all down.

"I don't care for bosses," he was quoted as saying. He would. Yet he'd say it in such a way that if you didn't work for yourself you wouldn't be offended.

The article concluded with an assessment of Patrick's future: bright, to say the least.

I put down the paper and picked up the phone.

Patrick answered.

"You little bastard," I said.

"Aw, come on, Swift," he said. "Don't you like a little surprise in your life?"

"I suppose," I grumbled. "How does it feel to be a super-star?"

"About like it felt to be a nobody. In other words, it ain't worth the paper it's printed on. Fortunately, I don't care. I am curious as to what kind of job offers might result, though. I've already gotten a call or two."

"You thinking of leaving us?"

"Nah. It's only a local newspaper, you know. The bigs won't be looking for me because I made the Sunday *Press*. Even if they did, I love saying no to the hard sell."

"I'll bet you do at that. Look, is the old lady around?"

"Sure enough. You want her?"

"Constantly. But just talking on the phone will do for the time being."

He laughed, made a scurrilous remark about our collective libido, and went to get Patricia.

"Loren," she said, "what'd you think, wasn't it a nice article?"

"Did you know?"

"Of course I knew."

"And you didn't tell me. I thought we were trying to base this relationship on the novel concept of honesty."

"I don't tell you everything, dear. It would be so tedious if I did. Besides, Patrick made me promise not to tell anyone."

"He and I have already discussed that."

"And?"

"As usual, he criticized me for not being joyful enough over life's little surprises."

"You aren't, you know. But . . . what did Mr. Campbell want?"

I took a healthy breath. Well, no point in beating around the bush.

"He wants me to do a job for him," I said.

There was one of those silences that you can never get used to.

"I see," she said finally. "And you accepted."

"Yeah. I can't turn down Ridley, Patricia. He's covered my butt for me. I owe him."

"Loren, I admire your sense of loyalty, you know that. It's a rare thing."

"But you'd still rather I didn't do the job."

She laughed. "You're incorrigible," she said. "Okay, let's sleep on it, all right? We've got plenty of time to talk things out."

"That we do."

"And a job might be the best thing for you right now. Anything you can tell me about it?"

"I'd rather not. Maybe later. What I'm hoping is that there's not going to be much to it and that I'll have it wrapped up in a couple of days."

"Want to see me tomorrow night?"

"Not only that," I said, and told her exactly what I intended to do to her body. She responded in kind. I loved it.

We hung up giggling like little kids.

The glow lasted for a while, but eventually it wore off. I didn't know if I'd convinced Patricia that the job might be a simple one, but I was far from convinced myself. I was, after all, an Outsider, and I always would be to those who were Virginia born and bred. I was a transplanted Yankee, come down to make his fortune off the good-natured Southerner. A twentieth-century carpetbagger. The enemy.

I could be well out of my depth before I began.

I poured some more Jameson over ice and got out the latest Travis McGee novel. It kept me up late, like they always do, but I didn't mind. It's become a very poorly guarded secret that Travis and Meyer are the finest fictional duo since Holmes and Watson. Guaranteed to distract your thoughts from weightier matters that are better slept on.

3

I HADN'T PLANNED TO GET UP EARLY ON MONDAY MORNING. IN general, Virginians don't like to deal with anything of importance before the day is well begun. Something to do with that thinned-out Southern blood, no doubt. I'd adapted nicely to local custom.

So I was still sleeping when Campbell called at eight.

"You know the boarding kennels on Route 20 South?" he demanded.

"Yeah, sure," I said.

"Meet me there in fifteen minutes." And he hung up.

I didn't like the sound of it, but the sheriff hadn't asked me, he'd told me. I went.

Route 20 heads south from Belmont, where I live. It passes through the last suburbs of Charlottesville, goes under the Interstate, skirts Piedmont Virginia Community College, and then heads into the woods. About a mile beyond the college, on two or three acres of open land, is the Blue Ridge Kennel. I pulled into its gravel drive. Campbell's cruiser was already there.

Ridley was standing next to his car. He motioned me to follow him.

We went around behind the main kennels. Back there were exercise yards and a couple of dozen fenced areas with individual animal houses. He led me to one of the latter.

Inside the fence, lying on the ground, was a pair of floppy-eared hounds. Their tongues hung from their mouths. They were obviously dead.

"Mine," Campbell said.

I didn't know what to say.

"Best hunting dogs I ever had," he said. "Poisoned."

I looked at him. His face was a deep red, almost maroon. The veins in his temple stood out like they were getting ready to detach themselves.

"I'm sorry," I said.

He reached out, took hold of my shirt and pulled me close to him. "We got to do something, Swift," he said. His voice was half strangling on itself.

"Easy, Rid," I said. "It isn't me." I paused, then added, "Don't let it get control of you."

He slowly released his grip. He looked me in the eye, started to say something, thought better of it. I looked down. He spun on his heel and walked quickly away without another word. I waited until he was out of sight, then returned to my car. The cruiser was gone.

A little shaken, I drove back to my apartment. I showered and shaved and had a light breakfast. I remembered to reinstate my answering service.

At ten, feeling somewhat better, I walked into Lester Beavans's campaign headquarters.

"Headquarters" may be a somewhat misleading word here, if it causes you to imagine a clean, well-lighted suite of offices staffed by comely young girls in red-white-and-blue straw boaters. After all, Beavans was running for sheriff, not the Senate. And even though Albemarle County is one of the country's most wealthy, county sheriff is somewhat of a hick job.

Beavans for Sheriff HQ was located on the downtown pedestrian mall. This is an attractive section of the old city center which had decayed, and was "renewed" a few years back with much hoopla and civic breast beating. For a while it was a popular spot. But then the city approved construction of one of those ugly, climate-controlled "malls," and the area began dying again. A couple of years later, wonder of wonders, a new round of construction was scheduled for downtown and things picked up again. With the fluctuation in real estate values, someone somewhere was grabbing a quick buck or two.

In any case, the latest rebound isn't quite in full swing yet. You can still rent space for cheap there. Which is what Beavans had done.

The office was a single room. It was on the second floor of a narrow two-story frame building that would be scheduled for demolition before long. The first floor had housed a boutique for a time. Then it was a store selling microcomputers. That disappeared with the Osborne. Now the building was empty. There was a *For Rent* sign in the window touting it as a sure-fire location. It was sure-fire only if you were into arson for profit.

Although on a small scale, it was a standard political campaign office. There were tables with stacks of handouts. Big posters on all the walls. The now familiar urban cowboy hat and broad smiling face of the candidate. It was a great face for a would-be sheriff, I had to admit. Open, friendly. He had that good ole boy look down pat. It conveyed the impression that this man was your personal buddy. Yet there was a toughness around the dark eyes that came through loud and clear, too. It said: I'm your buddy so long as we're on the same side. But if you're agin me, watch out, because I am not someone you should screw around with.

I especially liked the hat. Go get 'em, Les.

I wandered around, picking up handbills and gawking at posters. Many of the handbills pushed one of Beavans's campaign themes: conversion of the sheriff's office into a county police force. "It's time for professionalism," was the slogan. How Beavans qualified as a professional was beyond me, but the subject was timely. It was being hotly debated in local political circles and in the media. Ridley Campbell was known to favor keeping the current system, so Beavans had staked out a visible difference between them. In a sense, though, it was a non-issue. Because, should the county decide in favor of a police force, then the first offer of Chief would naturally go to the incumbent sheriff. The major advantage to a newcomer would be that he could staff the expanded department with people of his own choosing.

I'd been there a while before the other person in the room spoke. No hard sell here.

"Good morning, sir," she said. "My name is Ann. Is there anything in particular that we could help you with?"

The "we" was nice. This was a team effort.

"He's a good-looking man," I said.

"Yes," Ann said, "isn't he? But so is Governor Robb and look what he's done to us. It's not what a man looks like, but what kind of a man he is, don't you agree?"

I walked over and sat in a chair in front of Ann's desk. The desk was neat. Some In/Out baskets. A large calendar blotter. Various papers and notebooks. A phone with five extension buttons, of which four were apparently for future use. Behind the desk were a couple of gray metal filing cabinets.

Ann was young but not too young. Attractive but not stunningly attractive. Exactly the sort of person you'd want in a job like this. Old enough to be able to radiate a crisp sense of professional efficiency. Just pretty enough to be able to flirt a little if that was what the situation required. And that, I thought, was true American style politics, for both men and women. Cover your options. Be prepared to sell sex if you could, but deny that that's what you were doing if anyone called you on it.

In my case, Ann hadn't turned on the charm. At one time, that would have made me paranoid. I'd have worried that I was getting old and losing my appeal. But I've learned that things change when you're in a committed relationship. Somehow, you present a different face to the world. You give off unavailability vibrations that the opposite sex immediately picks up on. Curious, but there it is.

"I suppose I agree," I said. "But in my experience politicians all tend to be the same kind of man. Or woman," I added hastily.

Ann smiled at the gesture.

"Not Lester," she said. "Which is because he's not a politician. He's one of the peope. Basically, he's no different from you and me. Folks can feel that. It's why he's so popular."

Lester Beavans, working class hero.

"Popular?" I said. "I don't believe the people have yet spoken."

Ann leaned back and touched the right corner of her mouth with her forefinger. Under other circumstances, it was probably a very sexy mannerism. She looked at me with amusement of some kind.

"You seem a little jaded, Mr.—"

"Swift. Yeah, I guess I am. It comes with the territory, so they tell me. I'm a reporter."

"For what paper?"

"The *Press*."

"Oh. I don't think I've . . . heard of you."

Now she was doing her real job. There'd be a keen mind at work in her head. Old Les would want that in a frontperson. Any politician would. They were your first line of defense, there to keep away the vultures who wanted to pick at your flesh.

"I'm new to the field. Still trying to catch on. The *Press* has given me some stringer work. If I do good, I get a real job, oh boy. Want to help me get a real job?"

"I don't know," she laughed. "What do I have to do?"

"Just do what you do best."

I gave her a twinkly smile, but she wasn't having any. Ah, well. I took out my pocket spiral notebook.

"They asked me to do a background on Lester Beavans. All

35

you have to do is give me his life story. Dirty little secrets, that sort of thing."

I posed with my pen at the ready, trying to look expectant.

"Who gave you the assignment?" she asked.

"Berwyn Jones. Though I don't think he likes to be called Berwyn."

"Jonesy," she said with some fondness. "No, a Berwyn he is definitely not. A good man. And what does Jonesy wish to find out, Mr. Swift?"

"Call me Loren. Please."

"Like Lorne Greene?"

"If you wish. Different spelling, though. E–N."

"Okay, big fella. I'm Ann Luden, Lester's campaign manager. Fire away."

So. The campaign manager her own self. And a friendly one she was, too. But I still wouldn't want to tangle with her after hours.

"How well do you know the candidate?"

"Pretty well. Our families are both from the northwestern part of the county. They've been friends since forever. When Les needed somebody to handle his campaign, I took the job right off. Keeps me out of trouble, y'know?"

"What's he like in real life?" I made like I was taking newsworthy notes.

"Just about like he'd be if you met him during the campaign, actually. He's not a complex man, Loren. He didn't go to the University," she said in mock reverential tones. "Not that he's unintelligent. In fact, his mind is quick as a rattler. It's just not cluttered with a lot of book learning. Whatever he has, he's worked hard for it. Daddy never gave it to him. You should see him with the back roads folks; they love him. He loves them, too. He really does."

"I hope to see that. But what about his qualifications? To tell you the truth, I don't see any."

She shrugged. "We've had a peanut farmer and an actor for president lately. What are anybody's qualifications?"

"That's beside the point—"

36

"No, it's not. It's the basis of our style of democracy. Anyone who wants to can run for public office. It's up to the people to decide whether or not they can do the job. And if they don't, the people can turn around and pitch them out on their ear."

"But still, for sheriff. You'd expect to find some law enforcement experience there. Dogcatcher, anything."

"Do you know what Ridley Campbell did before he became sheriff?"

Actually, I didn't. Ann looked smug.

"You don't, do you? The answer is, he was in the Marine Corps. But the people have reelected him all the same, without him raising a sweat. I guess there's just no substitute for on-the-job training."

"Well, I don't know Ridley Campbell—"

"It's not important. The point is, if a man has the right characteristics, he measures up to his job."

"Like Ridley Campbell has?"

"Sure, like Ridley Campbell has. I'm not embarrassed to say that Ridley's done a fine load of work for a lot of years. Twelve, if I may be exact. Frankly, that's too long. He's getting stale. It's time for him to move on and let some fresh air in."

"Well, you may be right," I said. "We can all benefit from new ideas."

"You bet I'm right. Lester intends to take an antiquated county sheriff's department and turn it into a modern, efficient police force. And he'll do it, too. As long as the Board of Supervisors backs him up. Which they will."

"That seems to be a pretty touchy issue around here."

"It is. It's the one that'll get Les Beavans elected."

I did some scribbling, trying to decide whether Ann was a true believer or an extremely canny frontperson and nothing more. Or a little of both. I sucked on the butt end of my pen, a leftover habit from my smoking days. Portrait of the thoughtful reporter, working his way up to the tough questions. I wondered if she'd decided it was all an act.

"Okay," I said, "what is Mr. Beavans's political affiliation?"

"That's not relevant. He believes that the sheriff's office should be completely nonpartisan, as a police department would of course be."

"Just thought I'd ask. One always wonders where the money's coming from."

"Beg pardon."

"You know, who's financing the campaign, all that. Your candidate is spending a lot of money for a humble country boy. I know about all that nonpartisan stuff, but somebody has to be footing the bills."

"To the best of my knowledge, Mr. Swift, Lester is paying his own way. Of course, he does get some contributions. As I'm sure you know, by state law he must make public a list of those who give more than a hundred dollars. Which is no problem. Most of the people who support Les are plain folks. They aren't rich. I don't think anyone's kicked in more than two-fifty."

"Could I see a copy of the list?"

"Certainly. Just a moment."

She went to one of the filing cabinets, dug out a single sheet of paper, and handed it to me. It was a list of names and dollar amounts, and it only covered half the page.

"Keep it," she said.

"Thanks."

"No problem. We're honest here. And the press is our best friend."

I looked for some hint that it was a cynical wisecrack and didn't find one. The eyes were detached, but warm. The smile seemed genuine. I reminded myself not to let my suspicious nature get the best of me. I have to do that a lot.

"Well," I said, "I guess the next question is: When can I talk to the candidate?"

"Let me see."

She picked up the phone and punched out a local number, too quickly for me to catch it. I did try, but my P.I. reflexes were still a little rusty. She discussed my request with who-ever was at the other end, then asked me if tomorrow morning would be all right, here at the campaign office. I said fine.

She completed the arrangements. After hanging up, she made a notation on her calendar pad.

"Now," she said, "anything else we can do?"

I got up.

"I guess not," I said.

"Fine. See you tomorrow at ten then."

"Thanks again for your help. I'm looking forward to meeting your boy."

"Before long, he'll be yours, too, Mr. Swift."

I laughed. "Maybe he will. Maybe he will at that."

I spent the next couple of hours at the library. First, I went over the list of campaign contributors. I checked it against the local directory, looking for doctors, lawyers, businessmen —anyone who might have a lot of disposable income. I didn't really have much hope of coming up with anything. True to Ann's word, the biggest contributor was only in for two hundred and fifty dollars. If there was a money man behind the scenes, you wouldn't expect him to show on a list like this.

On the other hand, there might be a big backer who'd put up a small amount of money publicly, especially if he was going to be visibly involved in the campaign. Remote, but possible.

At the bottom of the list was the name Landon Gentry. Though I wouldn't have been able to pick him out of a lineup, I'd seen his name in the papers, off and on. Gentry was on the Albemarle County Board of Supervisors. He'd kicked in a couple of hundred bucks to the Beavans effort.

County supervisor in Albemarle is an elected position. It's also only part-time. But it's important. The county executive, who's full-time and appointed, takes care of the day-to-day implementation of policy. The supervisors make the decisions. They have considerable clout. And, as Ann Luden had pointed out, they would have the final say on the conversion issue.

Okay, so one of the county's top pols was backing the candidate for sheriff. Was there anything wrong with that? No. Was it even odd? No. Considering that Gentry was outspokenly in favor of the county police department, it would have been odd if he *wasn't* solidly pro-Beavans.

I pocketed the list of contributors. It hadn't helped much, but it wasn't a complete washout. If I ran out of leads else-where, I had the names of some people to talk to. Beginning with Supervisor Gentry. His money was riding on Brother Les. Perhaps he'd like to tell me why he thought he'd picked a winner.

The next step was to see what the press had to say. I staked out a microfilm reader and went through a few months' worth of back issues of the local newspapers, both daily and weekly. I read everything that had been written about either Lester Beavans or Ridley Campbell. I didn't find a single thing that I thought would be useful. So it goes. An average exciting day of detective work.

It was early afternoon when I left the library. Warm and sunny. Not much further I could do on the case, so I grabbed a quick lunch and went over to Patricia Ryan's house. She'd be at Hertford and Lee, I knew, the law firm where she works as a legal secretary. But I thought I'd pass a little time with her brother the computer genius. If he'd stoop to see me.

Patrick had his works out when I arrived.

"Hold on a minute, will you, Swift?" he said.

"No wonder you junkies are so sickly," I said. "You never get any sun. In here shooting up on a beautiful summer day. Life's passing you by."

He grinned as he turned the little bottle upside down and jabbed the needle through the rubber cap. The clear liquid was sucked up into the syringe.

"You mind if I don't watch?" I asked.

I looked away. It's not that I'm afraid of needles, exactly. It's just that they always remind me of sitting in an ugly room in Oakland, waiting to be shipped overseas. While I was there, I got shot up more times than I could count. They had vaccines for smallpox, cholera, hepatitis, you name it. None of them gave you a dime's worth of protection against bullets.

"Finished," Patrick announced. He was putting his stuff away. "Reprieved for another day. Good thing I remembered."

Patrick was only half-kidding. He's a brilliant kid when it comes to computers, but he's been known to be irregular about his insulin. You could chalk it up to absent-mindedness, or to the way he gets wrapped up in his computer projects, but I see it more as something else. Patrick is adamant about leading a "normal" life. He doesn't want to admit that he has any special needs, and in his mental image of himself he doesn't, in fact, have any. This can easily lead to missing a shot here and there.

"So what *are* you doing inside this afternoon?" I asked.

"A little of this, a little of that. New job I got. Some saber-metrics on the side."

"Say what?"

"God, you're a computer illiterate, Swift. When are you going to give it up and join the twentieth century?"

"When I decide that it's worth the price of admission."

Patrick was always riding me about that, being computer illiterate. I am, and that's a cardinal sin in his book. Not that I wouldn't admit to a certain fascination with the machines, especially since they've gotten compact enough to fit on the coffee table. Easy to use, too, Patrick says. Perhaps. I'll probably get into them when he convinces me that they really can handicap college football games.

"Come with me," Patrick said wearily, as if he were leading a small kid to the potty.

We went into his bedroom. A low, narrow workspace ran along two of the walls. It held three different microcomputers —an IBM, an Apple, and a North Star—and plenty of associated electronic gadgetry, racks of floppy disks, printers, and so on. Everything was within easy reach of someone in a wheelchair. Patricia had set the room up for him.

Patrick parked himself in front of one of the micros. He selected a floppy disk.

"Now pay attention," he said. "You might learn something by accident. This," holding up the diskette, "is the dude that runs the show. Ye olde operating system." He slotted the disk into its drive and closed the latch. "And so we boot up. This is a review question: What does 'boot up' mean?"

"Turning the machine on," I said.

"Close enough. Actually, you turn it on by giving it electricity, but it won't do anything for you until you activate core memory in the CPU here. That requires an operating system, in this case MS/DOS, which we've now loaded. It translates the programs I write into something the machine can understand. They're located over here." He pointed to a box adjacent to the floppy drive, similar to it but a little bigger and sealed up. "A ten meg hard disk. That means it stores ten million bytes of data. A lot. You need one, though, when you outgrow floppies. Now then . . ."

He went to work. It did look easy. Lines of print appeared on the computer's monitor and Patrick typed in what I presumed were responses. Nothing to it. As long as you hadn't grown up back in the dark ages of pencil and paper.

"Okay," he said, "we're ready. Over on the hard disk we've got my program and the data. Together they make a team. Like you and my darling sister."

"Very funny," I said.

"Only in this case you really can't have one without the other. You write the program, you gather the data, and then you bring the two together. Let them cohabit, as it were. And the result is, ta da: sabermetrics."

"This is where I came in."

"Actually, Swift, you'll be interested in this. Tell me, what is it about baseball that makes it unique and beloved of us all?"

"I think we've discussed this before. The game is the only one that's not played against a clock. It unfolds at its own sweet pace. It takes as long as it takes."

"True, true. But what else?"

"It's the only one where the defensive team has the ball."

"Also true. And?"

"It's played by teams, but all the action results from the performance of a single individual, the hitter."

"Okay. But you're missing the most important thing."

"Which is?"

"Statistics, Swift, statistics. Baseball is the most statistically complex sport ever invented. Think about it. It's not just a matter of points or goals scored and who scored them and who assisted. It's runs, hits, and errors. It's strikeouts and walks. Passed balls, bunts, and sac flies. Batting average and slugging percentage and e.r.a. Stolen bases versus caught stealing. Ratio of homeruns to at bats. And on and on.

"That's data. Tons of it, since people have been keeping detailed records of all this stuff for a hundred years. On top of that, there's the season. One hundred sixty-two games, plus the playoffs and the Series. Taken together, what do these things suggest to you?"

"Migraine headaches."

"Maybe. But how about profit?"

He had me there. I am a betting man.

"All right, Patrick," I said, "is this the long-awaited magical moment when you finally show me how to get the best of my bookie?"

"Could be."

"Don't tease me, kid. Gambling is serious business."

"Swift, you are many things to many people, but you are *not* a serious gambler. If you were, you would have learned the ins and outs of microcomputers years ago."

"That's what this sabrowhoosis is all about, right?"

"In a way. If you can't appreciate it for itself. Sabermetrics is simply the statistical analysis of baseball. It's a whole new ballgame, so to speak."

"Didn't we just agree that they've been keeping this god-awful mess of statistics for years?"

"We did. But no one ever applied statistical methodology to the data before. No one could have. Not without a computer. Oh, you could do primitive stuff. Answer questions like: Who had more career strikeouts, Sandy Koufax or Bob Gibson? But that's nothing. There's no analysis there. It doesn't help you with what you *really* want to know."

"Hmmm," I said. "I think I see. You're talking about prediction."

"For a P.I., you're not so dense at that."

"Thanks. Just what I need in my life, a smartass kid."

He punched my arm.

"Ah, come on, Swift. We still love you. You can't know everything about everything."

"Yeah, yeah. But let's keep it moving here. What's the payoff?"

"Glad you asked. The payoff is that because there are so many games, and because so much data is compiled about each one, we can do very thorough analyses of past performance, both individual and team. From them, we can extrapolate. For example."

Patrick gestured at the terminal screen. For some time now the computer had been waiting patiently to tell us something. In the center of the screen was the word TEAM. Next to it was a little blinking doodad called the cursor, which looked like an electric hyphen. It showed you where you were on the screen, and when you typed it moved, leaving a letter in its place. Patrick typed in BALTIMORE and hit the key marked "Return."

PERFORMANCE, the machine prompted.

OFFENSIVE, Patrick replied.

FIELD.

HOME.

GAME TYPE.

SINGLE.

TIME.

DAY.

"I can cut it off anywhere, you understand, depending on how specific I want to get," Patrick said. "So let's do it here." He typed GO.

There was a longish pause. Then, line by line, a table appeared on the screen. When it was completely filled, the word MORE printed at the bottom. The cursor continued to blink.

"Voilà," Patrick said. "How the Orioles have fared offensively so far this year in single day games played at Memorial Stadium."

I just gawked. It was all there. Number of hits, runs, home-runs, etc. By game and by inning. By day of the week. Following a day game, following a night game, following a double-header. According to opponent. Against lefties, against righties. As much data as you could possibly want.

"Ah, how do you keep track of all this stuff?" I asked. I didn't know what to say.

"The computer does it. I subscribe to a service that sends me a weekly summary of what's gone on in the majors. I update my files from that. You didn't think I entered all this by hand, did you?"

I shrugged. How the hell could I know what he did? Patrick laughed at me, the illiterate.

"There's a network of us," Patrick said. "Sabermetrics freaks. We pool ideas, compare notes. Send information to each other over the phone lines. That's what the modem is for, remember?" He pointed to a little box with a couple of tiny lights on the front marked DC Hayes 1200. "High speed data transmission.

"Some of the people I communicate with write down what they discover and put it out in book form. I think there's even one guy who sells his stuff to ball clubs. For me, it's just a hobby. But if you wanted to turn a profit, well, look here. In single games the day after a night game, Baltimore only averages a run and a half against lefthanders. I'd say that was statistically significant. Now all you have to do is find a lefty who does well against the O's and the next time he pitches in that situation you bet the family farm."

"Wait just a minute here," I said. "What if the Orioles get their run and a half and Boddicker hangs a shutout on the other guys?"

Patrick grinned like a gargoyle. "It's an inexact science," he said.

"Thanks a lot for nothing."

"It's not nothing. It's an edge. You play the percentages, over the long run you make out."

"But in the meantime, I lose the family farm."

"You're really a hopeless case, Swift, you know that? What

do you want? If the outcome of every game were known in advance, then they wouldn't bother to play them. And you wouldn't have anything to bet on."

He pulled out his floppy disk and shut down the infernal machine. Damn kid had an answer for everything.

"You know," I said, "it's a good thing I never make any bets with you. You ever back anything's not a sure winner?"

" 'Course I don't. The rest is for the fools."

"Okay kid," I said. "I surrender. If you can suffer the presence of fools, and never make a losing wager, I believe you will go far in this world. What do you have in the way of cold beer?"

"Right," he said.

He wheeled into the kitchen while I flopped on the living room sofa. A minute later he came out with a couple of Stroh's and iced glasses from the freezer. He was my kind of fellow after all.

It was warm in the Ryans' house—they were by no means wealthy enough to afford central air—but not oppressive. The windows were open and there was good cross-ventilation. A small oscillating fan was going. Still, it was the kind of day when beer tastes as good as it ever does. We sucked it down in silence for a while.

"So," I said, "what were you saying earlier about a new job?"

"Oh yeah," he said enthusiastically. "Got a new job today. You won't believe this, but it was because of that silly article in yesterday's *Press*."

"Sure I believe it. It may have been silly, but it was free advertising. And that's the name of the game."

"I suppose. Anyway, this guy saw it and he called me yesterday morning. Guy by the name of Howard B. Scott. You ever hear of him?"

I shook my head.

"Me neither. He's not one of *the* Scotts, I don't think, the ones who founded Scottsville and own about ten thousand acres around here. Or if he is, it's a different branch of the family. But he is from the area. And he's doing well, far as I

46

can see. He imports Caribbean handicrafts. He spent a lot of time down there, setting it up, but it's to the point now where he can run the whole thing out of an office in Charlottesville. He prefers to live up here, so he does.

"So he calls me up," Patrick went on, "and we make an appointment to meet first thing this morning. By ten I had a job. The man does not fool around."

"What does he want?" I asked.

"Basically, he wants to computerize his operation. You know, keep track of shipments, do accounts payable and receivable, that sort of thing. Like any business. He's completely computer naive, of course, and that's where I come in. I explained to him how it all works. I've got a package in my library that will do more or less what he's after. Some friends of mine and I wrote the programs and we share them. But of course no package will exactly suit anyone's needs. Every business has its own little idiosyncrasies. A lot of people who are getting into computers for the first time don't understand that. They think you just plug the booger in and it goes to work for you."

"I know, you have to customize the package, right?"

"Right. First, I help him select the hardware, the computer that's ideal for his purposes. Then I install the program package. And then I customize the package until it's individually tailored to the requirements of Pan-Caribbean Imports, Incorporated. The end result will be simple to use, but getting it in place is a rather complex process. That's why we computer whizzes charge so much for our time."

"All this and modest, too," I said.

Patrick shrugged. "Why should I be? Today, there are maybe a half-dozen people in Charlottesville who can do what I do, and the demand for the skills is tremendous. Ten years from now there will be hundreds of us, but at the moment we're it. I plan to cash in before the competition floods the market. That's what starting a business is all about, isn't it?"

Yeah, I thought. That's what it's all about, though you couldn't prove it by me. Patrick had talent and he had ambition. I didn't have much of either. He'd start a business and

47

it'd make a million bucks. I never did much better than pay the rent.

Still, I didn't begrudge him his dreams.

"Sounds good to me," I said. "When do you go on the payroll?"

"I already am. Did some preliminary analysis today," Patrick said. "Mr. Scott does not waste time. You know, he and I have similar views on a lot of things. He's been working for himself for a long time, which is what I want to do. He's really quite an interesting guy, traveled a lot, very dynamic, full of ideas. I think you'd like him. Why don't you drop by the office and meet him?"

"Ah, I don't know. Successful people intimidate me."

"C'mon. It'd be good for you. Meet somebody new. Besides which, he could tell you about his business. I'm sure he wouldn't mind, and it might be what you're looking for. There's good money to be made in import/export. You don't need any special qualifications. You can do it out of your home. If you've retired from the detective game, you're eventually gonna have to find something else, Swift. Maybe this is it. What do you say?"

Poor Patrick. He had the best of intentions. But I'm no salesman, never have been. If someone can sell Third World trinkets to the American consumer, fine. I couldn't sell the gift of fire to the clan of the cave bear. Howard B. Scott wouldn't be able to change that.

"I don't know," I said. "I'm busy tomorrow morning."

"That's all right. We'll be out looking at hardware then anyway. Make it after lunch." He gave me the office address.

"We'll see," I said. "If nothing else comes up, I suppose it can't do me any harm."

"Oh, good."

What the hell. It pleased him. My engagement calendar wasn't exactly jammed up. Maybe I'd even do it.

"Now," I said, "how about letting me get outside another couple beers? I need to loosen up some more before your sister gets home."

IT DIDN'T GO ALL THAT BADLY, OF COURSE. IT NEVER DOES WITH
Patricia. She's one of those people who, when you say something, it's understood. Without a lot of haggling over what's
the exact meaning of this or that.

Actually, I was beginning to suspect that what she most
disliked about the detective business was the secrecy. She'd
prodded me to tell her what I was doing for Campbell. I
couldn't, except in the most general of terms. That disappointed her. So I said that if she wanted to know these
things she'd just have to become my partner. It kind of
popped out, jokingly, but after I said it there was an uneasy
silence for a moment.

Then she cocked her head and said, "Hmmm. And what
do you think that would do to your precious male ego, Mr.
Swift?"

I didn't know what to say. I finally mumbled something
about it not being the sort of thing that would be suitable for
her.

That got her going.

"What you really mean," she said, "is that it's an unsuitable job for a woman, don't you?"

Maybe I did, though I wasn't about to admit any such thing. It didn't matter. I had a lecture coming, and I got one. About how men's points of view are unconsciously shaped by a cultural attitude in which women are to be considered second class citizens. About how transforming this attitude should be first priority for all of us. About how the only thing for which I could be held at fault would be an inability to change.

Her points were well-taken, as they usually are. And the damnedest part of it is that when Patricia lectures you, you don't realize it's happening. It feels like a discussion. More than that, it feels as if you're talking about stuff that's been on your mind for years, but that you've never been able to express properly.

Later we made love—long and slow, the way I prefer it— but we didn't spend the night together. It was a night for sleeping alone and pondering the random events that bring people together.

In the morning I had to get up and be at a certain place at a certain time. It felt like I was working again. There was something familiar and comforting about that.

I was still in a good mood at ten o'clock, when I shook Lester Beavans's meaty paw.

He'd been waiting for me, and in the flesh he didn't look that different from his campaign posters. Same pleasant jowly face, same ready smile. He was even wearing that crazy cowboy hat, in his office in the middle of summer. I guess when you're creating an image you've got to stick with it, even if it makes you look like God's original bozo boy.

The one thing that the two-dimensional posters didn't prepare you for was his size. Les was one hefty mother. He had that double nature to him that you often find in very large men. On the one hand, you can see the soft spots, the excess pounds that have settled into place over the years. On the other hand, you realize that this person could still crush you like a box of corn flakes if he took a mind to it.

Then there were his eyes. Hard, black, oddly humorless for

someone who smiled all the time. I'd noticed it in the photos, and I noticed it even more in person. To me, Lester Beavans's eyes said that if you screwed around with him, he would hurt you—and perhaps enjoy doing it.

Don't prejudge, I warned myself. I returned Les's handshake with some gusto, but not enough to turn the ritual into a gripping contest. If we got into one of those, I'd end up with a pouch full of bone chips hanging from my wrist.

"Mr. . . . Swift, is it?" he said. "How you doing?"

"Fine, thanks."

"Ann," he said, turning to her, "how about getting us some coffee? You a coffee man, are you, Swift?"

I nodded and said, "Black, with sugar."

"And take your time, dear. We got to get us in some men talk first."

Ann left the office without saying anything. Despite her official status, she didn't seem offended at being used as a gofer. They probably had a relationship that went back for years, with as many strange twists and turns in it as an ancient folk tale.

I took out a pen and my trusty spiral notebook. Play the role.

Beavans smiled and winked at me. "Fine-looking woman, what do you say?"

"Not my type, I'm afraid, Mr. Beavans."

"Pity. And call me Les, will you?"

"All right, Les."

"Now, what can I do for you? You want my life story, or what?"

I let him carry the ball. Little or no prompting was required. The idea was to get him talking freely, then try to extract the important stuff.

We chitchatted for a while. About his childhood. Growing up in a hollow tucked back into the mountains of northwestern Albemarle County. The changes that had gone down since he was a kid. Those sorts of things.

As we talked, I found that, despite my reason for being there, I was warming up to brother Les. It was hard not to, though I couldn't erase the sight of those two hounds, lying

51

there as if they'd died licking the dirt. Lester Beavans, with his quick smile and aw-shucks manner, was a true good ole boy. These are the boys who, if you mess with their women on Saturday night in a country roadhouse, will kill you in a heartbeat. Just go out to their pickups, pull the pump action 12-gauge off its rack, and blow you away.

Other times, however, the good ole boys are the nicest, friendliest, most helpful people you'd ever want to meet. A lot of them are my neighbors over in the Belmont section of Charlottesville. They migrate to town from the backwoods and dying farms of the South, and they stay on, preserving the values they were raised with.

To me, the good ole boys are a strange paradox. On the plus side, they represent much of what is best about this country. Loyalty to family and friends. The spirit of neighborly cooperation. A willingness to tackle the toughest job without first having to form a committee to study it. But then there's the dark side. The racial and sexual discrimination, the hard drinking and the easy violence, the broken homes and battered children.

I number a few of the good ole boys among my friends, primarily ones with whom I have the war in common. But being a transplanted Northerner, I realize that I can never be truly admitted to the club.

My conversation with the man who would be sheriff drifted closer to the present.

"You married?" I asked.

"Nope."

"Ever been?"

"Yeah, I made the big mistake once."

"Me, too. There don't seem to be much percentage in it."

He laughed. "You ain't lying there. I don't reckon I'll get caught again. There's too many live ones swimming around these days."

At this point Ann rejoined us, bearing coffee. It was easy to see how the guys back in the hollows would love their Lester. But it was hard to imagine that he was Ann's type, never mind her seeming commitment to the campaign. She was a tough, intelligent lady. Nothing simple country about her. Maybe I could use that later on.

"You want to liven up that coffee?" Beavans asked.

"You got any Irish?"

"No sir, none of that foreign stuff here. Just fine American Jack Daniels if you please."

"Sure, go ahead."

"Say when."

He spiked the coffee. A taste for me, considerably more than a taste for himself. With his bulk, he'd be able to handle it and then some.

"Tell me," I said, "is your ex-wife still around?"

"Now what would you want to know about that for?"

There it was. He'd said it in a nice enough way, sure, but behind the question was the inbred suspicion of outsiders, the implied warning not to get too close. Above all else, country folks will survive.

"Family background," I said casually. "You know."

"Yeah," he said after a moment's pause, "Connie's around. Still lives up to Free Union. But I'd prefer you didn't go bothering her, if you don't mind. She's nothing to do with this campaign here."

"Fair enough." I didn't need Les's permission to visit his ex-wife, but I didn't need to let him know that I was going to do it, either. "You have any kids?"

"One boy. Teenager now. Good looking kid." He smiled. This was okay territory. "Helluva ballplayer. Youngest ever to start for Western Albemarle. I think he might make the majors. That'd be nice for my retirement years."

"That's exciting."

He shrugged as if it were nothing. "You never know about these things, do you, Swift? They tear up their shoulders, what do you call it, the rotator cuff, I don't even know what the sumbitch does. When they do, it's all over in a day. I tell you, I ain't counting the money yet."

We drank some coffee. Ann had been busying herself with

the files, but I'd have bet my slender bank account she hadn't missed a word.

"So you've lived here all your life, Les," I said.

"Most of it. I went south for a little while there. To make my fortune, so to speak." He laughed.

"Where's south?"

"Florida. Got tired of winter, you know? Figured I'd see what it was like to be warm all the time. Found out there's no place like home."

"What part of Florida?"

"Boca Raton."

"Fancy. You make your fortune there?"

"Well," he said, "I can't say as I did badly. Went down there as a auto mechanic. Now that might not sound much to you, but it seemed like everyone in Boca had a Cadillac or something. And they paid good American dollars to have me keep them cars running.

"I done other things, too. Down Florida, you realize straight away that there's a lot of old people, with a lot of money, hanging on to their last years. And they're willing to spread that money around if you can do something for them. So I learned enough about sailing I could crew on the weekends. It's not a bad deal. You keep them company and do the little jobs they're too good for. In return, you get free food and drink, and if they get the mood, they throw the cash at you. Wouldn't want to spend my life at it, but I made out okay, like I said."

"Sounds pretty nice to me."

"Yeah, but there's no challenge to it, you understand. It's not like what I'm doing here."

That naturally got us on the subject of his campaign. We chewed on that for a good bit. Beavans had been guarded when discussing his past, but the present was different. Here his considerable enthusiasm came out.

"Why are you qualified to be sheriff?" I asked at one point. "You're primarily a car mechanic, aren't you?"

"Sure, but it don't make no nevermind. I'm qualified because

I know the people of this county. I'm one of them. I know what folks want and I know what they need and I know what they *don't* want. What qualified Ridley Campbell, anyway? That hitch in the Corps?"

"I suppose you have a point."

" 'Course I do. Besides which, everyone knows I stand for a professional county police force. I intend to staff that force with the very best people I can find."

"How can you hope to handle a modern police department?"

"Mr. Swift, when you're talking about staff, you need the trained men, you need the guys who can go out there and keep the peace, who have the knowhow to solve such crimes as we get around here. But at the top you don't need all that fancy cop school stuff. What you need is a leader, you know what I mean? Someone the men will look up to. Someone they're happy to work for. That's what you gotta have at the top or the whole rest of it falls apart. And that's the type of man I am. I can lead. I'll get in the modern equipment, sure enough, but I'll also make damn certain there's loyalty and hard work in my department. The best of the old and the best of the new, that's what I believe in. It's going to make me the next sheriff of this wonderful county, as well as its first chief of police. Depend on it."

What could I say to that? It was a rousing speech. Campaign rhetoric, of course. And spoken in the hope that it would be published in the daily newspaper. Yet there was no denying the man's drive. When he said he'd take the election, there was no doubt in your mind that Campbell was in for a tough fight. Beavans had the smell of a winner.

"Well, I thank you kindly, Les," I said. "As I told Ann, I'm doing this story on spec, so there's no telling when they'll put it in the paper. Or if they will, for that matter. But here's hoping. I need a steady job."

"Glad to oblige," he said. "The free press, that's one of the great things about this country."

"I just hope it's great enough to find a place for me in it."

"Oh, I'm sure you will. And you vote come November, now."

He winked and grinned that grin. We shook hands. I grinned back, couldn't help it. The man's good cheer was contagious, even with someone as politically cynical as myself.

Ann was all smiles, too. We said a round of goodbyes and I left.

It was late morning, warm and sunny. The pedestrian mall was beginning to fill with people. Soon the lunchtime crowd would arrive. Secretaries and lawyers and real estate brokers and local government bureaucrats, all the performers in the business district circus.

I found myself a bench under one of the mall's tasteful shade trees and sat down. Beavans's office was a short block away. I decided to watch for a while. See who came and went.

First to go was Lester himself. He came out about ten minutes after I'd left. He walked among the people, smiling and touching his hat. It looked like he knew everyone. Eventually, I lost sight of him.

I continued to watch the building, but no one else entered or left. About twelve-thirty, Ann emerged. She locked the door that provided access to the second-story office and hung a little sign on the knob. Then she looked purposefully up and down the mall. I was pretty well-concealed by the milling mob, and she didn't spot me. Satisfied, she walked briskly up a side street.

I'd been on the bench for an hour and a half. I was bored. Since I had no concrete plans, I decided to find out what Ann did on her lunch break. I tailed her.

She walked out to Market Street and turned east, never looking back. When it became evident that she was headed for the downtown parking garage, I sprinted back to Clementine, my old VW, which I'd left on the street.

I picked her up as she exited the garage. She was driving a dark Chevy Cavalier. My own wheels are not exactly the most inconspicuous in the world, but she wouldn't know them. I kept Clementine at a discreet distance.

We headed east. Traffic was fairly heavy, as it usually is. Charlottesville's road system was designed to handle about half the number of vehicles that it has to. The congestion thinned a bit after we'd crossed the Rivanna River. We were following U.S. 250, the old route to Richmond that's been replaced by the Interstate. It's amazing, really. A few minutes after leaving the busy city center, you're cruising through rolling farmland, where few of the houses were built after 1900.

I admired the scenery.

About five miles out, Ann stopped. She turned in at a small motel, one of those that makes its living catching the overflow from town during prime tourist season and on football weekends at the University.

Interesting.

I went past the motel a safe distance and turned around. When I got back, Ann's car was parked in front of one of the units. Well short of the motel, I hung a left onto a county road and positioned myself on the shoulder to observe the proceedings. My view was considerably hampered by a stand of tulip poplars, but that's the way I wanted it. I could barely see what was going on; anyone looking back my way would be hard pressed to tell they were being watched.

A couple of minutes later, a gray Ford T'bird parked next to the Chevy. A tall, skinny guy in a blue three-piece suit got out of it. He looked quickly around and hurried into the motel unit.

Well, well. On her lunch hours, or at least on *this* lunch hour, Ann played at hot sheets.

Was that any concern of mine?

I suppose not. My basic belief is that between consenting adults, anything goes. Live and let live. Otherwise, we're apt to end up in the strait-laced cultural nightmare people like Ronald Reagan seem so comfortable with. For real. Most of us, I think, would rather not. I'd rather not.

So Ann bedded some well-dressed fellow instead of scarfing soup and salad. So what?

Well, for one thing, the motel rendezvous probably meant they were doing it on the sly. That there was a wife and maybe some kids involved. Now I'm not keen on sneaky sex, where an innocent party stands to get hurt by it. But again, it's none of my business. Men and women are going to do what they feel compelled to do, and they are going to deal with the consequences in their own way. So be it.

The other thing was that I was on assignment. It was entirely possible that there were people who so coveted Ridley Campbell's office that they'd stooped to killing his pets and threatening his family. If they had, I wanted to help nail them. I didn't care what Ann and Mr. Upwardly Mobile did to each other's bodies. But I did care about what I'd been asked to do. In that context, Ann's lunchtime lustiness might be of use to me. And if by using it the sidewalk became a little safer for Ridley's son, then I'd use it.

I waited.

They took less than an hour. Ann came out first. It was hard to tell at a distance, but I would have said that she looked great. Calm, self-assured, well-exercised. She got into her car and drove off like she was totally on top of things. I let her go. I already knew where to find her.

Her yuppie boyfriend didn't look so terrific. His movements were nervous and jerky. But then, he'd be the one with the wife and kids in my scenario.

People's tawdry little secrets, I thought. The only thing that keeps them secret, especially in a town this size, is that hardly anyone gives a damn. The most cursory investigation by someone who wants to know will generally bring all the scum quickly to the surface.

The lover headed west, back toward Charlottesville, and I followed. He exited at McIntire Road and took that to the new County Office Building. He parked in the lot they covered the old high school football field with. So did I. His parking spot didn't have a name on it. Neither did mine.

If he knew he was being tailed, he didn't let on. His walk picked up some authority as he approached the building. I followed him up to the third floor and halfway down a bright clean corridor before he went through a door. I stopped in front of it, but I already knew what it was going to say.

Albemarle County Board of Supervisors.

I wasn't ready to lay my last dime on it, but I would have placed a sizable wager that I'd been following Landon Gentry, the Beavans campaign contributor.

Well, I thought to myself, there is no time like the present. Not ever. Seize the moment, for it will not come your way again.

Actually, in my present circumstances, I had little choice. That was one of the things about living in an overblown small town. Too many people knew who you were. So, sooner or later, someone among the people I'd be talking to would recognize me. They'd know that I was a former P.I. and that I might well still be one. My "cover," such as it was, would forever after be suspect, and my investigation would be hampered.

I went into the supervisors' office.

It was a small one, with a number of doors leading off it. One of them was marked "County Executive," the others were unidentified. The man I was following wasn't in the outer office, but a secretary was. Betty Anders, by the nameplate on her desk. She had blond hair that was teased and sprayed until the north wind wouldn't ruffle it. She also had a highly reflective smile which she turned on me without warning.

"May I help you?"

"Yes, is Supervisor Gentry in?"

"The supervisors don't keep regular business hours."

"Yes, I know that. But I saw Mr. Gentry outside. I thought he might have stopped into the office for something."

"Who may I say is inquiring?"

"My name is Swift. I'm a newspaperman."

"Oh. Well, I have our press releases here somewhere. . . ." She rummaged in her desk, didn't come up with anything.

"Please, Ms. Anders," I said, "don't bother. We have all of that stuff. I'm not really interested in position papers, anyway.

It's the human angle I'm after. A personal interview, if I might. What our public servants are really like, that sort of thing, you know? Do you suppose the supervisor could spare me just a few minutes?"

"Well . . . I'll see." She picked up the phone and punched two numbers. It *was* Gentry. She repeated my lies to her boss. A twice-told tale becomes the truth, doesn't it? Something like that. She hung up.

"Supervisor Gentry will see you if you can keep it under fifteen minutes," she said, gesturing at one of the unmarked inner doors.

"Thank you much, Ms. Anders. You've been most helpful. I'll not run overtime."

She nodded and busied herself with something or other. Didn't flirt with me even a little, and me a rising media star. I pushed through the door.

Gentry was seated behind a fake oak desk, scribbling furiously, looking official. They cultivate that look, politicians. I think they may practice it in front of their mirrors after slapping on the Aqua Velva.

When he'd finished writing, he stood up, flashed a quick official smile, and shook my hand. He was about four inches taller than my five-ten, but a lot skinnier. He couldn't go more than one-fifty, a good twenty pounds less than me. In his early thirties, clean shaven, brown hair a politically acceptable length. An angular, unremarkable face. And he was a nervous man. One of those types who are always fiddling with a pencil or jiggling their foot up and down. He had a tic under his left eye that fired away every now and again. He was very fortunate that someone like Ann looked more than once in his general direction. Maybe she did it because she'd been asked to.

"Mr., ah, Swift, did she say?"

"Loren Swift, yes." I bowed slightly and we sat down.

"That's a nasty case of the sniffles you've got there," I said.

"Damned summer cold. I just can't seem to shake it. It may be an allergy, but I've never looked into it." His speech was herky-jerky, too, like his gestures. "I don't suppose you want to talk about the state of my sinuses, though. Who is it that you work for?"

"I'm free-lancing at the moment. The *Press* is going to take me on if I can produce some decent stringer work."

"That's nice, but there aren't many lively stories out of this office."

"No juicy scandals? Not even a little innuendo?"

"I'm afraid not."

"A political office without a story. That's hard to believe. Sort of like Ed Meese without food."

He laughed in the manner of someone who never finds anything very amusing.

"How about Lester Beavans, then?" I asked quickly.

If the question had caught him off guard, he didn't show it. At least I don't think he did. With his level of nervous energy, it would have been hard to tell.

"What about Lester Beavans?" he repeated back.

"Friend of yours?"

"I know him."

"He's the one I'm doing the story on, Supervisor. His campaign manager gave me a list of his contributors. It's a modest list. Your name's on it."

He snuffled and cleared his throat. "Yes, I gave a few bucks. I'd like to see him sheriff."

"Why?"

"Because he's the right man for the job. Ridley Campbell's a dinosaur, Mr. Swift. He still thinks sheriffs ride on horseback and rescue damsels in distress. Lester's for a modern, efficient police force, which is exactly what this county needs. He's got my vote, and I don't mind committing a little of my money as well."

And if you're getting laid out of the deal, so much the better, I thought.

"What about his lack of experience?" I said instead.

"I don't think it will matter. The man's a leader, that's what counts. I feel that a real man grows into his responsibilities. Lester Beavans will do just fine."

Gentry appeared to be as much of a believer as Ann or the

61

man himself. Hell, maybe Les *was* perfect for the job. Maybe Campbell was only reacting to a couple of coincidences and the threat of his first strong opponent in years. But then there were his dogs. They weren't playing dead.

"Anything else about Beavans that you think the public ought to know?" I asked.

"Let's see," he said. "Well, you know that he's divorced, right? There's a lot would've forgotten their duty under those circumstances. Lester Beavans is not one of them. That boy of his has never wanted for anything. Even when Les was living out of state, he kept those child support checks coming. The man is solid, Mr. Swift. I wouldn't hesitate to depend on him."

I got up.

"Thank you, Mr. Supervisor," I said. "You've been most generous with your time."

"You can thank me by giving Lester your vote in November," he said.

"Sorry," I said, "but I live in the city. I'm not eligible."

"Oh well, tell your friends. Goodday, Mr. Swift."

On the way out, Betty Anders looked up. I smiled at her, but she was already looking back down.

The downtown mall is only a couple of blocks from the County Office Building, so I strolled over and filled my belly at the imitation European sidewalk café. I watched the girls in their summer dresses. It was more pleasant than watching Beavans's campaign HQ had been. If only you could do it for a living.

After lunch, I made a couple of phone calls.

The first was to Sheriff Campbell. I told him I had nothing to report. He told me he had nothing new to tell me. A very stimulating conversation.

Then I called Jonesy. We discussed the recent escalation in beer prices before getting down to business.

"What do you know about Landon Gentry?" I asked.

"You ready to tell me what you're really working on?"

"It's a story. Honest, Uncle Jones."

"I didn't think you were. Okay, but I've still got a functioning half-brain, you know. First you ask me about Lester Beavans and then about Landon Gentry. I'm going to have to assume a connection."

"The one contributes to the other's campaign fund," I said. "It's in the public record."

"Really. I didn't know that. Not that it makes me feel a Woodstein attack coming on. Should it?"

"How would I know, Jonesy?"

"I take it we're not talking about big bucks here."

"Two hundred is big bucks to some people."

"It's also very legal. I'm bored, Swift."

"Find a nice hobby. Writing novels, maybe. Look, can we skip the idle speculation?"

"Okay, okay. Landon Gentry. Highly successful real estate broker in the county. Ran for the Board of Supervisors six years ago. Got elected on his first try. Spent a fair amount of change to do it. Politically conservative, aren't they all? Rather a nondescript fellow, I'd say. If he's involved in kiddie porn or something, I'd be very surprised."

"He clean?"

"Come off it, Swift. Nobody's completely clean around here. You know that. The guy doesn't have any major scandals in the closet that I know of, but he's a politician, and he trades in land. Someone like that, there's bound to have been a questionable deal or two somewhere. It all depends on your point of view. The man who said, 'I am not a crook,' he really meant it. According to *his* belief system, he hadn't done anything wrong."

"Gentry says he's backing Beavans because of the county police force thing. That consistent?"

"Sure. Landon's a tough law-and-order man. He wants a bigger and better cop force. You find that a lot with guys who deal real estate. Private property's their bread and butter. They often think you need an army of goons to protect it."

"He a paranoid type?"

"Maybe some."

63

"I met him today," I said. "He's a nervous mother."

"I know what you mean. And it's getting worse. Politics will do that to you, though."

"Okay, how about his private life? He got a family?"

"Wife. Two kids. Nice people."

"He screw around?"

"It's said that he, ah, fancies the ladies. Most of them do. They think it's one of the perks that goes with elective office. I don't know who he's seeing at the moment, if anyone. Furthermore, I could care less. If you're building me up to some five-and-dime story about a supervisor who cheats on his wife, I'll kick your butt, Swift."

"Not to worry. Thanks, Jonesy."

"Not to worry yourself. It goes on the tab."

"I'll see you after the O's catch the Tigers."

"Agghh, don't remind me."

It was getting late in the day. I'd done some sniffing around, and I'd come up with nothing more than a philandering politician, if that's not redundant. No news at all, as Jonesy had pointed out. I didn't feel like pursuing the issue any further right now.

That was a change. It used to be that when I was on a case, I'd worry it night and day until I either resolved it or determined that it was beyond resolution. It wasn't like that anymore. And I knew it wouldn't be like that even if I got back into detecting full time. There was just more to life. Maybe I'd finally discovered that I was a workaholic and that it wasn't worth it in the long run.

I decided to visit Patrick at his new job. I'd more or less promised him that I would, in exchange for the free beer. It wouldn't do me any harm to meet the jolly trinket man. Besides, it provided an opportunity to knock off work without feeling at all guilty.

The address Patrick had given me was on Rose Hill Drive, a quiet street away from both downtown and the University. It turned out to be a small, two-story brick office building. There was a dentist in there, an insurance agent, an advertising consultant, a few others. Tucked away in a second floor corner was Pan-Caribbean Imports, Inc.

Patrick was in the outer office area. Hunched over a micro-computer, of course.

"Swift," he said. "The man keeps his promises."

"What, are you the secretary, too?"

The area had a couch, some chairs, a table with a coffee maker on it, a workstation for the computer, some filing cabinets. But no desk with a smiling receptionist behind it.

"Nah. Mr. Scott doesn't need one," Patrick said. "This isn't the kind of business where you get a lot of walk-in trade."

I pointed to the coffee maker.

"May I?"

"Sure."

I helped myself to a cup and sat on the couch.

"So, how's it going?" I said.

"Great. We picked out the computer this morning and loaded up on general software. He already had the work-station set up. I just moved in. I'm already well into the customization."

"Massa's in there?" I nodded toward a solid-looking wood door. It didn't say, "Office of the President," or anything like that on it.

"C'mon Swift, cool it, will you? There's no need to be hostile just because someone does something different from you."

"All right, I'll behave. Promise."

"Good. Mr. Scott's got one of his field men in there right now. They probably won't be too long. I've told him all about you, and he's interested in meeting you. I tell you, he's a comer, Swift. He is not at all a bad person for you to get to know."

"Hey, I'm here, aren't I? Don't go planning out my future for me, kid."

"Fair enough. So . . . what have you been doing all day?"

"Working on this thing that I can't tell you what it's about."

"Any luck?"

"Maybe, I don't know. I found out that there are still people who sneak off to motels on their lunch hour."

"You don't say."

"Tell me I shouldn't be surprised."

"C'mon Swift, what'd you think, there was a sexual revolution going on in this country? Oops, I forgot. You're one of that sixties generation; you *do* think that. Sorry, old pal. We young folks are a little more up to date. People still get married, you and my sister notwithstanding, and guys still cheat on their wives. It's always gonna be that way."

"That sounds like one of my lines."

He grinned. "Ah, you know I'm not a cynic; cynics don't start businesses. But I *am* a realist. People your age, they had a lot of grandiose ideas about 'relationships' and all that. Ideas that didn't work out. Sooner or later, you're going to have to face up to that fact."

"I'm only ten years older than you," I pointed out.

"These days, that's a very long time. Besides, you were a teenager in the sixties. It warped you. That and the war, of course."

"The war changed my life. I can't help that. It changed everyone's."

"Not mine. I was about two years old when Johnson sent in the troops. When Nixon resigned, I wasn't even in high school yet. It meant nothing to me."

I felt depressed.

"You're right," I said. "Ten years *is* a long time."

"Cheer up, grandpa. For someone who's lived through all the crap you have, you didn't turn out half-bad. I haven't approved of all of Patricia's boyfriends, you know."

"God, I give up. It's a good thing I don't have to live with you, Patrick. I wouldn't take this abuse on a daily basis. I'd smack you, wheelchair or no wheelchair."

He laughed. "You and who else?"

Come to think of it, maybe I wouldn't smack him. His legs might be useless, but his upper body was heavily muscled and fit. He worked out. A lot more regularly than I did.

The big door opened and two men came into the anteroom.

66

The second of them was medium height, five-eight or -nine. Stocky. Dressed in a beautifully tailored white linen summer suit. He'd be the boss. Mr. Howard B. Scott.

It was the other man, his field representative, who really caught my eye. He was about the same height, but with a lean, wiry build. You just knew that when he took off his shirt you'd see a lot of corded muscles and veins like ropes. He was obviously Latin American, right down to the brilliantined black hair and pencil mustache. He was wearing an electric green polyester leisure suit that he probably thought represented the pinnacle of fashion.

None of this was important, though. What was, was the sense of recognition that passed between us. I hadn't experienced it much since I'd moved out of the big city, but in an urban environment you develop that sixth sense or you get into very big trouble very fast. And you never lose it. It's the best early warning system you have. Sometimes it's all you have.

What it was now telling me was that this Latino dude was a heavy. Not some district sales rep. A pro. Mr. Fix-It. Hired muscle. Maybe with some brains attached, but muscle all the same. And what his sixth sense was effectively informing him was that I was a cop. Private or not, it didn't matter. Cop is cop.

"Mr. Scott," Patrick said, "this is my friend Loren Swift that I told you about. Swift, Howard Scott. And Mr. Martinez."

We shook hands all around. Martinez's was heavy with jeweled gold rings. It was also greasy. I refrained from wiping my own on my pants.

"Virgilio," Scott said, "call me Thursday, okay?" When he talked to Martinez, it was with a slight accent, as if they were used to speaking Spanish together.

"Virgilio Martinez," I said. "Watergate, right?"

Martinez laughed. I'll be damned if he didn't have a gold front tooth.

"No, no," he said. "That was Virgilio Gonzalez. And he was Cubano."

He didn't volunteer what *he* was.

"I call you, Mr. Scott," he said, and he left.

"Will you have some coffee, Mr. Swift?" Scott said.

"Thanks, I already have."

"Well, come into my office, then. I've been looking forward to meeting you. Young Patrick has told me so much about you."

"Only the good stuff, I hope."

"Of course. Come in, come in."

He ushered me through the door with one of those hand-in-the-small-of-your-back gestures. I could see why Patrick was taken with the man. He radiated a sense of controlled energy, of purpose. He was dynamic and he was rather charming. I had no doubt that I'd find he had a superior mind as well. Definitely Patrick's type of person. But I wasn't sure he'd turn out to be my type. It was exceedingly difficult to imagine him in a torn T-shirt, sucking on a cold Stroh's, caught up in the shifting rhythms of a classic Virginia/Carolina basketball contest.

His office was spare. There was a nice real oak desk. Some more filing cabinets. There were a few tropical-looking plants that I didn't recognize and some framed photos on the walls. Ocean sunsets, beach scenes, that sort of thing. Not the ones you get at K-Mart, that come with the frames you buy. Real ones. 11 × 14s and 16 × 20s. By some pretty fair photographers, to my eye.

Scott had a comfy executive chair for himself. It was leather, it tilted and swivelled, and I guessed that it would have some of those electric fingers inside. His visitors made do with straightback chairs that were simple but probably hideously expensive.

The boss was a man in his middle thirties. A little bulky, but looked to be in pretty good shape. Likely belonged to the town's top health club. He was clean-shaven and his hair was dark and conservatively cut. Dark eyes, too, and deep-set, somewhat mysterious in a nonthreatening way. A full round face, well-fleshed without being at all pouchy or jowly. You would never describe him as a good-looking man, but he did have that contagious energy. I could see him putting together a business deal. I could see a client coming in with a healthy wariness and leaving with a flush of optimism about what had just been agreed to.

We settled ourselves on either side of the desk.

"Who's the hired muscle?" I asked casually.

Scott laughed with what seemed like genuine good humor.

"You mean Virgilio, I take it. I assure you he'd be most offended by your characterization."

Either he was an honest man or he'd noticed that Martinez and I had instantly typed one another, in which case he was very sharp indeed. Since I had no reason to think otherwise, I assumed the former.

"He hasn't had an easy life," Scott went on. "His family had to leave Nicaragua with, shall we say, some haste. They arrived in Miami with a few hundred cordobas to their name. Under the circumstances, he's done extremely well, in my opinion. He's bright, and he's loyal. I employ him to help protect my interests."

"That's what you call a field rep?"

"Mr. Swift, am I on trial here?"

I was being an ass and I knew it. If the man wanted to hire Somocistas, that was entirely on his own head.

"I'm sorry. Patrick's told you what I do . . . what I used to do for a living?"

"Yes."

"You get into habits. You tend to turn conversations into interrogations. It doesn't mean anything."

"Perhaps it's time to make a career change."

"I've thought the same thing myself. As have some other people in my life."

"Good," he said. "Maybe I can tell you a little about the import/export business. I think it's an exciting one.

"We can start with Virgilio. You need someone like him, for security. He's a man not unlike yourself. I pay him to keep me secure, much as I might hire you to do the same thing. Of course, that's not all he does; 'field representative' is more than a mere euphemism, I assure you. But security is his primary function.

69

"You see, it's a very complex issue, especially when you're dealing with the Third World, as I do all the time. There's the matter of protecting your sources, for example. Third World people are very malleable, by our standards. A competitor of mine could move in on my suppliers, promise them the moon, and steal them away from me in a flash. I like to feel that I pay a fair price, and I wouldn't like to see that happen. Especially since the fly-by-nighters are often simply thieves. Virgilio helps me in this area. He speaks the language natively, of course, and so is much more effective than I could ever be.

"Then, too, there's the matter of personal security. Let's face it, as an American businessman moving about in the Third World, I'm a target. An inviting one. I'm fair game to everyone from common street criminals to revolutionary anti-capitalists. I believe in what I'm doing and I believe in my right to do it freely, but that doesn't mean I'm going to play it loose with my personal safety. I sleep a lot more soundly in the tropics knowing that I've got Mr. Martinez on my side.

"Does that clarify things a little?"

"Yes, it does," I said. "How did you get started in all this?"

"I got into the trade the way I guess most people get into things, by accident. I was down in Miami Beach, selling yachts for someone else. One winter I took a vacation trip to Haiti. While I was there, I bought one of these."

He pointed to a small cloth and hair doll that was sitting on his desk.

"I was wondering what that was," I said.

"That," Scott said, "is Pan-Caribbean Imports, in a manner of speaking. It's a voodoo doll, the very one that I bought on that first trip. I put it on my desk when I got back and one of my customers noticed it. He owned a string of gift shops and told me he thought an item like that would sell. He wanted to know where I got it. The rest, as they say, is history. One thing led to another and pretty soon I was supplying shops all over the South. Would you believe I've sold over two hundred thousand of these things? Authentic Haitian voodoo dolls. I wholesale them for four bucks. In Port-Au-Prince they cost me twenty-seven cents."

"That's a tidy profit."

"It is. Of course, I could just as easily have bombed. I'm a risk capitalist, Mr. Swift, and I love it. The American system offers an enterprising man the highest rewards in the history of the world. If he's willing to take some chances. Personally, I find the element of risk tremendously exhilarating."

"You appear to have taken a lot of the right ones."

"I guess I've done pretty well for a poor kid from backwoods Albemarle County. The voodoo dolls really got me going. They provided the seed money for company growth and diversification. I reinvested my profits and"—he gestured expansively—"well, today I'm tapped into markets all over the Caribbean and Latin America. I have a very smoothly running organization. That's how come I can operate the whole thing out of my hometown now."

"And travel when you want to."

"Yes. I still enjoy that aspect of it."

"Sounds pretty nice to me," I said. "I work for myself, too, but the business is not what you'd call booming."

"There's always room to expand for someone with intelligence and ambition," he said. "And the proper philosophy."

The way he said it, I got an eerie feeling, as if I were being probed for my openness to a job offer. I couldn't imagine why. I certainly wasn't ready. The buying and selling of goods for a living has never appealed to me, as I've said, no matter how much free travel you throw in. Then there was Scott himself. He was unquestionably a magnetic person, and no doubt a maker of profits. He was also an arrogant bastard, and he waved the flag of free enterprise and the American Way a little too vigorously for my taste. Now, I'm not an unpatriotic person. I like living in this country. I served in the army and all that. But your heavy duty flagwavers always put me off a bit. They make me feel like they're trying to convert me to something.

"I'm a little short on ambition," I said to change the tack. "And there are those who do not love me for my mind."

"A positive attitude works wonders," he said.

Yeah, yeah, I thought. And you can teach me all about it,

Norman Vincent. Right? Then I stopped myself. It wasn't fair to put the guy down for that. He apparently lived his principles, and they worked for him. Who was I to judge?

"You've probably got a point," I said. "Mine could use some improvement. I'll work on it."

"Good idea," he said. "It can't hurt. Meanwhile, what are you doing? Are you looking for a job?"

There it was again, in his tone of voice. The vague hint that he might be able to do something for me. If only I were more of a risk taker? Who the hell knew?

"Not exactly," I said. "But one of the things I've been thinking of going into is writing. I used to do some in school. A friend of mine works for the *Daily Press* and he asked me to write up a couple of stories on spec. If I do good, they'll consider throwing more things my way. It's a possibility." The lies rolled off my tongue before I really thought about what I was saying. It happens that way now and then. Perhaps it was a sign that I'd do well as, say, an investigative reporter.

"Sorry I can't help you there, but that's great. I certainly wish you luck with your journalistic career. It's an interesting field. And an important one."

"Maybe in Washington it is. But around here . . . Well, I don't want to take any more of your time, Mr. Scott. Patrick was right, I've enjoyed meeting you."

We got up and shook hands again.

"My pleasure, Mr. Swift," he said.

"Take good care of the kid, will you?"

"I don't think he requires much taking care of. He's a remarkable boy."

"He is that. Just be careful he doesn't wisecrack you to death."

"Consider me warned. And think on what I said, Mr. Swift. A man who's willing to take risks can go far in this world."

One last time. The open-ended invitation.

"I'll think about it."

"Good. Perhaps we'll meet again."

He said it as though he fully expected it.

"Yes, perhaps."

I let myself out. The heavy door closed behind me.

"Well?" Patrick asked.

"Interesting fellow," I said.

"Did he offer you a job?"

"Not exactly. But then, I'm not exactly seeking employment."

"Don't sell it short. There are a lot of interesting things to do with your life."

"Here we go. Kid lectures me on life's possibilities, now. I think I just remembered a very important appointment."

"Wait a minute—"

"See you later, kid. Don't buy any second-hand voodoo dolls."

Back home, Mrs. Detweiler was in her accustomed spot in the late afternoon sun.

"Mrs. D.," I said. "I just spent a very entertaining half hour with a bona fide pig capitalist. You shoulda been there."

"Ach, Swift, what you want to spoil an old woman's day for?"

"No, seriously, you would have loved it. A genuine exploiter of the Third World. Right here in our own Charlottesville."

She spat. She spat with such a studied disgust that it was a beautiful piece of theater. I'd have paid money if it weren't free.

"What's he do," she said, "run guns to the Guatemalan government?"

"Nothing quite so exciting," I said. "He buys native trinkets for cheap and sells them for dear."

"Even worse. I'll bet he told you he was helping upgrade a struggling nation's economy."

"Actually, he didn't, but it's only because we never got on the subject. I'm certain he feels that way."

"Don't believe a word of it. You can be sure that the money isn't going into the native artisan's pocket. It's the American capitalists who're getting rich, them and the corrupt local officials they've bought off. The bosses and the cops, Swift, it's always the bosses and the cops.

"And it isn't as if I haven't tried to tell people. But they just won't listen! Did I ever show you this?"

She pointed to the top of her head. There was a long scar up there. She'd acquired it during a labor demonstration in nineteen thirty-something.

"Yes, you've shown me before, Mrs. Detweiler."

"Miserable scabs," she muttered.

"I thought a cop gave that to you."

"Cops, scabs. What's the difference!?"

"I don't know. I've never met any scabs."

"When they start swinging their clubs, you don't ask who's on the other end. You get out of their way, if you've got any sense."

"Sounds like good advice," I said. "Looks as if you weren't quick enough that one time, though."

"Ach, we were tough in those days, it doesn't matter. The only thing that matters is the people. You mark my words, young Swift, some day the masses are going to have their say. And when they do, watch out."

"I will. When'd you say the revolution was, Mrs. D.?"

"The boy is hopeless. I treat him like my own son, he's hopeless. Get away with you, you're just trying to raise an old woman's blood pressure."

I gave her a big smile and walked down to my apartment. Mrs. Detweiler and I might not agree on everything, but there was no denying her basic humanity and the intensity of her commitment. I liked that.

It was a solitary kind of evening. I spent it with some Jameson and Travis McGee and Meyer in the Yucatan. I didn't see Patricia. It seemed like a good time to give our relationship a little breathing room. Since she didn't call, she probably agreed.

A quiet night, and yet there was something in the air, a steadily tightening screw of tension. I could feel it, as if a large invisible bear was beginning to give me the final squeeze.

I tried to ignore it, but as the hours passed it got worse. What? I went over the events of the past couple of days. Campbell and Beavans, Ann and Supervisor Gentry. I was on

74

a case, but still. Nothing I'd discovered should be provoking anxiety.

Was it the old occasionally reliable sixth sense sending a message? If so, what might the message be?

Toward ten I couldn't take it any longer. I put Travis down and went outside to smoke an imaginary cigarette. It's been years since I had a real one, but some of the associated habits are a long time in dying.

I stood out in the still night air. Then I heard it, far off. The first dull rumble of thunder. We hadn't had an electrical storm for so long that my body must have been finely tuned to the preliminary change in atmospheric pressure. Well, we could use the rain.

I chided myself for having momentarily given in to the nameless anxieties that came with the profession I was technically no longer engaged in. It was only a storm on the way. Relief for me. Relief for the parched red Virginia clay and the stubborn people who farmed it. I went to bed. I was awake when the first sheets of water hit the window, but I slept through most of the ensuing violence.

5

I PICKED UP THE PHONE BEFORE THE TENTH RING, I'M SURE. OR
somewhere in there. My head was a little fuzzy from perhaps
one too many fingers of Jameson, and I was sweating furiously.
I'd been dreaming about the Yucatan. I was trapped at the
bottom of a pit, and crazed Maya Indians three times my
size were throwing huge boulders down at me. Under the circumstances, I should have been grateful for the interruption.

I didn't let it show.

"Yeah," I said.

"You sound great, Swift. You always this alert first thing in
the morning?"

"Jonesy, what in the hell time is it?"

"Eight. Isn't that when we were supposed to place the
wake-up call?"

"Sure, sure. What's up?"

"You gonna remember this?"

"I'll try. What's 'this'?"

"Look, I've got to go out of town for the morning is why
I'm calling you at this lovely hour. Workingman, you know.

But I thought you'd want to hear it if you were still on Les Beavans's tail."

"It's possible. What you got, Jones?"

"Well, I turned up a guy you might want to talk to. He lives right in your neighborhood." He gave me a nearby Belmont address. "Guy by the name of Dewey Morris. He was Albemarle County Sheriff before Campbell."

"He knows Beavans?"

"That he does. It would appear that Mr. Morris and Lester are not exactly tit buddies, to say the least. I believe they had a run-in or something a few years back. When I told him I had a man doing up a story on old Les, Morris said, 'Send him over, I'll give him a story.' Think you can handle it, Scoop?"

"Sure. I love cops, as long as they've had their shields clipped."

"If it's news, let me know what he's got to say, okay? I've got to run, now."

"I will."

"That's two cases of Moosehead, pal."

"If it pans out. One for the legwork if it doesn't."

"Swift, you're a hardass."

I waited until nine, then gave Dewey Morris a call. He said to come over for coffee at ten.

It was another warm day, cloudless after the night's hasty soaking. The mimosas were all still in bloom along my street, their pink and white flowers like feathers. I'd had a solid breakfast and I was enjoying the day. The rock-hurling Mayas couldn't touch me here.

I got to the Morris house in under five minutes. It was a small white frame number, pre–World War II, in the state of preliminary decay you often see in Belmont. A house I knew I'd feel at home in.

As I did. Dewey Morris answered the door and immediately led me into the kitchen and sat me down at a gray wooden table. Partly gray, actually. The top coat of paint was peeling away to reveal a layer of white beneath it. I wondered how many times its color had changed over the years, and what had made someone want to cover up a nice chunk of maple, or whatever it was, in the first place.

"There you are, Mr. Swift," Morris said, putting a king-size mug of coffee in front of me. We quickly got ourselves on a first name basis. I looked him over.

He was maybe sixty and well-preserved. Tall, lean in a way that made you suspect he hadn't always been. He had the feel of a man who'd carried a lot more muscle in his younger years and had never run to fat, had merely dropped the weight as it became a burden to him. All that remained now was the gristle and sinew. He was a good-looking man, in the sharp-featured Appalachian tradition. It didn't hurt that he still had a full head of thick white hair, either. Well, maybe it hurt *me* a little, as I touched my thinning crown, but that wasn't his fault.

We chatted for a bit: the drought, how it was going to affect the summer's crops, how we couldn't imagine farmers hanging on these days, that sort of thing. Virginians are a leisurely people. If you get to the point too soon, they think it's rude. It probably is.

After a decent interval, I gave him the struggling reporter cover story and asked him how long he'd known Lester Beavans.

"You gonna put this in the paper, are you?"

"That depends," I said. "Do you have something to tell me that you *don't* want to see in there?"

"Hell, no," he said.

"In that case, I'll do my best. If they decide to print it, then they will. You never know, though. Newspapers some-times go a little easy on public figures."

He snorted. "Not so's I've noticed."

"Probably not. But in the past few years, things have changed. Nowadays, everyone's terrified of lawsuits. We've got a huge surplus of lawyers out there and they've got to scratch up business somehow. Otherwise people would get the idea they're unnecessary. So libel suits are way up."

He snorted again. "Lawyers! I never had much use for 'em myself."

"Me neither. Unfortunately, they put the fear of God into editors. But tell me about the candidate for sheriff."

"And believe me, I hope he stays that way. Let him run all he want, just don't let him win."

"You don't care for the man."

"Hah! That don't say it at all."

"Well, let's start at the beginning, if we could. How long have you known him?"

"Oh, Lester and me go back a ways. About, let's see, must be close to twenty year now. He was only a kid then, you understand. Taking cars for joy rides, small stuff. I chased him a few times, back in the county. He loved a chase, but we all did as kids, huh? There wasn't that much to it. That was all before he went . . . mean."

"He went mean? Why?"

"Can't say. It happens to some, you know? Happened to Lester around when he got twenty. He knocked up that Shifflett girl, then married her. That changes a man, sometimes. You run crazy and free when you're a teenager and all of a sudden you're a adult with a load of responsibility. Babies and whatnot. There's those can't handle it, right from the gitgo."

"Lester Beavans among them?"

He nodded. "Or either, *some*thing done it to him," he said. He wasn't really looking at me anymore. "You know, you take a lot of your big men, like Lester, they're just as peaceable as can be. It's like they know what they can do to you, so they don't have to go proving it all the time. Which is good for us. Because there's always some damn fool thinks he's got to challenge him. Show off for his girlfriend and whatnot. Most of the time, luckily, the fool will realize he's made a mistake and back off. Or the big man will ignore him, or convince him that it ain't worth fighting about, whatever it is. Once in a great while, the fool won't know when to quit. In that case, the big man will be obliged to put him quietly to sleep with one punch. And that's the end to it.

"Then you got boys like Lester Beavans."

"He's different?"

Morris rested his elbows on the table and leaned in toward me. His eyes were bright with . . . I don't know what with.

"Swift, he's a bad one. Now I suppose you can't print that in your paper. But it's the truth. That boy is just plain bad."

"He seemed pleasant enough to me," I said.

"Sure he did, what you expect? That's his act, old buddy-buddy to ever'one. But I know better."

"You have a run-in with him?"

"More than one. But just let me tell you about the one." He was into it now. Whatever he had to say, he believed it and he wanted me to believe it. His eyes glistened as he reconstructed the past.

"It's been fifteen year now," he said. "Somewhere in there. But I remember it like it were yesterday.

"I had to go to the hospital to take the boy's statement. Collie Green. Not a nice fella himself, you understand. We'd been around some times, me and him. Bar fights, the usual. Collie was a hellraiser. Loved to scrap. Night he got into it with Lester Beavans was his last fight ever.

"You wouldn't believe what I seen in that bed. I didn't believe it myself. Let me tell you, I was a good bit bigger in them days as I am now. But I couldn't've did that kind of damage. Lester like to broke ever' bone in that boy's body, and I mean *ever'* one. It were way beyond settling an argument. Just looking at him, you could tell, this boy been worked over by someone en*joyed* what he was doing. Collie never did walk right again, not to this day."

"Beavans do any time?" I asked.

He shook his head wearily. "You know how it is. Any bar fight, ever'one involved has forty-eleven of his buddies to swear the other guy started it. You end up with one guy's word against another's and that's nothing. Besides which, Collie Green wasn't about to testify. The experience put the true fear to him for all time. He come up a deacon in the Evangelical Baptist Church, if I'm not mistook."

"And Beavans walked."

"Yeah, he walked. Now, you tell me. Is that the kind of man ought to be sheriff?"

"It don't sound like it."

"You gonna print the truth on him?"

"I honestly can't say, Dewey. I'll write it, but it's the paper decides what goes into print." I felt like a heel. That can happen when you assume identities other than your own. Among other times. "You're right, though. The public deserves to know what sort of man they're voting for."

Well, at least I could see that Jonesy got the story. He'd probably do something with it.

"What happened to Beavans after the incident with Green?" I asked.

"Well, it weren't in the papers or nothing, but the story got around some. Didn't nobody pick a fight with him after that. Them hill people, they probably thought *more* of him after he done it. Lester, he stayed out of any big trouble, far as I know. The people retired me from my job. That's when Ridley Campbell first got voted in. Then the boy drifted down south someplace. I lost track of him 'til I seen him running for my old spot."

"I heard he wound up in Florida for about five years. He get into anything down there?"

"I wouldn't know."

"Well, I guess that's about it, then," I said. We got up. "Thanks for the story."

"They won't print it," he said.

I was looking at an old man. He still had an inner toughness to him, but he was old, and holding onto what remained didn't matter as much.

"If they don't," I said, "I'll see the story gets out. I promise you."

"They won't print it because they're scared. Everyone's scared of old Lester. Hnhh. Them as don't scare easy seem to gone out of fashion these days. Let me tell you one other reason folks got to be scared. Lester never could get to where he had two sawbucks to rub together, you get my meaning? He's got some friends in high places, people who're staking him to this campaign. If he's paying his own way, I'm the president of U-V-A."

"You have any idea who Les's friends might be?"

"Nope. But they'll be rich, and if they do something for him, he's gonna do something back. I been sheriff. Don't nobody give a dime without they want a favor in return."

"Thanks for the tip," I said. "I'll see what I can dig up."

I turned to go, but he put a hand on my arm. He didn't hurt me, but somehow in the gesture he communicated the physical strength and presence of the man he'd once been. I found myself wishing I'd known him back when.

"Swift," he said, his face close to mine, "if you go up against Lester Beavans . . . watch your ass."

He cocked his head. I suddenly felt that he knew I was no newspaper reporter.

"I will," I said.

"Good. No offense, but . . . you're no match for him."

Heading down the road in Clementine, I was glad to be outside again. I'd enjoyed Dewey Morris up to a point. At the end, he'd rattled me. That shouldn't have been the case—Campbell after all was going against Beavans, not me—but it was.

Beyond having been rattled, I'd picked up my first solid information about Lester Beavans's character. That information made one thing quite certain: namely, that I was in some very unpredictable waters and that I didn't really have a decent set of oars.

What Morris had told me hadn't come as a great surprise. I'd felt from the start there was something nasty behind the candidate's good ole boy grin. Then again, having a hunch and knowing can be two different horses.

It was time to decide. If I got any deeper into this thing, I could undoubtedly find myself in more trouble than I wanted. My debt to Campbell didn't mean I had to risk my neck. I could chuck it.

On the other hand, I'd said I'd do a job, and it wasn't done yet. I don't like to walk away from unfinished business.

Then there was my curiosity. It was up now, and it was tickling the devil out of me.

And there was the moral issue. Suppose Beavans was as unfit for the job as Dewey Morris believed. Now, I don't have a huge sense of civic responsibility, but I do think there are people we'd be better off keeping out of public office. Not to mention that I had something of a personal stake in the outcome of the race. It was entirely possible that I'd be having dealings with the Albemarle County Sheriff's (or Police) Department in the future. If so, I'd a whole lot rather deal with Rid than Lester Beavans.

In the end, my subconscious made the decision. Before I quite realized what was happening, I was out in the country, pointed toward Free Union. I was still on the case.

Free Union, in northwestern Albemarle County, still has a country store. In most other ways, it's changing fast. It's one of those places that twenty-five years ago was in the deep boondocks. Since then, a lot has happened. New people have moved to the area by the busload, creating an intense demand for housing. The overflow from Charlottesville began its inexorable spread out into Albemarle, eating up what were formerly farms and woodlands. Then there were those folks from the big cities who always wanted to live in the country anyway. They found high-paying jobs in town to which they commute from their mountain hideaways. Or they built their retirement homes.

Free Union has its share of tucked-away mountain hollows, as well as pleasant rolling hills and some nice farmland. It's a mix that you often find in the foothills of the Blue Ridge, and people like it. Add in that the area is a picturesque thirty-minute drive from Charlottesville and you can understand why land prices have soared in the past two decades.

The big acreages have been divided, and divided again. Fortunately, it's not yet to the point where they're building condos and shopping centers. It's still the kind of place where

83

you can stop in to the village store and ask directions to somebody's house and not get treated like Muammar Khadafy.

I did just that, in the hope of locating Connie Beavans. There were three old codgers in the store, and I soon learned more about the candidate's ex-wife than I'd bargained for.

First of all, her name wasn't Connie Beavans anymore. She'd been born a Shifflett (and would always be one, they said, hinting that it wasn't too terrific a distinction). Then she was a Beavans until she lost him. That, in their opinion, was probably her fault. Then she'd latched onto Dexter Brock and that was her name now, Connie Brock. It was generally agreed that she hadn't done badly with Dexter, by whom she'd had two kids to go along with the one courtesy of Beavans. It was also agreed that she'd been a real looker in her day but had let herself slide over the years.

Eventually, they got around to telling me where I might find her. There was a heated disagreement about the best directions, as there often is when you're in an area with lots of back roads. No one would give in and I finally had to take my pick.

It didn't turn out so bad. Ten minutes and only one mistake later I stopped next to a mailbox with *Brock* lettered in black on its side. When I did, a brown pickup that had been following me for the past couple of miles clattered past and disappeared around the next curve. The day was hot and very still.

The Brocks' home faced a hardpan county road, set back maybe a hundred feet. It was a two-over-two Virginia farmhouse, to which a wing had been tacked on in back, adding another two rooms. It had lapped siding, painted white, and the usual tin roof. There was a full-width open front porch. It was an old place, but tidy-looking.

Two children were playing in the front yard, a boy about ten and a girl a year or so younger. They stopped when I arrived and came over to check out my fancy wheels. No doubt they were more accustomed to late model jacked-up Chevies than Volkswagens that predated their births.

84

I got out.

"Hey mister," the boy said, "what you want?"

I looked for traces of Beavans in the kid's eyes, then suddenly remembered that this one wouldn't be Lester's. It was a strange kind of mistake for me to make. Reminded me that I might be a little out-of-shape as an investigator.

"Looking for your mama," I said. "She home?"

For a reply, the two of them turned and skittered off toward the house. I trailed after them, taking my time, enjoying the scenery. It was a lovely spot. The house was on a knoll, shaded by two huge old oaks. To the right was a pair of producing apples. Their fruit would be small this year because of the drought.

There were ridges on either side of the property. They converged at a distance of about a quarter-mile. Higher mountains were visible beyond. A small streambed passed downhill of the house. It was dry.

By the time I got to the front porch, a woman had emerged from the house and was watching me.

"Hi," I said, one foot on the lowest step. It's good form to wait to be invited up.

"Evening," she said.

That's Virginia country custom. They don't recognize afternoon as a time of day. It's either morning, evening, or night.

"What can I do for you?" she added after a decent interval. The kids were eavesdropping from just inside the door.

The codgers down at the country store had been decidedly wrong about Connie Brock. She wasn't a teenager anymore, but she wasn't on a slide, either. She was unattractive only if you prefer them young and inexperienced. I was looking at a mature woman in her early thirties. About five-eight and sturdily built. Big bones, broad shoulders and hips. Solid. She'd had three kids, but there was surprisingly little excess flesh on her frame. She stood as though, if you tried to push her over, she'd spring back up like one of those inflatable plastic clowns with sand in its base.

Her hair was wavy, shoulder-length, wheat-colored. Blue

85

eyes. Her face was sun-browned and somewhat lined. My guess was that for each line she'd learned a trick or two. She didn't wear makeup, and she hadn't smiled yet.

"I'd like to talk to you for a few minutes, Mrs. Brock," I said.

"What on?"

"Lester Beavans."

She smiled then. Actually, she busted out laughing. She had nice teeth. When she'd laughed herself out, she was still regarding me with amusement, one hand on her cocked hip.

"Our future sheriff," she said. She shook her head. "I don't believe I got anything to say about the man."

"You married him, didn't you?"

"Well, don't we all make mistakes?"

"What's so funny, by the way?"

"You wouldn't understand. Who are you, anyway?"

"Look Mrs. Brock," I said, "we could stand out here all day and trade questions back and forth without getting any answers. At the end of it I'd have sore feet, a dry throat, and fewer brain cells than I came with. How about if we at least sit down about it. I promise you that I do not come from the federal government with a new arrangement to enrich your life."

"Mister, you do have a way with the words, but don't nobody come in without I know their name."

"Loren Swift. I'm a newspaper writer."

"I should've knowed. How about some iced tea, Mr. Swift?"

"I'd be obliged."

She turned and I went up the steps after her. As I did, the brown pickup rattled slowly past, going back the way we'd come. Connie Brock glanced at it.

"Neighbors?" I asked.

"Never seen it before in my life," she said.

She led me into her kitchen. It was bright and airy. Though it faced south, the oaks helped keep the room cool, as did a breeze which rolled down the mountains and through the windows. Since the pickup had passed out of earshot, the only sounds to be heard were the buzzing of summer insects and the shouts of the children, who'd moved their play out back. I felt as if I'd found a little fold in time where the twentieth century was just now getting underway.

Connie Brock served iced tea from a glistening pitcher.

"Thanks," I said. I meant it. It was a hot day, and half the glass was gone before I realized I was gulping.

"Don't mention it. Now, what exactly is it about my ex-husband that you're interested in, Mr. Swift?"

"Well, he wants to be the next sheriff of Albemarle County. I think the people of the county have a right to know who it is they're voting for."

"You working for the *Press?*"

"Sort of." I gave her the cover story. She nodded.

"So that's where we'll read about it," she said. "Okay, just say Lester Beavans is a damn fool. That ought to do it. Anything else you need?"

"Wait a minute, wait a minute. I can't just go around calling a man a damn fool. Even if he is a public figure."

"Why not? It's the truth."

"Says you."

"Who should know but me? I was *married* to him, you remember."

She had me there. She'd know him better than any of the people I'd talked to. For some reason that hadn't yet sunk in. Or else I was beginning to confuse myself with an actual reporter.

"I assume," I said, "that one of the foolish things he did was to walk out on you."

That tore her up. She was the best audience I've ever had. Any old thing would set her to laughing. I wished my regular jokes were that good.

When she finally wiped the tears from her eyes, she said, "Excuse me, Mr. Swift. But that's a good one, that is. Lester Beavans, leave *me?* Lord, I run that boy off for fair. Don't let *no*body tell you no different."

If she was lying, she was a better actress than Meryl Streep. I believed her.

"Why'd you divorce him?" I asked.

"I told you, Lester's a damn fool. Listen up, now. The only things he cares about are cars and chasing tail. The day don't pass when that boy has two clear thoughts in his head at the same time."

"Pardon the obvious, but why'd you marry him, then?"

"You've met Lester."

I nodded.

"Then you know what a charmer he is," she said. "I fell for it. I was only sixteen, what did I know? Here came this big, handsome, charming guy with a smile as wide as your heart. Any of the girls would have died for him. I was supposed to figure out right away that his head was filled with boiled grits?"

I laughed. "I guess I didn't know much at sixteen, either," I said.

"There you have it. At least I got out before he done too much damage."

"You mean like five kids or something?"

"Yeah. We just had the one. Junior's a real nice kid, don't get me wrong. Real good-looking. And an athlete, Jesus. I love him very much, Mr. Swift. But he's like his daddy. Not bright."

She shrugged and refilled the tea glasses.

"Do you have any idea why he went to Florida?" I asked.

"Probably to get a thousand miles away from me."

"Come on, Mrs. Brock. I don't see you as a husband beater. Besides, the man must weigh two-eighty, or thereabouts."

"You don't understand. Lester gets nervous when he's around people who are smarter than him, especially women. He's afraid of them. He can beat the living hell out of just about anyone, of course. But whoever lets Lester beat him is a bigger fool than Lester himself. With Lester, all you got to do is outsmart him and he'll never lay a finger on you. Believe me."

I wanted to believe her, but I knew that I never would. I wasn't going to fight Lester Beavans, and I wasn't going to try to outsmart him, either. There was too much risk involved, and I knew what the man was capable of. She might have him

88

pegged in the context of their unique relationship, but that wouldn't necessarily carry over someplace else.

"He never beat you up?" I said.

"Never. Oh, he got mad a few times. He does have a temper on him. But when he did he'd just go out and get drunk with the boys or pick up some bargirl with less between the ears than he's got."

"What'd he do down in Florida all those years, do you think?"

"Beats me. Probably fixed cars. It's what he does best and he don't know much more."

"A friend of his told me that he never missed a child support payment while he was out of state."

"Well, I wouldn't say *that*, exactly. He did send money, but it weren't regular-like. I might get a check two months running, then not one for six months, y'know, and then like as not it wouldn't quite make up for the ones he missed. Let me tell you this, though. Lester does care about his Junior. I wouldn't never say that he don't. Couldn't nobody."

"The man has a good side?"

"I suppose you could call it that. He likes kids, and they generally like him, too. Just don't let him try and raise them up."

"How's Lester at managing money?" I asked.

"Terrible. Give him a checkbook and he'd screw it up so bad hell wouldn't take it."

"I expected you might say that. How do you think he's managing a political campaign, then?"

"I'd say he has some help."

Yeah, I thought. There's Ann. She's no dummy. And maybe Supervisor Gentry. And . . . someone else?

"Do you mean financial or organizational help?"

"Both," she said emphatically.

"I've met some of the staff, but they don't seem like financial backers. You have any idea who might be supplying the cash?"

"Mr. Swift, I don't know and I don't give a damn. When I heard Lester was running for sheriff, I had myself a right laugh and that was the end on it. If the folks in Albemarle County see fit to elect that fool, then . . . well, I guess it'll be what they deserve, somehow."

"I take it you don't intend to vote for him," I said.

She chuckled. "That about do it, Mr. Swift?"

"Yeah, I suppose so. I don't know how in the hell I'm gonna *write* this story, though."

"Write it, don't write it. It don't matter. Lester'll still be a mush head and the sun'll still come up tomorrow. We'll all keep on getting by. Even if we do have Lester's big butt holding down the sheriff's cruiser."

We said our goodbyes and I walked back to my car. I stood by the door for a minute, allowing the peacefulness of the setting to soak into me. I get out of the city too infrequently. Then I noticed that Clementine's left front tire was flat as a tortilla.

I bent down to look at it. I pulled out the cause of the flat: a bright new sixteen-penny nail, straight and unhammered. And half of it had been sticking out of the tire.

The fact that it was new was odd. But the other, that was impossible. If I'd picked the thing up off the road it would have been bent, or pushed all the way in, or mashed up against the tread.

No, someone had deliberately punctured my tire while I was talking with Connie Brock. And they wanted me to realize it.

I went back to the house and told her what had happened. She immediately called the kids in.

"Children," she said, "did either of you pound a nail in Mr. Swift's tire?"

She looked at them with a stern expression. She'd know their reactions. They both shook their heads dumbly.

"Okay, run along now." They did.

"Neither of them done it," she said. "I promise you. Besides, we both know they was out back while we was in here."

"Any other kids around here that do stuff like that?"

"Next nearest kids are half a mile away. They might could, but I think we would of heard something. Us or the kids, one."

"It is strange."

"Yes, it is. You got a spare?"

"Yeah."

"Need any help?"

"I can manage. I'm no Lester Beavans with cars, but I know how to change a tire."

"Well," she said, "I'm sorry it happened to you. It's really not that bad a neighborhood."

We laughed.

"I'll bring you some more iced tea," she said. And she did. She also kept me company, entertaining me with back country stories. One of them concerned the origin of her maiden name. According to her, during the Revolutionary War, a group of local orphans were moved from farm to farm, in order to keep them out of the clutches of the British. The children eventually came to be called "little shift-lets." Which stuck. So today Shifflett is one of the most common names in the area. It's as good an explanation as any.

In spite of the heat, it was the least unpleasant tire changing I've ever done. Lester Beavans shouldn't have cheated on this one.

On the way back to town, I thought about random vandals. I decided I didn't believe in them. But I couldn't decide what it was that I did believe in.

I also considered the mysterious Mr. Beavans. He'd come on to me like the last of God's own swell fellows. Ann and Gentry thought he'd make a terrific leader. Ridley thought he was trying to buy or intimidate his way into the office. Dewey Morris thought he was mean as a snake. And his ex-wife thought he was a buffoon.

Would the real Lester Beavans please stand up.

I'd been puttering around in my apartment for about five minutes before I realized what it was that was wrong. Things were out of place. Just a few, and not obviously so. They'd been moved.

Like the lamp on my desk. It sits on the left side, which is

91

most comfortable for me when I'm working there. Now it was on the right. The chair, which I always leave pushed under the desk, was pulled out slightly. My authentic Fillmore Auditorium Janis Joplin with Big Brother and the Holding Company concert poster was hanging a little crooked on the north wall. Things like that.

It was subtle, and it was insidious. Because the impression was not that the apartment had been searched, just that it had been rearranged.

Quickly, I checked the important stuff. The desk drawer was locked. I unlocked it. The Walther was still in there. I looked behind the sofa. The Police Positive was taped in place as it should be. From the look of the dust patterns, no one had even inspected the area. I got the ammunition box down out of the closet. Nothing missing, as far as I could tell. I removed the bedside table drawer and pried up the false bottom. My emergency cash supply was intact.

I sat on the edge of the bed, feeling very peculiar. My apartment had been broken into, yet nothing had been stolen. In fact, it appeared that the intruders hadn't even been *interested* in things of value.

Then I thought about the mysterious flat tire and my skin really began to crawl. It was the same thing. A very low-key but very clear message was being sent my way: *Swift, we can hit you any time, any place. You are not safe from us.*

I had no doubt that the people involved had shown their hand before. Ridley Campbell had received the message and now I had. So my newspaper cover wasn't holding up. Someone on the other side had decided that I was still in the detective business, and that I was working against them. Should they discover who I was working *for*, the next warning might be considerably more serious.

I called the sheriff after I'd put down a healthy shot of Jameson. I only misdialed the number once.

"Rid," I said, "they're on to me."

"Who is?"

"I don't know. The ones I'm supposed to be finding out about."

"You got something for me?"

"Not much more than I know they're on to me. Let's meet somewhere and I'll tell you about it."

"I can't right now," he said after a pause. "I'm wrapped up with some stuff."

"How about later?"

"Okay, tonight. Mac's, about ten. You come in there, you see any of my men around, or anyone you recognize at all, you walk to the bar and pretend you didn't notice me. Have a beer and leave."

"Got it," I said. "Now, one more thing, Rid. Can you make some contacts with the cops in Florida?"

"I suppose so."

"Get on the horn. See if they ever pulled Beavans in for anything down there. Try Miami, Boca Raton, Lauderdale, the whole area."

"You *do* have something."

"Not really. I think it's worth a shot, though."

"I'll have to do it quietly, make sure they report back to me personally. I guess it can be managed. It'll take some time, too."

"That's all right. See you tonight."

Later in the evening I called Patricia. I told her I would be tied up for the night and would try to see her tomorrow. That was no problem with her. She didn't quiz me too closely on what I was doing.

Then I slipped *Cheap Thrills* on the stereo and let Janis work me over while I waited nervously for ten o'clock. It seemed like it had never taken her so long to get through "Ball and Chain."

Before I left the apartment, I debated whether to carry the Walther in my jacket pocket. I decided against it, but only just. The situation wasn't yet quite life threatening, I didn't think. Still . . .

I decided to transfer the Walther to the drawer of the night table next to my bed. That drawer didn't have a lock on it, but I wanted the gun close to hand while I was sleeping. Who could say when my uninvited visitors might drop in again? I

93

considered my situation one last time when deciding whether to load the Walther or not. I loaded it.

Mac's is a small roadhouse on U.S. 29, just south of the Interstate, out where the town suddenly gives way to thickly wooded mountains. I like the place. It's a bar for truckers and construction workers. Students from the University never go there.

I walked in right at ten. Campbell was already there. He was seated at a corner table and was huddled in an intense conversation with one of his deputies. Per my instructions, I ignored him, parked myself on one of the barstools and ordered an icy Stroh's.

The TV above the bar was on. Atlanta against the Dodgers. Superstation WTBS. Now that the entire country is either wired for cable or has a dish out back, the Braves have truly become America's team. No wonder their boy wins the MVP award every year. The other guys don't get half the exposure.

Pascual Perez was on the mound for Atlanta, bouncing back after a short stretch in the Dominican slammer for possession of coke. The sweet white summer snow. It seemed like everyone was into coke these days. Doctors and lawyers and movie stars and all my favorite athletes. I'd tried it once. Someone gave me some at a party. It didn't do a thing to me. Nothing. Zip. I couldn't understand the appeal, why there were those who'd spend a small fortune on the stuff every week of their world. But then, there were a lot of things I didn't understand.

Coke or no coke, old Pascual was throwing BBs out there. The men in True Blue were swinging at the breeze.

Halfway through my beer, Campbell's deputy left. I watched the game for another five minutes, then looked over at him. He nodded and I went to his table.

"Tell me," he said.

I recounted the flat tire and rearranged room incidents. Campbell grunted now and then. I noticed that he was chasing shots of whiskey with his beers. He was somewhat in the bag.

94

It was showing only because he was letting it. Rid's one of those rare people who can sober up in an instant if he has to. Really sober up. I've seen it happen.

"Yeah," he said when I'd finished, "that sounds like them, all right."

"I take it as a gentle warning, Rid. They're obviously not convinced by the cover story. They've discovered I used to be a detective, which didn't take much doing, and they're assuming that I may be back in business. But they can't be sure. Just in case, they send a couple of low-key messages."

"Okay. You think they've connected us up?"

"I don't see how. Unless they've got spies everywhere,"—I looked around the bar somewhat uneasily—"which I doubt. If I stick hard to the cover, they may come around to believing it."

"They find out you're working for me, it could get a mite rough on you."

"The thought had occurred to me."

"You want out?"

I drank some beer. "I know what I *don't* want," I said. "I don't want to end up over at the Medical Center. Too many people go in there and never come out again."

"I can't protect you entirely, Swift. As you realize. You want out, I ain't gonna hold it against you."

I drank some more beer. It didn't help.

Finally, I said, "Ah, Christ Jesus. I never quit a job before. It don't feel right."

As I said the words, I realized in a rush that there were things about me that were never going to change, no matter if I stayed a P.I. or not, no matter what kind of situations I got into if I did stay with it.

Ridley's respect for me probably about doubled on the spot, but he wasn't the kind of man who would give it away, beyond a slight relaxation around the eyes and at the corners of the mouth.

"Thanks," he said. "If it gets heavy, I'll be there. Count on it."

95

I would. In fact, I'd stake my life on it. And if there's something you'd confidently stake your life on, then you've got ahold of one of the rare things of value.

"We better be careful, Rid," I said. "We might end up ushering in a whole new era of cooperation between cops and P.I.s."

That lightened things up. We could laugh about our unusual relationship. We could put aside the potential embarrassment it held for both of us. We could get down to business.

"Okay, what have you got for me?" he said after we'd relaxed and drank some.

I filled him in on what I'd learned so far. From Connie Brock and Dewey Morris and Landon Gentry. From my interview with Beavans himself.

"There's something there, Rid. I can feel it."

"But he ain't broken any laws, has he?"

"Not that I know of."

"Then we're still where we started. I can't go nosing around my political opponent because he's got a bad smell on him or because your furniture might've been out of place."

"What about the Collie Green business?"

"I've heard the story," he said. "But I don't think it does us much good. Fifteen years is a long time. People change, and all that. Plus, a lot of those boys out in the country, if they were around, they're *impressed* with what Lester done. They won't hold it against him."

"Yeah. And I suppose dredging it up might make it look like you're using one past mistake to crucify him. It could backfire."

"Might could."

"Ah well, what about you? You pick up anything from the Florida cops?"

He shook his head. "They're not back to me yet. But don't look for much to come of it. Nobody's gonna back an ex-con for sheriff. An ex-con ain't even *allowed* to run for sheriff. He'll be clean."

"You're probably right. Got any other ideas?"

"Leave me think on it," he said. "Maybe I can come up

with something. I got a favor or two I can call in from the feds. Get ahold of his tax returns, whatnot."

"That should be interesting. In the meantime, I'll see what I can do. If it comes to it, I can always try leaning on Gentry. He's boffing Beavans's campaign manager behind his wife's back, which makes him vulnerable. He might not know anything, though."

"Watch how you lean, Swift. I still represent the law."

Just like that, he'd distanced himself. There was a warning in the look he gave me. The air thickened slightly with memories of past times when we hadn't exactly seen eye-to-eye.

"They're threatening your family, Rid," I said.

That got to him. I could plainly see the conflicting emotions inside him. I could also see that he was close to becoming very angry with me.

"Swift," he said finally, in a tone that suggested he was barely keeping the lid on, "I am *aware* of the threat to my family. But whatever we do, we do it within the law. Otherwise we're no better than they are. Understood?"

Despite the beer, my throat seemed dry and I had to clear it.

"Understood."

We gave it a good silent drinking interval, enough to let the cloud pass.

"Something else that bothers me," he said finally.

"What's that?"

"These things that've been happening, it ain't gonna be Lester that's doing them."

"Right. 'Subtle' is a word I don't believe he's familiar with."

"Then you got your man behind the scenes. But it's damn straight he ain't dirtying *his* hands, either. Which means we got a certain inference to draw here. There's at least one other guy on the payroll. Probably more. Maybe a lot more."

"I agree."

"I don't like the heft of this thing, Swift. Just what in hell can these people be up to?"

He had me there. Whatever it was, I had to agree that it was beginning to look like something big. I decided to do some thinking out loud.

"Well," I said, "it appears that someone is trying to buy the sheriff's office, along with maybe some key people in local government. What comes immediately to mind is protection for an illegal activity. Which could be anything. Gambling, stolen cars, pot farming, any damn thing. How's that grab you?"

"Makes sense," he said. "The question is: What the devil can we do about it?"

"Keep plugging away. Look for an opening. Go for it when we find one. I hate to say it, but that's not a lot."

"It ain't."

"The sonofabitch might win," I said after a pause. "You'd better prepare yourself for that."

"I'd rather not."

"How about if you change your position on the county cop thing? Right now, that's the biggest difference between the two of you. You could say you've had a change of heart, that you might be in favor of a police department. That way, you'd undercut the main issue he's running on. Wouldn't cost you much."

Ridley had been looking progressively more morose, until I mentioned changing his position. That perked him up.

"I can't," he said firmly.

"Why not? What the hell difference does it make? If you're sheriff when they convert, you'll be the first chief of police. Just like Beavans expects to be."

He stared at his beer for a while, then chased some whiskey with it. Our conversation was taking a turn away from the strictly professional. That's something he doesn't ordinarily encourage; he's a cop, after all, and we're not really friends. On the other hand, it was one of those nights. Give us another few rounds and we might start singing the old Hank Williams pain songs together.

"You believe in anything, Swift?" he said finally.

Coming from Campbell, it was a question out of deep left field. Not to mention that I had no easy answer for him. I wasn't sure I *did* believe in anything.

"I don't know," I said. "I believe in being as good as your

word. Does that count? I believe in love while it's happening, but not when it's gone."

"I guess I meant in terms of what you do for a living, though you did answer that some. Me, I've seen a load of crap in my life. But what should I expect, considering what I do. You don't see the good side of people that often." He shrugged. "I wouldn't change it. It's what I do. It's a job that needs doing, and I'm good at it. The people have always voted me back in, so they must agree.

"And there's the thing of it. The people always get to have their say. That's the way you oughtta run local law enforcement, to my way of thinking. Now they want to do away with it and bring in some appointed chief of police who won't ever have to answer to the people he's supposed to serve. If he's a bad one, tough. I can't support that kind of change, Swift. It's forced on me, I'll find a way to live with it. But I won't help to make it happen."

"Even if it means Beavans wins?"

"Even so. I never was much for that lesser of two evils stuff. You know, do something that goes against your grain in order to prevent something worse from happening. That might be a practical way to live and all, but it ain't for me. Once you sell yourself out, you ain't gonna be worth a damn no matter what you prevent."

I shook my head slowly. "Well, I'll be damned," I said. "Grass roots democracy. You're a bit of a surprise, Sheriff."

"Swift," he said, "there's more things you don't know about me than you'll ever know."

I laughed. "Next you'll be telling me that you favor gun control," I said.

"I do. If people couldn't get handguns, we'd have less murders."

"Okay, Sheriff, that's enough for one night. You've convinced me that you're a character of real complexity. More my poor brain couldn't take. Do we need to plan any more strategy?"

"Nope. We just need to *get* something."

"You do whatever you can, then. I'll keep poking around.

Maybe I can convince my man over at the *Press* to start asking some questions. Maybe he could do it without turning Lester into a martyr."

I got up. It had been a strange evening.

"Give me five minutes," I said. "I don't want to be pulled over on a DUI."

"You okay?" He smiled, just a little. *He* was okay.

"I'll make it. Home is close."

"Drive slow."

"My VW doesn't know any other way. I'll call you if anything comes up."

"Thanks, Swift," he said.

He ordered another round as I left. It was between him and himself now. I didn't need to know the outcome.

6

It was the U.S. Cavalry to the rescue. The troopers were mounted on ten-speed bicycles and they were all pedaling away like maniacs. Each bike had a whip aerial with a red white and blue pennant fluttering from it. One guy had a trumpet, of course. He was blowing the solo from "Penny Lane." The lead bike had a flashing blue cop light mounted on the handlebars, along with one of those traffic bells that you ring with your thumb. The lead rider, furiously ringing his bell, was Ridley Campbell.

I don't know how long it was before I realized that the bell was actually my phone, ringing out there in the real world. I've never understood how it is that dreams can integrate sudden outside events into their logic so easily. There's a lot of things I don't know how they work.

Like the call itself.

I groped around and got ahold of my phone before the caller gave up.

It was, of course, Ridley Campbell. You explain it.

"Swift," he said, "you awake?"

"I am now," I mumbled. "What time is it?"

"Seven. I got a lot to do today."

Seven? Jesus. After last night, how could the man be functioning effectively at seven in the morning?

"Look," he said, "something happened yesterday that I didn't find out about until I got home. You oughtta know. My wife got a birthday card in the mail, one of those joke cards. On the front is a pistol, pointing straight out at you. You open it up and it's a side view of the gun with this little flag coming out of the barrel that says, 'Surprise.' Under that is the Happy Birthday message. Nobody signed it."

"So?"

"So my wife's birthday is in February."

"Oh, shit."

"Yeah, I reckon they just wanted to make sure I been getting the message here."

"Well, there's no mistaking this one."

"Right," he said. "First thing I'm gonna do is send Betty and the kids out of town for a while. They can go stay with my sister down in Carolina. That ought to be far enough. Then we got to get these sonsofbitches, Swift."

"I'm trying."

"I won't tolerate threats to my family."

"Take it easy, Rid. We've still got a pretty empty basket. If you fly off the handle now it could end up costing you the election. You can't go after your opponent until you've got something so solid it'd interest the Albemarle Commonwealth's Attorney."

I could almost hear him grinding his teeth.

"Let me work on it another couple of days," I said. "I'll think of something."

He muttered to himself and hung up. In truth, I didn't know what it was I was going to think of. The opposition looked to have all the good cards and they were playing them very close to the chest. Bringing the bastards out into the open would require a creative line of attack. And I was short on creative lines of attack right at the moment. While trying to conjure one up I fell back asleep.

The phone woke me again, at a somewhat more decent hour. It was Jonesy.

"Guess what?" he said.

"Katherine Graham called. She wants your bod."

"Swift, you know, you really have the knack, how to hurt your fellow man. But alas, the *Post* does not yet wish to contract for my inimitable services. Their loss. Actually, my very own editor called me in. Wanted to know what you're up to."

"Well. That didn't take long. What happened?"

"Nothing much. Ann Luden, your favorite campaign chairperson, talked to the editor yesterday, while I was out. He knew you only through your previous notoriety, of course. Had no idea you were looking to join our tribe. Ann mentioned my name."

"You get in trouble?"

"Nah. I told him you were a friend of mine and you were trying some feature work on spec. He said to remind you that you're not to advertise yourself as a courageous *Press* reporter. Consider yourself reminded."

"Thanks," I said. "There's a story here, Jonesy. I don't know what it is yet, but I'll find it. Meantime, did you know that Lester Beavans almost killed a guy with his bare hands about fifteen years ago?"

"No, I sure didn't. That's a bit before my time. Who told you?"

"Your buddy, Dewey Morris. You might want to talk to the guy. It seems like the sort of thing the voting public ought to be aware of."

"Hmm. That kind of story's a tricky one, and the courts aren't sticking up for us like they used to. But I'll check it out. There wouldn't be any further clues coming, would there?"

"Not yet. You'll be the first to know, Jonesy."

"Sure. Catch you later, old man."

I pulled myself together over a cup of coffee with some Jameson splashed in it, thinking about what I ought to do next. I couldn't think of anything. That was the rust showing once again. A good investigator improvises when he's at a loss. I'd misplaced the ability.

Fortunately, the phone rang before I had a chance to get good and down on myself.

"Mr. Swift, this is Ann Luden, down at Lester Beavans campaign headquarters." I love the way Southern women can turn a simple statement into a question.

"Hi, Ann," I said brightly. "What can I do for you?"

"We—Lester and I—we wondered if you could come by again. There are some things we felt we should share with you."

Like maybe five of Les's closed fingers?

"That would be fine," I said. "Where?"

"Same place. Say, in an hour?"

"Okay, swell. Should I bring my lawyer, or a large dog of some kind?"

She laughed. Maybe it was genuine. No, probably not. The game was getting rough. She wouldn't be in a playful mood.

"That won't be necessary, Mr. Swift," she said. "Goodbye."

I had time to shave, shower, dress and wonder whether now was the time to start packing a gun. Then I thought: to go see the candidate for sheriff? That was ridiculous. Wasn't it?

There was a sign on the street-level door to Beavans campaign HQ that said *Back At*. Underneath was a little clock with movable hands, set at noon. The door, however, was unlocked. For me, presumably. How nice. I let myself in and went up the stairs. I hoped they weren't intending to keep me until twelve.

Ann Luden and the candidate were sitting behind the tidy desk. Les's face still beamed at me from the four walls, but the flesh and blood model wasn't exactly ready to burst into joyful song. Ann was looking dour as well. I guess I have that effect on some people.

I went over to where they were sitting. They'd thoughtfully provided a chair for me at the very spot. I seated myself in what I hoped was a jaunty manner.

"Y'all burn the toast this morning?" I asked either of them.

"Mr. Swift," Beavans said, "I understand that you've been talking to my ex-wife, who I thought I axed you not to bother."

"And how would you understand that?"

"Connie told me."

That was too much. I cracked up.

"Swift," Ann said, "I'm glad that you think this is a comic situation here."

"No, you're not."

"Okay, I'm not. Would you care to share the joke with us?"

"The joke is that Connie Brock wouldn't voluntarily give this clown the right time of day."

I immediately regretted saying it. My intention was not to make Lester Beavans madder at me than he already was. There was unhealth in that. But it had gotten said. Beavans took it in stride. Because of his position, he couldn't get too overtly hostile with me unless we were alone back in the woods somewhere. I wasn't about to let that happen, ever.

"Swift," Ann said, "there is no point in name-calling, as I'm sure you realize."

It looked as if Ann had been appointed spokesperson, with Les there to lend credence to the whole thing, as well as to serve as a physical reminder that I'd better be a little careful where I was treading. I let out a greatly exaggerated sigh.

"Okay," I said, "let's take the gloves off, shall we?"

"I don't know what you mean," Ann said.

"Sure you do. The reason you know I talked to Connie Brock is that you've been having me followed. Let's take it from there."

"Swift," Ann said, "we're running a legitimate political campaign here. We do not engage in activities such as having people followed. That's more in *your* line, is it not?"

Beware of people who describe themselves as "legitimate."

"If you mean detective work, that's my *former* line," I said.

"Loren Swift," Ann said as if reading from a cue card, "Charlottesville's one and only private cop, shows up at our office claiming to be a reporter. He then goes off and talks to people closely connected to the candidate, some of whom he was specifically requested not to bother. This behavior has us asking ourselves some questions. Isn't that odd?"

"You mean questions like: 'What's a nice fellow like him doing in a place like this?'"

"The logical assumption is that you are working a case for someone." It was another question.

"I'm self-employed."

"Swift," she said, "the editor of the *Press* was emphatic about your relationship with them. It doesn't exist."

"Not yet it doesn't, but give me a shot. I told you I was working on spec. If I do a good job on the campaign, who knows what might come of it? Did you talk to Jonesy?"

She shook her head.

"Why don't you?"

"I don't believe that will be necessary. I assume that Mr. Jones will back you up in this matter."

"I don't need backing up," I said. "I just need a little help with my new career. It's not easy, at my age."

"I doubt that we can help you."

"Okay. Then is there something that you want?"

She sighed exaggeratedly and spoke to me as if addressing the world's premier airhead.

"We would like for you to file your story, if that's indeed what you're doing, and move on to something else. Please. I'm sure even you will understand that it doesn't look good for us to have an *ex*-private detective hanging around our campaign. People's attention is easily misdirected."

"But what if I'm not finished?"

"Swift," Beavans said.

"Behold, the great man speaketh."

"Swift," he said again. "I don't need to be worried about whether you're poking your detective's nose into my business. Kindly tell that to whoever it is employs you."

"Is that a threat?" I did my best to look amused. It wasn't easy, dealing with a human trash compactor.

"I don't threaten people," he said. "I'm a busy man. I got a lot to do to get myself elected. I just don't have the time to fool with you, like I said. Is that so goddamned hard to understand?"

I got up.

"Lester," I said, "you've made your point. You too, ma'am. I think you're both terrific people, and I'll miss you when you're gone, and I do appreciate your having me down here to talk things out like this. Now, if you'll excuse me, I've got myself a story to work on."

I left. We didn't bother shaking hands. Whatever agreement we'd made didn't require that to seal it.

At the downstairs door I turned the little sign so its *Welcome* side was facing out.

I walked over to the same bench I'd occupied after my last visit to the downtown mall. Nearby was one of the black cast-iron sculptures that decorate the area. It was of a bag lady; you find them even in small-town America these days. I contemplated the sculpture while I thought about what to do now. I hoped indecision wasn't becoming a habit. It's a difficult one to break.

Okay. They'd delivered some nonverbal warnings yesterday. Just in case I was extra dense, today they'd added a personal message. So far, they hadn't gotten nearly as heavy with me as they had with Campbell. That made sense. They couldn't know for sure whether I was doing newspaper or detective work. And Campbell was the real target. Besides, every threat is a calculated risk. You have to play it off against the potential gain and against the increased possibility of exposure. I wasn't going to merit serious attention until I somehow ceased to be small potatoes. There was also the likelihood, in their minds, that I would scare off at the first hint of unpleasantness. As most people do.

It wouldn't be good to get too cocky, but I figured I was safe from bodily harm for the time being. That still left the question of what my next move should be.

There weren't many choices. I'd satisfied myself that there was something shady about the Beavans campaign, but what did I have that would convince a disinterested third party? Flat tires and rearranged furniture? No chance. Until these people made a horrible mistake out in full public view, Ridley and I were powerless.

That left me with only one clear line of action. Try to provoke them into making that mistake. I might be able to accomplish that by becoming highly visible, by being a nuisance to them. The idea failed to thrill me, but it was all I had. (I didn't even want to *consider* that what you do with a pesky fly is to swat it.)

Beavans came out a few minutes later. He'd pulled himself together in the meantime and was all smiles again. He walked the mall like it was private turf, shaking hands and tipping the good ole boy hat. I followed him, making sure he knew I was there.

I trailed after him for the rest of a highly uneventful day. He had lunch with a bunch of men in conservative suits, none of whom I knew. I ate in the same restaurant. The food was lousy. Then he drove down to Scottsville and addressed a women's garden club. He was courteous and cooperative, if not particularly eloquent. They listened like he was Robert Redford. I sat in the back of the room, pretending to take notes. After that, he went back to campaign HQ for about half an hour. I waited on the mall. Then he drove out to Crozet, the largest town in the county, excluding Charlottesville. He parked at a modest brick rancher in a subdivision and went inside. Since the mailbox said *Beavans*, I deduced that the candidate was now at home. I let him be. He knew what I'd been doing.

I returned to Belmont.

When I got home, Mrs. Detweiler was right where I expected her to be. She called me over.

"Look at this, Swift!" she said, brandishing the afternoon *Press*.

I took the paper. The lead story was about a guy who'd been fished from the reservoir that morning. Dead from a single bullet to the heart, with his nose missing. The man was a John Doe for the time being, since no identification had been found on him. He was described as around thirty, five-ten, wiry build, and of Latin appearance, possibly Mexican, with a prominent scar on his right cheek. Anyone who thought they knew him was urged to contact the police. All in all, it was a rather unusual occurrence for Charlottesville. But then, strange things are happening everywhere.

"Thanks, Mrs. D.," I said. "That's just what I need to read about today."

"You *do* need to read about it. Everyone needs to be made aware of the problem."

"What problem, Mrs. D.?"

"For God's sake, Swift, migrant labor. The migrant labor problem! You didn't realize the problem we have around here?"

"Uh, I guess I didn't."

"Well, listen up. You think of illegal aliens, you think of Texas, you think of southern California, right? Think again. We've probably got as many per capita here in Virginia as any of those other places. Haitians, Dominicans, Mexicans, Jamaicans, you name it. Anywhere there's poverty, the capitalists go in and lure the unfortunates up here to pick the apples and the peaches, the field crops, whatever's in season. They pay them nothing, of course. If the laborers complain, they get shipped home. Or they end up like this poor fellow here."

"You think this John Doe was an illegal alien?"

" 'Course he was. What else would he be?"

"I don't know. Anything."

"Swift," she said as if patiently lecturing a moron, "can you tell me where Charlottesville's barrio might be? We don't *have* a Latino minority living here. What do you think, someone shot a Spanish professor from the University and dumped him in the reservoir without his credit cards? Sometimes I think you haven't learned anything at all from me."

"I see your point," I said.

"It's disgusting. They think they can get away with murder around here."

"The migrants?"

"The bosses, you creep! Money's the only thing that matters to them. Profits. The cost in human life isn't even figured in!"

"But suppose he was running drugs?" I said. "There *is* a

109

lot of grass and cocaine floating around this town. And the missing nose might be symbolic."

"Even worse! Who do you think controls the drug traffic? It's the same people, the ones who are getting rich from exploiting the poor. The same cops protect the big drug importers as protect the big orchard owners. You think anyone could import drugs or human beings without official cooperation? Hell, no! Every once in a while, they throw the public a scapegoat, sure. But the profiteers keep on profiting, you can count on that."

"Yeah, you're probably right. But I think it's in human nature to want to get one up on the other guy."

"Nonsense. The only reason it seems predetermined is that we have a society based on profit instead of people's real needs. It doesn't have to *be* that way!"

"Enough for today, Mrs. D. Tell you what, next time I talk to Ridley Campbell, I'll ask him what he makes of John Doe."

"It's not important. The important thing—"

"—is the system. I know, I know. We can discuss the Revolution later."

I left her grumbling to herself and walked down to my apartment.

Nothing had been moved today. I hadn't expected them to visit me again, but I was relieved all the same.

After a light supper, I called Patricia.

"Hi, stranger," I said.

"Hello yourself. Are we going to get together soon?"

"Well," I said, "something has, ah, come up."

"Loren, don't you put on that tone with me. Are you avoiding me?"

"Patricia, I am not avoiding you. I am not seeing someone else. I am not trying to prevent discussion of those things that are important to us. Will you trust me about this?"

"Does it have to do with Ridley Campbell?"

I paused.

"Yes," I said finally. "I think it's better that I kind of keep to myself for a while."

"What is this? Do you think you're protecting me from something?"

"I didn't say that."

"You sure as hell implied it, and I resent it. I thought I made it clear that I don't need to be insulated from your affairs. You know what's wrong with you, Mr. Swift? You just can't escape your old set ways of thinking. Even after being exposed to me for nearly a year, there's an important part of you that still sees women as basically helpless, with you as the great protective white knight."

"Maybe," I said. "But you told me yourself that ingrained patterns of behavior are very difficult to deal with."

"With you it could be impossible."

"What does *that* mean?"

"It means that you have to take a good, long look at your ability to change. If you can't, we can't make it."

"Oh come on, Patricia. Aren't you being a little rigid yourself?"

"Perhaps. But I can't start bending now. If I do, I'm just going to make the same mistakes I made in my marriage. I won't go through that again."

"Which leaves me where?"

"I don't know. Think about yourself. Think about me. Think about us. See what you come up with. We can see each other when you think it's safe." She said the last word as if expelling an unwanted mouthful of dirty water.

"Okay. I'm sorry—"

"Skip it."

There wasn't anything else to say and we hung up. Patricia Ryan was one stubborn Irish lady, and when she didn't want to move, you couldn't budge her.

I didn't want her to be sucked into the case. Yet I didn't want us to break up over it, either. So there it was. Somehow, Patricia and I seemed to find ourselves in more no-win situations than people who loved each other ought to. I didn't know what I could do about it except drink some beer and let it ride.

I went to the refrigerator and pulled out a Stroh's.

111

7

THE FOLLOWING MORNING I WAS UP EARLY. BY SEVEN I WAS parked within eyeball distance of Lester Beavans's house. His car was still out front. I settled in to wait.

As I sat there, I thought about the strangeness I'd gotten involved in.

I was certain that there was something of questionable legality going on. There was nothing unusual about using money to try to influence an election, of course. That was one of the constants of American political life, from top to bottom. The use of intimidation is also far from unknown, but I tend to associate it more with the closely controlled ethnic wards of the big cities. It was rife in Boston. Not so in rural Virginia. Probably the payoff isn't so generous down here.

Still, political leverage in Albemarle County could be profitable. In a fast-growing area, favorable treatment by the pols could readily enrich someone in, say, the land business. That made me think immediately of Landon Gentry. He was already a supervisor, no doubt using the office to line his pockets. Did he have his eye on some bigger prize? Maybe. Yeah, he just might.

Whoever the man behind the scenes was, I found myself wanting to know the full extent of his designs. What grand scheme necessitated poisoning animals and threatening innocent bystanders? I wanted to look the guy full in the face before I helped Ridley squash him.

I kept my keen detective's eye on Lester's house and, sure enough, around nine the candidate stepped out into the morning sunshine. He looked well-rested and well-fed, and about as big as half of next week.

Swift, I thought, you are out of your mind. You are trying to annoy a man with a violent temper who could break each distinct bone of your body without generating a single bead of sweat.

I told my wiser side to shut up. This was all I had. I tailed Beavans until he either led me to someone or got mad and made a mistake. Or else I sat on my duff and did nothing.

You are not satisfied doing nothing, I told myself.

Beavans got into his car without a glance in my direction. I cranked up Clementine and we began our little procession.

He took old U.S. 250 into Charlottesville. It's still a pleasant route, following the C&O railbed through mostly bottomland. Cornfields and horse farms, with a scattering of antique shops, nurseries, and mom-and-pop groceries. In twenty years, as the subdivisions continue to multiply and Crozet becomes a populous bedroom community for Charlottesville, it will degenerate into a miserable traffic-choked two-lane road. If there's any scenery left, people will be too busy dodging accidents to enjoy it.

Coming from the west, as we were, you're well into Charlottesville almost before you realize you've left the country behind. The city's like that. If you approach from the north, then there's a whole motel–fast-food–shopping-mall strip to fight your way through. Yet from any other direction it sneaks up on you. Country one minute, city the next. Makes it very easy to find clean air and open space.

Beavans headed straight for downtown. He parked in the

parking garage. I followed suit. Although he might have been aware of the orange VW on his tail, he totally ignored me as I tracked him to his office.

I staked out my trusty bench and prepared for the inaction. I've never minded waiting for things to happen. It helps if it's a sunny August day and there are beautiful women strolling past with some regularity. But I can take it at any time. P.I.s—cops of any kind, for that matter—have to do a lot of sitting around, of course. You know that before you get into the game. Yet some never adapt to it. They go bonkers and quit the trade. Or they turn to drinking on the job. I ran into a lot of that kind back when I lived in Boston. Irish kids from Southie who couldn't make the regular force and thought the private game was a way out of the life of poverty.

Me it doesn't bother. Maybe that's the sign of a low I.Q. I don't know. I prefer to think that I have a rich imagination. I do things like replay my most memorable sexual experiences. I try to recall the words to early 1960s rock and roll songs. I make lists: the ten worst movies of all time, my favorite Italian baseball players (Johnny Berardino!), people who did time because of Watergate. I compose terrific poems and short stories that I never write down later.

Time passes.

Whatever I'm waiting for either happens or it doesn't.

In this case, I was simply waiting for Lester Beavans to come back outside. When I interviewed him, I'd noted there were no back stairs. He was obliged to exit the way he'd entered. That made the job a lot easier than it often is.

Beavans proved me right by reappearing shortly after eleven. He failed to acknowledge my presence and headed for the parking garage. I followed at an indiscreet distance.

We were on Market Street, half a block from the garage, when a stocky fellow in sport shirt and leisure slacks stepped into my path. He'd been lounging against a fast-food storefront. Now he was evidently going to have a chat with me.

"Hi," he said.

"Excuse me," I said, "but I already gave."

I made to push past him. He put a hand gently but firmly on my arm.

"Uh uh," he said.

Ahead of us, Beavans was turning into the garage. As he did, he looked over his shoulder. A tiny smile creased his face, then he was gone.

"Look," I said, "would you mind?"

For an answer, the stocky fellow pulled out his wallet and flipped it open. A Charlottesville city cop's badge winked up at me. It might have been real or it might not have, since I didn't recognize the guy. It didn't matter. I'd been had. I couldn't afford to treat him as if he were bogus. I couldn't afford to have "Interference with a Police Officer in Performance of His Duties" written into my record.

I gave up the chase.

"Okay," I sighed. "What've I done?"

The stocky man shook his head slowly and turned down the corners of his mouth.

"Nothing, yet," he said.

"Then why the attention?"

Beavans's car pulled out of the parking garage and turned away from us. The candidate didn't bother to check us out. I watched as he took a right at the next light. That could lead to the east-west Interstate, or south into the sticks, or just loop back to the other side of town. He might be on his way anywhere.

"Just wanted to find out what you was up to," my companion said. I'd almost forgotten about him. "We got a complaint that a law-abiding citizen was being harassed. We don't like to hear that kind of thing."

"I'm a reporter," I said.

"Big deal. I'm afraid that don't give you the right to annoy people going about their legal business."

I wanted to rearrange his smug face for him, but I didn't. Instead, I stepped past him without another word. He didn't care. I was some clown he'd never met before and wouldn't mind if he never met again. He'd go back to his stupid cop job; I'd try to pick up the thread of the case again. It would be pointless to make any more of it than that.

I walked up the parking garage ramp and got into Clementine as if I had a purpose. I even had my key out. Then I put it back in my pocket. The long hot afternoon was stretched out in front of me and I had nothing to fill it with. Not the ghost of an idea.

Time passed, but my view of the concrete wall in front of me remained the same.

Finally, I went back to the fast-food place. They had a telephone there. I noted that the stocky cop was gone. And here I thought he'd been hanging around because of the cuisine.

I put in a call to my answering service. The lady with the suggestive voice told me that two people were trying to get ahold of me: Ridley Campbell and Patricia Ryan.

I phoned the sheriff first. Business before pleasure, and all that. I also wasn't sure that my current mood was right for discussing whatever Patricia had on her mind.

Campbell came on the line and told me to stay put, he'd get right back to me. I guarded the pay phone. No one tried to take it from me. About two minutes later he called back.

"Swift," he said, "we got us a development here."

"So I gathered," I said. "A break for our side?"

"Depends how you look at it."

"You have to get out of the office to tell me?"

"Uh huh. We can't afford to take chances no more. Anyways, this is it. The Miami cops got back to me this morning. They're the only ones had anything at all on Lester Beavans. Drunk driving. Once."

"That ain't exactly gonna knock him out of the sheriff's race."

"Right," he said. "I was kinda disappointed myself. But we figured the guy couldn't of had much of a record, didn't we? So I wasn't gonna slit my wrists over it. Then we all of a sudden got very lucky."

I felt my stomach tighten. If we'd gotten lucky, that could only mean some disturbing news was on the way.

"The car he was driving," Campbell went on, "it wasn't his. He might of been drunk, but his buddy was all the way passed out. Guy by the name of Joseph Bidwell. Owner of the car. He was asleep in the back seat and didn't wake up until they all got down to the station. Naturally, I had the Florida boys run a scan on the Bidwell character. Guess where our friend Joe is at the moment?"

"The slammer."

"Very swift."

"I went to detective school. The punch line coming now?"

"Yeah."

"Okay," I said, "I'll bite: What is brother Joseph in for? Child molesting?"

"Nope. Possession of cocaine with intent to distribute."

Well, I had to admit that it made sense. There was more money to be made in cocaine than any other business, with the possible exception of oil. Check this out: the price of gold, on the world market, is currently running around four hundred dollars an ounce, U.S. On the street, cocaine will bring *seven times* that. That's two-eight-oh-oh dollars. Per ounce. Many people find that to be sufficient incentive to consider a life of crime, even in a town the size of Charlottesville. Or maybe I should say, especially in a town like Charlottesville. Lately, the place I call home seems to have become a hotbed of cocaine abuse. At least, according to the newspapers. The town is full of affluent, well-educated people, which somehow makes it fertile ground for the powder peddlers. Charlottesville has even been dubbed the "Aspen of the East."

Reaction to this has been predictable. People have been tripping over one another in their haste to express moral outrage in tones louder and more strident than their neighbor. Meanwhile, life goes on, and with it the real problems involved: public ignorance as to the true effects of the drug; a law enforcement effort aimed primarily at the user, who is extremely unlikely to be a threat to society; absurdly harsh punishments for simple possession (especially if you're poor and/or black), which create criminals where there were none;

and the conspiracy of crooked cops and judges and lawyers and politicians, which gets them rich by allowing the mega-buck industry to continue operating.

Naturally, no one wants to touch issues like these with a ten-foot pole. It's a whole lot easier to scream for the blood of the "dope fiends." And safer.

In any case, if Lester Beavans were somehow mixed up in the cocaine racket, it would explain a lot of things. Most obviously, where the campaign funds were coming from. There was also the matter of what Les's backer was up to in the long run. If you were into major league drug dealing, then buying the sheriff was one of the most sensible investments you could make. And there was something else, too. It gave me the creepy crawlies to think about it, but there it was.

"You think John Doe ties in?" I asked him.

"Could be. You cut off a guy's nose before you kill him, I'd say that was intended as a message to someone."

"I take it you're assuming it's the same guy who sends messages like phony birthday cards."

"I am."

"Jesus, Rid, it just keeps getting worse."

"You want out?"

"You have to keep asking me that, don't you?"

"I ask you," he said patiently, "because I mean it. You're not obligated to risk your neck for me. If we're into cocaine dealing and murder, it's official cop business now. You take a hike, ain't nobody gonna say one word against you. Leastways me."

He was right, yet he wasn't.

"Sure," I said. "Official cop business. And what have you got? An unidentified stiff in the reservoir and some joker in the Florida slams nobody ever heard of. That's nothing. Lester Beavans may not be able to tell coke from baking soda, for all you know. You're guessing. I happen to be guessing the same thing. But together our guesses add up to a quick spit in the wind. They don't make anything like a case, as you will be well aware."

"So?"

"So you need me. Until we get something more solid than what we have, there still isn't a damn thing you can do."

He cleared his throat. "Well," he said, "I wouldn't say as your assistance would be . . . unwelcome."

The man's pride was hard and deep. He'd mainline coke himself before he'd admit to needing the likes of me.

"Thanks for the vote of confidence, boss," I said.

"Watch your mouth, Swift."

"Easy. This is no time to start getting on each other's nerves."

"All right. Forget it."

"I will. Now, my plan to shadow Beavans has run into a snag." I related how Lester had ditched me earlier. "Anything you can do about that?"

"Hmmm," he said, "I don't know. If I go to the city cops, I'll be pretty much out in the open from then on. And so will you, little brother."

"You're right. Don't do it. I'll figure out something better. If nothing else, I can rent a car and try to tail him under-cover."

" 'Course that'd take away the getting him mad end of it."

"Yeah, but there's still the possibility he might lead me somewhere important. Beats fingering my belly button."

"Give it a shot," he said. "I got something else in the popper, too. I called in that favor from the FBI. They're gonna get me Lester's tax returns for the past seven years."

"Aaaah. That would be very nice."

"It would. I told them as fast as they could manage it, please. So maybe by Monday. You know the feds. Even the President don't work weekends. I'll let you know soon as I got something in my hands."

"That ought to do it, then. I'll work on rigging a way to let Lester know we're closing on him."

"Good." He paused. "Swift," he said, "you carrying a gun?"

"No."

"Well, maybe you ought."

"Maybe I ought."

We left it at that. But he was right, and I knew it. We'd passed the point of no return. We were in a hardball game with some very talented players. They weren't going to tolerate my presence indefinitely.

I called Patricia. Bob Lee, her boss, answered the phone himself. He told me Patricia wasn't there, that she'd called in sick. I thanked him and phoned her at home.

"Loren," she said as if out of breath, "where have you been? I've been trying to get you all morning."

"I had to get up early. What's the matter?"

"Can you please come over here right away? Please?"

"Sure, but what is it? What'd I do?"

"Not you, Patrick. It's Patrick."

I tensed myself, preparing for the worst. Patrick was a paraplegic, and diabetic. You never knew.

"Loren," she said, "he's gone." Her voice caught a little on the last word.

"What do you mean, 'gone'?"

"Gone. Disappeared. I don't know what I mean. Could you please come over here?"

Five minutes later I was holding her in my arms while she sobbed away her fear for Patrick and her frustration at having been unable to get in touch with me for so long.

When she'd cried herself out, more or less, I sat her down at the kitchen table. I fetched the bottle of Irish whiskey I insisted she always keep on hand. I placed the glass in front of her. She sipped at the whiskey as if it might suddenly start climbing up her nose.

"Now," I said, "tell me."

I could see her gathering it all together. She paused for a moment, then out it came.

"He called Wednesday night," she said, "around seven. He said he was going to work late and then spend the night at a friend's house. I didn't think anything of it. Yesterday he didn't check in, but you know me, I'm not a worrier. When he hadn't showed by bedtime, I decided I'd give him a good talking to when he got home. Then I thought, look at me, acting like the poor kid's mother. He's over twenty-one, after all. He really doesn't have to account for his time. I went to bed feeling a little foolish. When I got up this morning, it was obvious he didn't come in last night, and I realized I hadn't been foolish at all."

"Okay," I said, "what have you done so far?"

"First thing I called Mr. Scott, as soon as he got to his office. I still thought that, maybe, Patrick would turn up there. He didn't. Mr. Scott hasn't seen him since Wednesday. He said Patrick had told him he was going to a friend's house that night to work on some new software. That was the last Mr. Scott's seen of him. He's very concerned, too."

"You tried the hospitals, right?"

She nodded. "Both of the ones in town. Waynesboro, even. Nothing."

"Have you called the cops?"

"Yes. There's no record of an auto accident or anything like that. They said that if I wanted to come down and file a missing person report I should, but that they thought it was really a little soon for that."

She'd said the word "soon" with some bitterness.

"Yeah, they have to say that. They won't be much help, anyway, since he's not a minor. Adults are allowed to do a lot of things, including disappear, as long as there's no sign of kidnapping. The cops can't be bothered. Damn!"

"Loren," she said, "I know something's happened to him, I just know it. I'm his sister. I'm . . . scared."

"I trust your feelings," I said. "But we're not going to get a great deal of official assistance on this, at least not for a while. We're going to have to do it ourselves."

"Bob will let me take the time off. . . . Oh, for Christ's sake, listen to me! My kid brother's missing and I'm worried about *work!*"

I put a hand on her arm.

"Patricia," I said, "I'm a professional. And as a professional, I have to tell you this. Nine times out of ten a missing person isn't actually missing. Chances are, there's a logical explanation for it all. As you say, Patrick's free to do what he wants without consulting you. On the other hand, I know you and

I know you don't frighten easily. So I have to treat it as if he is missing and does need finding. In that case, we'll find him. But bear the other in mind, can you?"

"Loren," she said, "I *know* something's wrong."

She looked me straight in the eye, and I felt like I'd been whacked with a hammer. My professional judgment was that she might be right and she might be wrong. My personal judgment, however, was clear and steady. She was his sister and she was a woman whose insights I'd learned to respect. She would know.

"What are the medical implications?" I asked.

"He can get along pretty well, considering," she said. "He's learned to do without a catheter and all that. The one thing he needs is his insulin. If he doesn't get it, he'll, he'll . . . Oh God, what could have *happened* to him?"

I got her to drink some whiskey, before she broke down again.

"Patricia," I said, "we'll find him. I'm good at this and I've got you to help me. We *will* find him. Now, would he have some insulin with him?"

"I don't know. It depends on where he is. Yes, he normally keeps a supply near him."

"Where does he get it from?"

"People's Drug Store, usually."

"They know him there?"

"Of course. Everyone knows—oh, I see what you mean. We ask them to keep an eye out for him."

"Right. You take care of that, will you?"

When they're in a state like Patricia's, start them doing something. It takes their mind away from their anxiety, and they often find reserves of strength they never knew they had.

"Of course," she said.

"Okay. Next, his friends. Who's the one he spent Wednesday night with?"

"His name's Paul. That's his best friend. I've tried calling him. No one's home."

"Keep trying. Find out what they were working on. Do you know how to operate Patrick's microcomputers?"

"Some."

"If you don't," I said, "get Paul to help you. Go through the stuff on Patrick's desk. There may be a clue on one of those floppy disks in there."

"I'll try."

"Patricia, if there's anything there, you'll dig it out. That's the way you find someone. You keep digging. Eventually, it pays off. It's virtually impossible for someone to vanish without a trace in this society.

"Now, how about Patrick's other friends? The hacker network. You know their names?"

"Most of them."

"Call the ones you do. Find out from them the ones you don't. See if they know anything or have heard anything. If not, put them on the alert. Ask them to keep talking to one another. The more help we have, the better.

"What about girls? Could Patrick be more involved with someone than you know?"

"I don't think so. He has a number of female friends he seems to get on well with. But he's sexually dysfunctional, you know. I doubt that he has a . . . serious romantic interest."

"He may be dysfunctional, but he's still a young man," I said.

"What do you mean?"

"I mean he'll still have a sex drive, even if it can't be carried to completion. I'd ask around."

"All right."

"And by all means, get down to the cops and file that missing person report. It can't hurt. Now, don't worry about accomplishing everything in one afternoon. Some people won't be at home, you know. I've just made a lot of suggestions so you won't run out. I'll meet you back here at six. Whatever's left we can work on together."

"What'll you be doing?" she asked.

"I'll start by spending some time with Scott and take it from there. He might have seen or heard something he didn't realize was important right then, and it might head me in the proper direction. I'll put Ridley Campbell to work, too. He'll have his staff watch for Patrick's van, and whatever else he can do."

I regretted saying it as soon as it was out. So far, we'd avoided any reference to my current case. I'd just as soon I hadn't mentioned Campbell's name. But now, there it was, and she picked up on it instantly.

"Lord, I haven't even asked about you," she said. "Are you okay? What's happening with Ridley?"

"I'm okay," I said. "It's still going on, but this is more important. I can go back to it later."

"Look Loren, I'm sorry about last night. I was out of line, but I was too damned stubborn to admit it until right now. Maybe I was already thinking about Patrick."

"It seems to have healed itself," I said.

"Feels that way to me, too."

We kissed. Not passionately, but with tenderness. A kiss between two people who had more important things to do than hurt each other. We just kept cracking and mending the bond.

"I'll need a photo," I said. "You should carry one, too. Patrick's memorable if you see him in his chair, but if you saw him in the van, you wouldn't know."

"Of course," she said. "I should have thought of that, shouldn't I?"

"Not necessarily. If you don't have many, or you only have one good full-face picture, I'd suggest getting some copies this afternoon. In case we have to circulate them. The camera shop ought to be able to get them to you by tomorrow."

"Good idea."

She went to her room, rummaged around, and returned with a couple of decent snapshots.

"This okay?" she asked.

"Fine."

"I also have this one." She showed me a framed head-and-shoulders shot. "I'll get it duplicated."

"Okay, let's get to work."

* * *

Clementine coasted to a stop in the parking lot of the office building on Rose Hill Drive.

I'd called ahead to make sure Howard B. Scott was in. Then I'd tried Patrick's computer buddy, Paul. He wasn't home yet, but his roommate said he'd be back in an hour. To the best of the roommate's knowledge, Patrick hadn't spent Wednesday night over there. That wasn't entirely unexpected, but it was bad news. I told Patricia to keep after Paul until she got ahold of him. There was still a chance he'd know something of importance.

Finally, I'd made a call to Ridley Campbell, to let him know what was going on. When I'd finished, he said of course he'd put out a bulletin on the van right away. And he'd see what else he could pick up, though what with Lester Beavans and John Doe he had his hands pretty full. It felt like he thought Patrick would probably turn up on his own.

Then he said, "Look, Swift, I understand what the kid means to you. And I understand how you got to give it first priority and put my problems on the back burner for a while. But don't forget what you got yourself into, okay?"

"Ridley," I said, "I'll get back to it when I can. I *told* you that, for chrissake!"

"Calm down, will you? That ain't what I mean. What I'm saying is, our friends won't know that you've dropped out of the action for a while. They may have plans for you. While you're wrapped up looking for Patrick, they could catch you off guard. Clear?"

I didn't say anything. I hadn't even thought of that.

"What it amounts to is, be careful. All right?"

"Okay."

He was right. Goddamn him but he was right. All I needed was to be out hunting for Patrick and run afoul of Lester Beavans and his wrecking crew. Nevertheless, it was a possibility and it had to be prepared for. Before visiting Scott, I'd gone to my apartment. I'd clipped the little holster to the back of my belt and slid the Walther into it. Then I'd chosen my longest, baggiest sport shirt and put it on. You wouldn't notice the gun unless you went searching for it. I was armed now, but I silently implored Les and the fellas to stay out of my way for a bit. I'm not a pacifist. I'll fight if it's necessary, and I'll even initiate violence if I feel that I have to. But I don't like it. My ideal world is a boringly peaceful one.

I went up to Pan-Caribbean Imports. We met in Scott's spartan inner office. He sat across the desk from me.

"Mr. Swift," he said. "I've been terribly concerned. How can I help?"

"Well," I said, "you appear to be the last person to have seen him."

"But how is that possible?" he cut in. "He was on his way to a friend's house. They were going to . . . program or something."

"He apparently never got there. At least Paul's roommate doesn't think so. We haven't been able to talk to Paul yet. He's the one Patrick was on his way to see."

"But people don't just disappear on their way from here to there. Not in Charlottesville. I don't understand. What can I do to be of assistance?"

He seemed genuinely agitated by the turn of events. Maybe he'd had time to develop a real fondness for Patrick. That could be a help. He wasn't my sort of fellow, but he was a man of intelligence and resources.

"Tell me everything you can remember of Wednesday," I said, "up to the point you last saw Patrick."

He leaned back in his leather executive chair and stroked his chin. It took him a few moments to pull his thoughts together.

"I got into the office late," he began. "Noonish or thereabouts. I had some business that I needed to finish up at home. When I got here, Patrick had been working all morning."

"How'd he get in?"

"I'd had a key made for him. He was the kind of person you just . . . trusted, you know?"

I nodded. Yeah, I knew.

"Is," I said.

"Pardon?"

"*Is* the kind of person you trust."

"Oh God, of course. I'm sorry."

"Please go on."

"Well, I'd had the key made on Tuesday," he said. "I don't keep to a regular schedule, and we both thought it would be a good idea if he had access to the office until he completed the project. Anyway, I arrived around noon and Patrick was keying away. He told me that he thought things were going really well and that he'd probably be able to start giving me some hands-on instruction by the end of the week. I told him that was great. We talked about setting up an instructional schedule and about some further modifications that I'll need to make to my inventory system in order to have everything come out right. They didn't amount to a great deal, so I said no problem. Then I went into my office and worked pretty much straight through the afternoon."

"Did anyone else come in that afternoon?" I asked.

"No, no one."

"Did you get any calls?"

"Is that important?"

"I don't know. It could be. I'm just winging it here. I guess what I really meant to ask is whether Patrick got any phone calls."

"Well," he said, "there were several calls, back and forth, between me and one of my offices in Florida. I'm trying to work out the details on a shipment of coral jewelry, as it happens. Patrick had nothing to do with it, and I hadn't even discussed it with him. No need to. As far as him getting any calls, I can say definitely that he didn't. There's only the one phone in here, as I'm sure you've noticed. He didn't use it that day."

"Meaning he didn't make any, either?"

"Correct. Not while I was here."

"So during the whole afternoon, you didn't talk to each other."

"I can't say for positive. We may have exchanged a couple of words when I went out there to get coffee. Nothing of substance, though."

"Okay. Did you talk with him later in the day?"

"Yes, I did," he said. "Late in the afternoon. Maybe around five."

"What about?"

Again he gave it some thought. He struck me as someone who'd want to get details exactly right. I found myself revising my opinion of him slightly upwards. I should probably put more stock in Patrick's judgments.

"Vertical markets," Scott said.

"What?"

"Vertical markets, that's one of the things we talked about. It's something he's very interested in. You see, Patrick has an extremely good business sense. That's unusual for someone in his field. Computer people generally care little about what lies outside their area of expertise. It's especially true among hardware people, those who know what makes a computer tick, and can take one apart and put it back together. Their work is so complex, I guess it doesn't leave much room in their heads for outside interests. Patrick's not like that, though. I'm sure you know that."

"Of course," I said. "But what's a vertical market?"

"Oh, nothing very complicated. It's just a fancy modern way of saying specialization. Take a company like IBM. They're generalists. They want a slice of every part of the computer market. They manufacture hardware, develop software for it, provide service for their machines, everyhting.

"They've always been the model for the rest of the industry. As smaller companies entered the marketplace, they patterned themselves after IBM. Probably unconsciously as often as deliberately. The result was a glut of companies offering the same products. Payroll systems, accounts receivable packages, inventory control. That's attacking the horizontal market. Patrick does that to some extent, or I wouldn't have hired him. But he's smart enough to realize that ultimately there's too much competition in the horizontal market. The big guys will eventually eat the small businessmen for lunch.

"Here's where the vertical market comes in. Someone like

Patrick, what he does is identify some special need that's not being filled. Then he moves straight up the market, filling it for everyone before the competition develops. By the time he has any rivals, he's into a new vertical market."

"You mean, something like programs specifically for the needs of private detectives," I said.

"Exactly."

"And that's what Patrick intended to do?"

"Not private detectives, I don't think. But he talked as if he were working on something specialized."

"You don't have any idea what it might have been?"

"I'm sorry, no. We talked mainly in generalities. He did say that he'd received a number of inquiries since the article in the newspaper. Perhaps one of them set him off."

"All right," I said. "What else did you'all talk about?"

He shrugged. "Baseball. Girls. It was sort of informal."

"Anything there that might be a clue as to where he is?"

He thought about it. I looked at the placid scenes pictured on his walls. Photos of life as it ought to be.

"No," he said finally. "I don't think so."

"What happened after you finished socializing?"

"I went back in my office and took care of some odds and ends. Then I went out for dinner."

"Patrick was still working when you left?"

"Yes. I asked him if he expected to be working late, and he said probably for a couple more hours."

"When was this?"

"About six-thirty, I'd imagine."

"Then you went out?"

"Yes. I went to a restaurant for dinner. I wanted to come back later myself and attend to a couple of things."

"And did you?" I asked.

"Yes."

"When?"

"I don't know. Eight-thirty. Possibly nine."

"Was Patrick still here then?"

"No."

"Did he leave you a note? When he'd be in on Thursday, what he had planned, anything like that?"

"No," he said. "That wouldn't have been like him. He worked very independently. He'd tell me when he finished things, but that was about it."

"How late did you work, Howard?"

"An hour or so."

"You didn't hear from him during that time?"

"No, I didn't. When I was done, I locked up and went home."

"Patrick's van," I said. "Was it in the parking lot when you got back from dinner?"

The question seemed to confuse him.

"I don't know," he said. "I guess I didn't notice. Why would it . . ."

"It's a long shot," I said. "Someone may have picked him up and he may have come back for the van later."

"I don't think so. No, the van was definitely gone, now you mention it. I'd have thought it odd if I'd seen it and then not found him here."

"Okay, so what do we have? Patrick left here sometime between about six-thirty and nine and hasn't been seen since."

"It's not a lot," he said, "is it?"

"It's not. How about you, you got any personal theories?"

"I wish I did. The only thing I can think of is that something might have come up while I was out. Somebody called him and—"

"Who would call him here at night?"

"Perhaps one of his friends. The other possibility is that *he* called someone and they made some plans."

"Could be. Can you find out if any long distance calls were made from this phone that night?" This wasn't too strange a suggestion. Charlottesville lies near a line dividing area codes. Many "local" calls wind up as long distance.

"I'll try," he said. He made a note on a memo pad in front of him.

"Anyway," I said, "we still have the problem that he called Patricia around seven and said he was going to spend the night at Paul's house and then never did. Why would he do that?"

"What if something came up between seven and the time he left?"

"Possible, but I don't see it. He would have called to let his sister know the change of plan. He would also certainly have called Paul, which I don't know yet if he did."

He shook his head. "Nothing makes any sense," he said.

"Nope, nothing does. All right, Howard, I think you've told me about all there is that might be of any use. I'll think on it, and if any other questions occur to me, I'll call. Meanwhile, if you remember anything else, no matter how trivial it might seem, get in touch. You can phone either me or Patricia. My answering service will take the message if we're both out."

He was silent for a long moment. Then he said, "You will find him, won't you, Swift?"

"I'll find him. I'm going to keep at it until I know he's okay. Which I'm sure he is. There's no record of an accident. He's not in any of the local hospitals. And as long as he's got his insulin, he's pretty self-sufficient. I'm assuming that there's a logical explanation here somewhere, and that we'll be hearing from him soon."

"I hope so."

We shook hands and I left.

The next step was to canvass the building, which I did. Most of the people there were nine-to-fivers, but I did find one guy in a real estate office who'd worked into the evening on Wednesday. I asked him if he knew Patrick's van and if it had been in the lot when he left. He said he thought it had been. I asked him what time that was. He said eightish. I asked him if he'd seen or heard anything else unusual that evening. He said no. I thanked him for his help.

No one else in the building had seen or heard anything. I wasn't surprised.

So that was it. It wasn't much, but it was something. I was closer to knowing when Patrick had left the office. Not much before eight, not after nine. Later on, that might prove to be a valuable thing to know.

Now all I had to do was find out in which direction he'd headed.

I stood in the parking lot, next to Clementine. I reached out for the door handle. As I did I saw, out of the corner of my eye, a brown pickup passing by on Rose Hill Drive. I froze and withdrew my hand. A wave of paranoia swept over me. It probably wasn't even the same pickup, but it triggered the memory of how I'd felt in Free Union and in my rearranged apartment. That memory meshed with Ridley's words of caution and suddenly I didn't trust anything or anybody. Not even my faithful VW.

I walked slowly around her. Crawled underneath. Propped open the engine compartment and peered inside.

What are you looking for, Swift? Bombs? A punctured brake line? A directional transmitter?

I didn't know.

I finished my inspection. She looked like my car, nothing more. Gingerly, I opened the door and got in. I turned the key in the ignition. The engine started. It didn't blow up. I felt relieved and somewhat foolish at the same time.

Nevertheless, this had to stop. I couldn't afford to be worried about the Beavans crowd while I was searching for Patrick. I didn't want to check my car for tampering every time I used it. I drove to the downtown mall.

The little clock in the door said that they'd be back in about fifteen minutes. I decided it was worth the wait.

In actuality, Ann Luden appeared in about ten minutes. She unlocked the door and went up to campaign HQ. I went up after her.

"Swift," she said. "What—"

I held up my hands, palms out. "I surrender," I said.

"Swift, what are you doing here?"

She was standing with hands on her hips. Once I'd thought her an attractive woman.

"I told you," I said. "I surrender."

"To whom and for what?"

"To you, to the candidate, to whatever shadowy figures are lurking in the background of this campaign. For the duration."

That was stretching things a little, but I certainly didn't want to put a time limit on my nonparticipation.

"Swift," she said, "I don't have an idea in hell *what* you're talking about. If you're not going to make sense, get lost, will you?"

"I hope I don't have to get lost to keep your people from following me."

"Aaaaagh! We have *not* been *follow*ing you! The only following I know of is what *you've* been doing to Lester."

"Okay, maybe you're not following me anymore."

"Dear God. Look, Swift, you are being a very large pain in the butt. I really have plenty of things to do that are more productive than this. So if you don't mind . . ."

"And if I do mind?"

"That's tough. I have neither the time nor the inclination to trifle with you."

"Shucks," I said. "I guess I'm not really wanted."

"The man has a brain after all."

"But I did come here to tell you something, Ann. I'm finished. I'm not going to dog Lester's campaign any longer and I'm not going to do the story that you've had such trouble believing in. There are some considerably more important things in my life at the moment. So you're free of me. I'd just like to be left alone, too."

"Mr. Swift, it will give us great pleasure to leave you quite as alone as we've already been leaving you. Now, is that it?"

"That's it."

"Good."

She turned her back on me. Without a single kind word of farewell. So it goes.

"May the best man win," I called out as I left.

She ignored me.

I eased out of the office and had started down the stairs before I realized that I wasn't alone. The stairwell was narrow. Down near the bottom, it was being filled from wall to wall by the bulk of Lester Beavans. He looked up at me. His eyes were like two holes poked in a midday blue sky, nothing beyond but the emptiness between the stars.

"Swift," he said, "I thought I done told you I didn't want to see you hanging around no more."

For some reason, my legs felt like they belonged to someone else. Someone who weighed about forty pounds and had trouble kicking a football without cracking his ankle. Beavans was too big for me to pass unless he turned sideways. He seemed entirely disinclined to do that.

"Ah well," I said, "you see—"

"Swift," he said, "I am a patient man, am I not?"

I nodded. He was whatever he said he was.

"Speak up, son."

"Yes," I said, "you sure are. Patient."

"And do you think I might now be losing my patience with you?"

"Yes, I suppose you might."

"And what do you think I will do if I lose my patience?"

"I don't know. I reckon you might get angry."

"You reckon right. I don't like to get angry, Swift. It makes me sometimes do things without thinking about them. You know what I'm saying?"

Suddenly I realized how silly all this was. I was in a public place with a candidate for office. For sheriff, no less. He might growl at me, but he sure wouldn't bite. I'd just been unglued by the power of his physical presence.

My legs returned to their rightful owner and I started down the stairs.

"Look Les," I said, "I've just had a pleasant chat with Ann. I'm out of your hair. My journalistic career is on indefinite hold. Right now, I don't care if there's a story in this campaign or not. If there is, somebody else can get it. That's the truth. So I'll make you a deal. I lay off you, you lay off me."

I stopped just above him.

"How about it?" I said.

He looked dubious. He cocked his head to one side and stared at me as if trying to dissect my intentions.

"Mind if I slide on past?" I said.

He turned aside. I think he was perplexed at how quickly

the atmosphere of intimidation had dissipated. He wouldn't want to feel like he was losing his touch.

"We ain't never *did* nothing to you, anyway," he said after me.

I was almost out the door. I just waved back over my shoulder without turning around.

Next I decided to hit the service stations. I took out my map of Charlottesville and drew a little circle around the office building on Rose Hill Drive. I made the diameter half a mile. That'd do for starters.

It stood to reason that if Patrick had suddenly decided to take a trip somewhere, he would've wanted to start with a full tank of gas. Maybe the van's tank had already been full. Okay, then I was wasting my time. But maybe it hadn't been; Patrick was notorious for ignoring such things. In that case, I could probably locate the station where he'd stopped. Patrick is someone you might remember, and he's chatty. The attendant would likely recall him, and I might pick up some hint as to where he'd been headed. I could also find out whether he'd been alone.

The job isn't as large as it might sound. There aren't but so many stations in Charlottesville. Many are entirely self-service. Those I could eliminate right away; Patrick never liked to hassle with pumping his own gas. I could also eliminate those that closed before eight.

I was still left with quite a few inside my little circle, but a manageable number. It was a pretty good time of day, too. Few stations stay open after ten, and almost none are all-nighters, so the evening crews for the most part would be in place. It'd take some time, but I figured I could cover the circle by the time I had to meet Patricia. If I didn't find anything, I could widen the circle.

I didn't find anything. I drove and I talked and I showed pictures, and I got a very polite nothing.

I arrived at Patricia's house right at six. Hot, tired, and

frustrated. She was already there. We made some sandwiches, opened a couple of beers, and sat at the kitchen table to discuss our progress.

I ran down the things that I'd tried and plans I had for the future. At one point, I thought she was going to start crying. She was looking at me as if I weren't there.

"What is it?" I said.

"Oh Loren," she said, "it's just that I keep seeing Patrick in the van in a ditch somewhere that no one can find him. I couldn't bear that."

"Don't," I said, but I couldn't stop her from thinking her thoughts. I'd had the same vision myself. I was able to push it out of my head most of the time.

Then she cried a little. I let it run its course. There was nothing I could do. Patricia would have gotten furious if I'd started giving her any phony reassurances.

Later, she went over what she'd done. Gone to the cops and filed a missing person report. They were sympathetic, cooperative, and seemingly helpful, as I knew they would be. They would also not follow up with any serious energy.

She'd been to Patrick's regular drug store and talked with the pharmacist and his assistants. They all knew Patrick. None had heard from him recently. All were very concerned and promised to let her know if he showed up. If they couldn't get her, they were to phone me. She'd also talked with Patrick's doctor, on the outside chance that he might be contacted. That was an excellent idea, and one I hadn't thought of.

She'd gotten ahold of Patrick's friend Paul. The two of them had planned on getting together Wednesday evening to work on some programs they were developing. Patrick had mentioned he might stay the night if the work kept them up late. Not surprisingly, he'd never shown up. Paul wasn't concerned at the time. His friend had been known to become distracted and space out prior commitments. Now Paul thought we had good reason to worry, though. He'd promised to help in any way he could. For starters, he was coming over around eight to sift through Patrick's diskettes with us. As far as he knew, and he should know, Patrick didn't have any current projects that would suddenly call him out of town. But it was worth a look.

After talking with Paul, Patricia had tried a couple of Patrick's other cronies in the hacker network. They had all expressed concern, but had told her the same thing: if anyone knew anything, it would be Paul.

She'd also asked everyone if Patrick had a girlfriend that she might not know about. No one thought so.

That was about it. We'd both run down our afternoons, and even in retrospect they amounted to little. Though we'd done the small things that needed to be done. We cracked another couple of beers and enjoyed a few minutes of silence.

Then Patricia said, "Loren, I want you to tell me something."

"Sure," I said. "Shoot."

"I want you to tell me what you were working on for Ridley Campbell."

"C'mon, Patricia, this isn't—"

"No! I don't want any of your song-and-dance about it. This is pre*cise*ly the time that I want to hear it. The whole thing. If I'd known a little more, it might not have taken me so long to find you today."

She had that look that she gets. When she does, if you get in an argument with her, you will lose.

"Okay," I said, "I understand your frustration earlier in the day. But I'm with you now. I won't leave you until we find out what's happened. I don't understand—"

I stopped because it was hopeless. She turned the green eyes on me full force. She could use them to shut you up any time that's what she wanted.

"Loren," she said. She said it evenly, too evenly. Inside the bomb was ticking away. "My kid brother is missing and you are, for better or worse, my man. His disappearance has coincided with you working on something for Campbell that's so nasty you don't even want to see me while you're doing it. Now all of these things may bear no relation to one another. Yet there's that one chance that they're somehow connected.

So long as that one chance exists, I have the right to know what you've been doing. I can't make it any plainer than that. Now, will you please tell me."

Her words were a full bucket of ice water in the face. Damn me for not considering the possibility. But I hadn't.

I didn't think there was anything in it. I had no reason to suspect that the Beavans crowd knew of Patricia's and my relationship. In addition, it was pushing things to imagine that they'd get at me through Patrick. Why not just deal with me directly? Which they'd already done to some extent.

Still, I had to give it some consideration. There might be dark corners and mysterious connections in the campaign for sheriff that I knew nothing about. The thought made me uneasy.

So she was right. She did deserve to know.

"Patricia," I said, "I'm sorry. I truly am. This is the first time I've been involved in something dirty since a couple of days after I met you. I haven't been at all sure how to handle it. Probably I've done it all wrong. Enough said."

Then I told her everything. The whole story, from my first meeting with Campbell in McIntire Park up to the moment I slipped past Lester Beavans on the stairs earlier in the day.

"So you see," I said at the end, "if there's cocaine involved, we're dealing with some ruthless characters. They're not the type who would go after someone like Patrick when they could just as easily have me. Or Ridley, for what it's worth."

"Jesus," she said, "using cocaine money to gain control of Albemarle County politics. Is it possible?"

"Yeah, it's possible. Very large money is involved here. If that's what's happening. It looks probable, but there's still a lot of speculation on our parts."

She shook her head. "It's all so hard to believe. This isn't New York City. It isn't Miami or L.A. or even Nashville. It's Charlottesville–small-town–Virginia."

"No matter," I said. "It's still 1980s America. We're the most drug-dependent society in the history of the world. If cocaine abuse is suddenly a national epidemic, it should come as no surprise."

"I guess I felt like it was something that happened . . . other places."

I laughed. "Happens in the finest of homes. What they should do is legalize everything. Start from scratch."

"Loren!"

"Nah, it's a good idea. If everything were legal, we'd very quickly find out if we deserve to survive as a culture or whether, given the candy store, we'd spend all our time in it."

"I don't think it's worth the risk."

"You're just admitting that we may be hopeless."

"That's your point of view," she said. "Anyway, this is all irrelevant. What I care about is whether my brother could have somehow gotten mixed up in this ugly business."

"I don't see how."

"I don't either. But we're both saying that it's a remote possibility. Don't you think that's enough to mention it to Ridley Campbell?"

"I do. Plus I'll make sure that Rid keeps me informed of any developments while I'm not working directly for him. In fact, I'll do it now."

And I did. Ridley didn't think there was much chance Patrick had fallen in with dope dealers because of somebody wanting the sheriff's job. But he did agree the two of us should keep in close touch.

"Nobody's seen the van," I said.

"Nope. I got all the men looking."

"I checked with Ann and Lester today. They weren't thrilled to see me. I told them I wasn't gonna bother them anymore. Asked if they'd mind returning the favor."

"Good idea," he said. "They still watching you?"

"I'm not sure. I hope not anymore."

"You're slipping, boy. Used to been, you'da *known* something like that."

"I realize that," I said. "Believe me, I do. I thought it was like riding a bicycle, but it ain't. You don't use your skills and you lose them fast as your eye for the hard breaking ball."

"Didn't know you played."

"A little. I always had trouble with the curve low and away. If you can't hit it, you get left behind."

"Good thing you like detecting."

"Ha ha. Nice, Sheriff. You're a real untutored wit, you are."

"Easy on the fiddy-cent words, Swift."

"Yeah, I've noticed your sluglike mind. See you, Ridley."

Shortly after I'd finished talking with Campbell, Paul arrived. He and Patricia and I worked late into the night, sifting through the stuff in Patrick's workspace, looking for some new development project that Paul didn't know about. Paul was skeptical. He didn't think Patrick was the kind of person who would keep a juicy new job all to himself. Still, he agreed it was worth a try.

We looked hard.

At one point, I mentioned to Paul that Patrick's current employer thought he had some sort of new project in the fire.

"Vertical marketing, he called it," I said. "Something to do with finding a niche no one has filled, then running with it."

"Sure, we've talked about that," Paul said.

"This guy seemed to think Patrick had a specific application in mind."

Paul thought about it.

"He may have been talking about the real estate thing," he said. "We've been conceptualizing a package that would do everything from searching MLS listings to displaying plats to projecting tax advantages. It's a wide open market, and if we could wire into all the real estate offices in this town, we'd have a license to print money. But we haven't even begun to develop the software yet."

"You don't think he's off somewhere connected with that."

"Nope. He would've discussed it with me first."

"Patrick's boss also said he's received a lot of inquiries since the newspaper article. Any chance one of them led to a sudden trip?"

"I just don't think so, Mr. Swift. If there was a query that really turned him on, I would've heard about it. We're not jealous of each other's successes. We share things. When he gets excited, he calls me. I'm his best friend."

"Okay," I said. "Let's keep looking anyway."

By midnight we were only halfway through the diskette library and we hadn't found anything. We decided to knock off. Paul agreed to return in the morning to pick up the search again.

Patricia and I went to bed.

It was strange, the two of us lying there on our backs, next to each other but not touching, wrapped in our own thoughts. We didn't even try to make love. Now me, I think that sex is great for reducing tension. But Patricia would have thought it horribly inappropriate, I could tell. I respected that and I let her be. When she wanted physical contact, she'd let me know. In far less time than I thought it would take, she was asleep.

I lay awake for a long time, trying to make some form of sense out of an event that was so entirely without it. Patrick had now been gone for better than two full days. What were the conditions under which such a thing could happen?

Not many.

First, obviously, he could have had an accident. He could have lost control of the van, piled into a ditch somewhere, and remained undiscovered. It was possible. It was, however, unlikely. The circumstances would have needed to be special: he would have had to be uninvolved with another vehicle; it would have had to occur with no witnesses in sight or within earshot; and he would have to be someplace where days could pass with no one noticing what had happened. Unlikely. Such conditions are associated only with accidents late at night on remote back roads. Patrick, by contrast, had left Scott's office before nine. To the best of everyone's knowledge, he'd been headed for a friend's house within the city. An accident in town simply couldn't escape notice for so long. And even if he had detoured out into the boonies for some reason, it was still damned difficult to go off the road without leaving some sign that would be discovered before the next day was out.

The accident theory was lousy. I couldn't discount it completely. But it was lousy, and besides, it wasn't something I could profitably pursue.

There was also the possibility that Patrick might have left town, on business or whatever. I didn't like that one any better. If he had, there was almost no chance that he wouldn't have told his sister where he was going. Plus his luggage was still in his closet and there didn't appear to be a lot of clothes missing. Plus he hadn't been to the drug store for extra insulin. I didn't like it, but if that was what had happened, then he didn't need finding and he'd get in touch with us when it was convenient for him to do so.

Another possibility was that Patrick had been the victim of some random crime or other. In that case, he would almost have to be dead, with his body concealed somewhere. And the van would have to be on its way to some used car dealer in Carolina who operated on the fringes of the law. There was little hope there, and nothing that I could actively do to help. The only way we'd ever find out anything would be if the van were traced. It would take the cops to do that.

What I ended up with was a great deal of unlikelihood. I was forced to take Patricia's suggestion seriously, that Patrick had in some way run afoul of the people I'd been investigating. There was no evidence that that had happened, but there was no evidence that it hadn't. I looked at it and it looked improbable still. What would they have done? Killed Patrick because I was annoying their boy? Snatched him in order to use him against Campbell later on? It didn't make sense any way I put it together. If big-time drug profits were at stake, then the people involved were certainly capable of holding a paraplegic kid against his will. But why? The puzzle had some very sizable missing pieces.

Yet there was a difference between this improbability and all the others. It was one that I could look into. It wouldn't be the place where I'd want to put all my eggs. But, starting tomorrow, I could at least take some preliminary action.

I fell asleep before I could determine what form that action should take.

8

SATURDAY MORNING PATRICIA AND I WOKE UP WITHIN MINUTES
of together. We held each other for a while. I murmured small
words of encouragement and she pretended to believe them.

Over breakfast, we made some plans for the day.

"Why don't you stay here with Paul," I said. "There's no
need for the both of us to hang around."

"Okay," she said.

"That ought to take at least the morning. I got the impression he still had a ways to go."

"I think he does. And that's just the floppies. Patrick's got
a hard disk, too."

"Yeah, but I think it's mostly baseball stuff on there."

"Who's to say he hadn't decided to try and make some
money off his baseball knowledge?"

"Good point. Stick with it as long as you need to."

"Sure," she said. "But I pretty much agree with Paul. I
doubt there's anything in that room that he doesn't know
about."

"Well, we won't know until we know."

"Right. After that, I'll start contacting his other friends.

Actually, I could begin doing it during. Paul won't need me to be with him every second. He's aware of what we're looking for."

"Fine. If you've got any time left over, you might start canvassing the drug stores. Make sure every pharmacist in town has his name and has seen a picture. Make sure they know who to call if he comes in. While you're at it, let the city cops know what you're doing. It'll show them you're seriously concerned, it'll be a courtesy to them, and they won't be surprised if some druggist does call.

"Meet back here at six again?"

"Six. But you haven't told me what you're going to do, Loren."

"I'm not positive myself. I'll widen my search of the service stations, knock on doors around Rose Hill Drive. But those are real long shots. They're not enough. I suppose I'm going to end up taking your advice."

"What advice?"

"To look into the possibility that Patrick's disappearance is connected to the job I was doing for Campbell."

"Oh." She looked at me as if trying to read my mind.

"You did suggest it," I said.

I felt myself going on the defensive. I didn't know why I was doing it, but Patricia had that effect on me sometimes. She'd give me that certain look and off I'd go. One of the things I'd decided was that she might possibly be more intelligent than I was. Not as clever, certainly, but maybe more intelligent in the intellectual sense. Even if I did have one semester of college to her none.

"I know I did," she said finally. "You're not going to involve me in any of that, are you?"

"Patricia, why should I involve *you* in it? *I'm* the one who was working on the case. You've got more than a day's work to do as it is."

"None of it the slightest bit dangerous."

"*Some*body's got to do those things."

"Loren, you're dividing up the work along certain lines."

"It's a matter of convenience."

"I think it's more than that."

"You think I'm still trying to keep you separated from the seamier side of my life," I said. "Is that it?"

She nodded.

"Well, so what if I am? I'm experienced in dealing with these things and you're not. You're entirely unequipped. It's logical, my way."

"Let me just remind you," she said tersely, "that we're not in a logical situation anymore."

"I know that."

"Loren, I will do what you say. I will get done the little tasks that need to get done. But you are going to have to rethink the way in which you relate to people outside yourself. Mostly me."

Lady, I thought, you not only make me rethink the rules, you get me asking myself what game I'm in the middle of.

"I don't know what to say to you, Patricia."

"Just say to me that we are in this thing together and that we must not hesitate to ask things of one another, no matter the consequences."

"That's a lot of words. Can I just say yes?"

She smiled. "That will be fine. I'll check with your answering service from time to time. If something comes up and you can't get me, leave a message with them. Whatever it is. Okay?"

"Okay."

"Let's find something today."

"Let's."

I started out with service stations again, widening the circle by half a mile. If the guy who'd been on duty wasn't there, I got a name to check back with. When nothing panned out, I returned to Rose Hill Drive and began canvassing the neighborhood adjacent to the office building. Banging on people's doors, asking if they knew the kid in the wheelchair and his

145

van. If they did, had they seen it leave the area on Wednesday night? If they didn't, had they seen anything at all unusual that night?

It was a miserable, tedious job, carried out for hours under another merciless August sun. But it paid off.

I found a jogger. So help me, I will never make fun of them again. This guy lived on a quiet street off Rose Hill, and I found him doing quiet, Saturday around-the-house chores. He told me that every day, when he got home from work, he'd run a couple of miles. On Monday, he'd noticed Patrick pulling himself into the van. He'd been ready to offer assistance with the chair, but then noticed that Patrick had the routine down well, so he'd jogged on. He saw the kid on Tuesday, once again as Patrick was leaving the office. And he saw him again on Wednesday, but it wasn't when he was jogging. It was later, when he was walking to the nearby convenience store. The van came out of the parking lot and turned right. That was the way you'd turn if you were headed toward the By-pass, out of town.

What time?

He wasn't sure. Probably about nine. Definitely after dark. Was he alone? I held my breath.

Sorry, he couldn't say. It was dark. The van had turned away from him. Besides, he had no reason to want to be checking the van for passengers.

I thanked the jogger and immediately called Campbell. He promised to redouble his efforts to locate the van. Then I went to the city cops and pleaded my case for half an hour. They were considerate and made sympathetic noises, and they promised to help look for the van. But as yet there was no evidence that any law had been broken. Until there was, they couldn't launch a full-scale investigation.

It was frustrating, but I understood. The cops deal in crime, not conjecture. If they fully ran down every crackpot's speculations, they'd never get anything done. I left the cop station knowing full well that if Patrick were somewhere findable, then there was a ninety-nine percent chance it would have to be Patricia and I who found him.

Back on the street, I thought it over. I could continue to do the little things that every investigation requires. The kind of things that had gotten me the scanty facts I already had. At best, I could reasonably hope to improve my understanding of the events of Wednesday night only slightly.

On the other hand, I could give in to the gnawing feeling I had that there was something very evil going on and that Patrick had been sucked into it. If I did that, I would at least know where to begin.

I mentally tossed a coin, making sure that it came up tails, then got in my car and drove to the nearest supermarket. There I picked up a case of Moosehead. Then I drove to Jonesy's place.

Jonesy lives in Belmont, like I do. Our apartments are not dissimilar. Both are in old frame family houses that have been converted in the past ten years. Whereas I live in a basement, Jonesy's an attic dweller. Not exactly luxury digs, especially for someone with his ambition, but then the *Press* isn't overly loose with the salary money.

I figured there was a good chance Jonesy would be at home. Since he's gone on the day shift, he gives the paper a weekday nine to five and not much more. Besides, the Orioles had a big afternoon game with the Tigers and it was on TV. Jonesy is a fanatic Bird fan. As the summer wears on, his habits become more and more predictable. Especially if Baltimore is in the thick of a pennant race. They usually are.

He was in.

"Berwyn Jones, I presume," I said at the door.

"Swift," he said, "you are the penultimate answer to a thirsty fan's prayers. Do come in."

I followed Jonesy into the apartment. He's a slight man, a couple of inches shorter than me and a good deal lighter. I picture him as the classic kid who gets beat up a lot in elementary school and develops a way with words as a defense.

Jonesy's TV dominates the living room. It's one of those big twenty-some-inch models. He's wired for cable, plus he subscribes to all the options the company offers. Claims it's the only way to survive in a cultural backwater like Charlottesville.

The TV was on. Morris and McGregor were warming up. We cracked a pair of beers.

"Long time no visit," he said. "Business or pleasure?"

"Business," I said.

He sighed. "What else? I don't think you enjoy my company anymore, Swift."

"I promise an uninterrupted afternoon of beer and sports-talk someday soon," I said. "Just let me get a few things straightened out."

"That's your life, Swift, and you don't even realize it. There's always something that needs straightening and there always will be." He reached over to the TV and turned off the sound. "I'll shut it up, but I won't kill the picture. Too big a game." He leaned back and stretched out his bony legs. "You now have my divided attention."

"Good. I want to buy some coke."

He laughed most heartily. "Nose candy? You? C'mon Swift, you're a juicehead!"

"Nevertheless, I want to buy some coke."

He stopped laughing. "What is this?"

"I told you. It doesn't sound that complicated to me."

"Swift, it may not be complicated, but it's pretty goddamn off the wall. Since when did you turn into Frosty the Snow-man?"

"I don't see that that matters. I'm looking for a connection. I expect you can point me to one."

He got up, walked around his chair twice, and sat down again. The Tigers were batting in the top of the first. Mc-Gregor looked sharp.

"I don't like this," he said. "I've known you for a couple of years and I've never even seen you smoke a joint. Now you expect me to believe you're into *cocaine?*"

"I don't care whether you like it or not," I said. "Will you help me?"

He stared at me while he thought it over. I could see the wheels turning inside his head. After they'd turned, it was presumed that a fat news story was about to pop out here.

"What's in it for me?" he said.

"I already bought you a case of Moosehead."

"You're too kind."

"I could arrange to bring another."

"Can it, Swift. You're working on something. I get two calls in the past week asking about local political figures. Then you come looking to get your nose greased. Sure. I'm not a moron, even if I do work for the *Press*. Let me put it this way: I don't really care what the local pols are running up their noses, but if there's more to it than that, I want to know about it. You dig?"

"I dig."

"So what are my chances of being dealt in?"

"If there was anything to be dealt into, your chances would be poor."

"You make this a difficult friendship, Swift."

"You make it tough for a fella to get high, Jones."

I smiled winningly. He wasn't about to let it bowl him over.

"I don't know," he said. "Suppose I give you what you want, are we talking the possibility of a payback at some future point?"

I shrugged. "We're talking a man who wants some drugs, as far as I can see," I said.

"All right, already," he said. "I get the picture. You don't want to talk about it. At all. It must be pretty damned important to you. Let me think."

He thought. I watched Morris retire the side in order. He looked sharp, too.

"Okay," Jonesy said. "This is obviously a touchy subject. What I'll do is, I'll do the talking for both of us. I'll give you what you want. But so help me, if I don't get something better out of this than a stupid case of beer, then don't bother me ever again. I mean it, Swift. I really do."

I smiled winningly again.

"Now," he went on, "what you're asking ain't quite so simple. There's coke dealers and guys who deal some coke. Since there's so much coke in this town, there's a lot of the latter. It's a pyramid. Bunch of small-timers at the bottom. Probably one guy at the top. We don't think any of the mobs control the trade in Charlottesville. Yet. In between, you got your middlemen. They aren't easy to locate, but give me a few days, I'll get you a name."

"I need a name today. A street dealer will do."

"That's easy. What kind? College kid?"

"Give me a scuzzball if you got one."

"What, you want to get burned?"

"Maybe."

"Jesus," he said. "Okay, it's your funeral. Francis Fench."

"Francis *Fench*?"

"That's his name. I think it might even be Francis Xavier Fench."

"Address?"

He gave me an address off Cherry Avenue.

"Black guy?" I asked.

"Naw." He described Fench. "Looks more like a sixties relic. He lives in a black neighborhood because he thinks it's cool, or because he thinks the law's less likely to hassle him. Hell, I don't know."

"Okay, Jonesy. Thanks."

I got up. The Tigers had two on, one out. Scotty was struggling.

"Just remember the deal, you bastard."

"Thanks, Jonesy."

As I left the apartment, Jonesy turned up the sound on the TV. I heard the whoosh of a beer being opened, then the crack of a bat followed by no hometown cheering. The Tigers were up to something.

I hadn't wanted to treat Jonesy that way, but I'd had little choice. I needed to get across clearly that I didn't want him even to speculate on what I was doing, much less start poking around himself. The fewer details he had, the better. I'd make it up to him someday.

Right now, I needed to meet Francis X. Fench. I drove to the address Jonesy had given me and parked half a block away. I walked to a two-story green frame apartment building with small outside porches on each floor. There were a lot of people in the street, it being a summer Saturday. The people were all black. They looked at me, some with disinterest, some with hostility. I tried to look like a nice guy.

I went into the green building and up to the second-floor rear. There would be a balcony out back, too, I imagined. Something for a hasty exit. I knocked on Fench's door.

He wasn't in. Or at least he wasn't answering the door. I didn't feel like breaking and entering yet, so I left.

I walked back to my car. No one had trashed it. I got in, rolled down both the windows, and tilted the seat back a little. I sat in my personal pool of sweat and I waited.

The people of the neighborhood looked my way from time to time. I kept on trying to appear friendly. One thing I really didn't need right now was trouble because of the color of my skin. But I didn't want to miss Fench, either. Maybe I should have asked for the name of a student.

After a while, nearly everyone lost interest in me. If I was a cop, I obviously didn't want anyone in sight. That was all most folks ever cared about. The only human contact I had all afternoon was with a couple of young kids who came over and peered into the car like it was a display case in the museum of interplanetary artifacts. They wanted to know what I was doing. They didn't really care; they knew I wasn't after them. It was just kid curiosity.

I told them I was waiting for a friend of mine. When they asked who, I told them a girlfriend. When they asked if she was black, I said, what else? They thought that was very funny. I told them I was only kidding, ha ha. I didn't want their big brothers wondering what black girl. They asked me if I wanted to see them do Michael Jackson. I said sure. They did him, and they were good. Then they got bored and went someplace else.

At six I got out of the car and walked up the street to a public phone. I called Patricia and told her I wouldn't be home. She demanded to know what I was doing, so I told her, without naming names and places. Naturally, she wanted to know how I'd decided on this particular course of action. I told her it looked like our best shot at the moment. Then I took a deep breath and told her what I'd learned from the jogger.

"Oh God," she said. I could feel her straining to keep the hysteria at bay.

"It's bad," she said, "isn't it?"

"I don't know. It's not really much more information than we had before," I said lamely.

"Don't, Loren."

"All right."

"Have you been to the police?"

"Yeah, first thing. They're maybe a little more concerned, but I wouldn't wait on them. Ridley'll do his best to help, though."

"It's up to us, isn't it?"

"I think for the most part. Right now, we need the answers to some questions we haven't asked yet. I'm hoping this character I'm after will get us started."

"I—I guess it's as good a plan as any."

"Hang on, Patricia. I'll be home as soon as I can."

I hated to leave her like that, but there was nothing else to do. We hung up and I walked back to the car.

I waited. It was a long wait and it was hot. Making up lists of Italian ballplayers didn't help. I was too personally involved in what I was doing.

Eventually, it got dark. I didn't like that. I wasn't afraid, since I had the Walther, but I still wanted to avoid trouble. One way to do that is not to sit alone in a car after dark in this neighborhood. I pleaded silently with the P.I. gods to keep me out of the path of any Saturday night mean drunks in the vicinity.

Fench arrived about ten-thirty. The street wasn't particularly well-lighted, but I recognized him immediately. He was white, for one thing. Short and wiry, with a ponytail halfway down his back. A sixties relic, as Jonesy had said. Hard to miss. He didn't look my way.

I followed him into the green frame building. He was well

up the stairs when he heard me come in after him. He turned instinctively. Whatever he saw, it made him take off for the second floor. I took off, too.

If he'd had another second's head start, he'd have beaten me. As it was, he was just turning the key in the lock. I whipped out the Walther. When he saw it, he froze.

"Inside," I said.

When he hesitated, I added, "Slowly. And don't even think about trying me. I really don't care if you live or die."

It's an act that I have difficulty carrying off. Someone like Lester Beavans, for example, would have seen through it instantly and squashed me like a cockroach. The act works well with punks, though; they have an ingrained respect for guns. Fench didn't hesitate any longer. He opened the door and moved inside. *Very* slowly.

I kicked the door shut behind us.

"Stop," I said.

He stopped.

"Look mister," he said, "what do you want?" His voice was furry and he had to clear his throat once.

"Lie down," I said. "On your stomach. Arms stretched out in front of you, legs spread. *Now!*"

He obeyed.

"Look," he said. "I've got some money. You can have it. . . ."

I knelt down and put one knee in the small of his back. I pressed the barrel of the Walther against the base of his skull. It's one of the most horrible feelings in all the world. I know. He made small whimpering sounds and filled the air with the stench of his urine.

"Fench," I said as coldly as I could, "I am not interested in you. I am not interested in your money. I am not interested in how you made it. I only want one thing from you. I want to know who supplies you with coke. If I do not know this five seconds from now, I am going to turn your brains to oatmeal."

"Johnson," he yelped.

"Nickel Johnson?"

"Nickel *Johnson.*"

Johnson was small-time. He dressed like a big city pimp. He drove a long black Cadillac. The cops knew he was into drugs and prostitution but hadn't quite been able to put him away yet. Or hadn't wanted to. He wasn't much more than an overblown punk. In the drug pyramid, he wouldn't be more than middle level. And that would be as high as he'd be allowed to rise unless he could figure a way to bleach his skin. Either side of the law, the racial pecking order was the same.

Small-time. Not the best fit to my purposes.

"And who supplies Johnson?" I said.

"Hey man, I don't know. Jesus, I'm only a street dealer—"

"Five seconds. Four, three—"

"I don't know!" he squealed. "I don't *know!* For Christ's sake, I don't *want* to know!"

I let him blubber and drool for another few seconds. He didn't crack and start spouting names. Maybe he really didn't know any more. It was possible. Even if he did, if he hadn't told me by now, he wasn't going to. I withdrew the gun from his head and eased off his back.

"Okay, Fench," I said. "You've been most cooperative. Now there's just one other little thing. If I find out you've told anyone about our little chat, you're through. Next time you don't even see me. I find you on a dark street some night and you never know what hit you. Believe me, you won't be able to hide from us. We straight on that?"

I liked the "us." It was a nice touch. It'd scare him good.

"Sure man, sure," he said. "Just leave me alone. I don't tell nobody."

"Good. Now, you lie there peaceful like for five minutes. I even think I see your face before I'm out of this neighborhood and you're gonna be very, very sorry, y'dig?"

"Right, sure."

"Have a nice evening, Fench."

I walked back to my car. The last thing in the world I expected was for Fench to tail me out of the building, but I didn't take the chance. I made a U-turn, away from the apartment building, and drove a block before I switched the lights on. If Fench was watching, he wouldn't get much. One Volkswagen looks exactly like all the others in the dark.

When I got back to Patricia's, she was waiting up for me. We sat down and cracked open some beer.

"How you holding up?" I asked, taking her hand.

"Okay," she said. She attempted a weak smile.

"Let's compare notes," I said. Better to talk about something else.

We went over our days. She and Paul had plodded through the rest of Patrick's library of floppies. Nothing unexpected had turned up. She'd then covered the drug stores. All of the pharmacists in town were now on the lookout for Patrick, though none had yet seen him. Those two jobs had taken her up to dinnertime. Which reminded me that I hadn't yet eaten. I got some cold chicken out of the fridge and washed it down with another beer. I added a jigger of Irish whiskey for dessert. I was still a little keyed up from my encounter with Fench, and the alcohol helped take the edge off.

After she'd talked to me, Patricia had begun tracking down Patrick's friends, female and otherwise. That was good; she was realizing the value of keeping busy. But nothing had come of it.

I then told her what I'd done since six o'clock. I didn't pull any punches when I came to the part about trashing Francis X. Fench.

"Um," she said, "that's a side of you I've never seen, Loren. Thank God."

"Why?" I said. "Are you afraid I might brutalize you?"

"If it's in you, it's in you."

"C'mon Patricia. Sure it's in me. It's in everybody. If I was a randomly violent person, you'd know it by now. There are just certain situations in which it's all you have. Dealing with punks is one of them. You've got to quickly convince them that you are tougher than they are and that you are capable of absolutely anything in the very next second. Otherwise, they'll eat you alive."

"I suppose."

"Patricia, I want to find your brother. If in order to do that I have to lean on some half-wit street punk, then I'll do it without thinking twice. Do you disapprove?"

"No."

"It feels like you do."

"No," she said wearily. "I don't. You have to do the kinds of things you know how to do. Part of what you think you're picking up is probably your own disgust at what you sometimes get forced into. But the biggest part is: I'm tired, I'm worried, I miss Patrick, and I hate living in a world full of people who make profit off of other people's misery."

It was undoubtedly the most negative thing she'd said to me since I met her. Normally, she had an unforced optimism to her nature that was unshakable. It was one of the things about her that I didn't want to see change. I felt a strong need to reach out to her.

"Patricia—"

She shook her head. "No, don't," she said. "Let's just go to bed, okay?"

"Okay."

We went to bed and made love for the first time in a week. I've heard it said that it's the body's natural response to conditions of great stress. Whatever, Patricia was tentative at first, then became transformed. She clawed at me as if trying to turn us both inside out. At one point, she cried out with a combination of pleasure and anguish that tore at my soul.

It was an experience unlike any I'd ever had. For half an hour after it was over, I continued to see exploding suns in front of my eyes. They whirled and danced and then were swallowed up by the dark.

9

When it comes to Sunday mornings, I'm as boring and conventional as any man around. I like to sleep late, linger over breakfast, read the paper if I have the energy to go and get one, accomplish nothing of importance.

On this Sunday morning, Patricia and I dragged ourselves out of bed with serious sex hangovers. The day did not stretch out before us with promise. We'd already done most of what we could do.

Neither of us referred to the previous night.

"Explain to me what you're planning," she said over coffee.

"I'm not sure," I said. "But I started with your suggestion that Patrick's disappearance might tie in with the sheriff's race and all that. Now at this point we suspect that there are drugs involved. So it seemed logical to try and find out who controls the local drug scene. Maybe if we knew that, the next step would suggest itself. I didn't think it would work to start with Beavans. The only alternative was to start with street drugs and try to backtrack to the source. Fench deals on the street. He told me who his supplier is. I can now try to get the name of that guy's supplier, and so on. It's kind of a long shot, but somewhere along the way I'll come across some answers if it all ties in. The main problem is that the higher you go in the pyramid, the tougher it is to get people to talk."

"And your next target is Johnson."

"Right. Fench fingered him. Considering the circumstances, I doubt it was a lie."

"And how do you expect to get him to talk?"

In truth, I didn't have any idea. I had hoped that the morning light would get my imagination moving. Wrong again.

"Dunno," I said. "How about you?"

"I thought you didn't want me involved in this end of things."

I shrugged. "I don't, but you already are. I'm finally beginning to realize that."

"Okay," she said. "How about Campbell? Could he do something with Johnson?"

"I doubt it. First of all, he'd be putzing around in the city cops' territory. Where drugs are involved, that's dangerous. If any of the cops are on the take, they get angry. If they're not, they get angry anyway, because they want to get sole credit for the big drug bust. It can be good for your career. And the second thing is, the probable cause is just too thin."

"The second also goes for the Charlottesville police, I presume."

"Right. I'm sure they already have him pegged. They aren't going to want us mucking up whatever plans they have, just to get us the next name up the ladder."

"How about us trying to set him up ourselves?" she asked. "Get him into a compromising situation and then trade our silence for his information."

"Mmmm. That's very tricky, dear. If the cops did it, it'd be entrapment. If we did it, they'd more likely look on it as collusion in a criminal activity. The cops are *seriously* unappreciative of such stunts. If they found out, they'd likely fry our butts, and the prospect of jail has never appealed to me. At the least, I'd get my license pulled for all time."

"I could do it," she said matter-of-factly.

"Do what, exactly?"

"I don't know. A phony drug deal. Whatever you do."

I laughed.

"Don't laugh at me."

"I'm sorry, Patricia. I admire your courage, but you're completely naive where things like this are concerned. It's rather difficult to imagine you posing as a small-time drug dealer."

"You don't think I can act?"

"I don't know if you can act or what. But acting to a docile theater audience is one thing. Acting to a man who's attuned to the slightest false note is another ball game altogether. And if you fail to convince him, he's bound to have someone on hand whose sole function is to bring pain into people's lives. I don't like it."

She looked defeated.

"There must be something we can do," she said.

"I don't know," I said. "I've got some contacts. I'll put out the word that I want to meet with Nickel Johnson. If he agrees, I'll try to figure out a way to get him to talk to me. It's all I can think of right now."

"It doesn't sound too promising."

"You never know."

You never did. I'd earned a certain cachet in the local black community as the result of a previous case, when I'd helped put away the would-be killer of a popular basketball player. In truth, I doubted that that would help me learn the name of Johnson's supplier. I was more inclined to agree with Patricia's assessment of the situation. Still, I needed to try. I called a friend whom I was certain would be able to get the message to Johnson.

What did I want to talk about? I was asked.

Business, I said.

Okay, I was told, Johnson will get the message. But don't hold your breath waiting for a reply.

I wouldn't.

Then we were left with Sunday to fill.

We filled it with more of the same. Talking to Patrick's friends, though by now we were out among acquaintances. Driving around, knocking on doors. I expanded the circle of service stations again and talked with a procession of faceless pump jockeys. Nothing. We then divided up the town's fast-food restaurants. There was a chance Patrick had stopped for something to eat on his way to wherever. That didn't produce anything, either. Still, by the end of the day half of Charlottesville knew the kid was missing and had agreed to keep its collective eyes open.

And it was becoming progressively more difficult for me to keep the lid on my own anxiety. Something had happened to Patrick, that much was sure. My instincts were telling me with increasing certainty that it was the worst, that Patrick *had* somehow become entangled in my earlier investigation. It became more and more likely as Patrick became harder and harder to find. Because this is a simple truth: for the most part, only professionals can make someone vanish without a trace. And the only professionals I'd been involved with recently were the ones in the shadows behind Lester Beavans. But where was the connection to Patrick?

We went to bed early, after another cold supper. We'd become easily irritated with one another. It might have been better to sleep apart, but I didn't even consider it. Patricia was distant and unaffectionate. She stayed on her side of the bed, I stayed on mine. It was a bad night for her. She tossed and turned a lot, and in the morning she looked haggard.

We had breakfast and a couple of cups of coffee and some desultory conversation.

"Why don't you go to work?" I said finally.

"That's not funny," she snapped.

"No Patricia, I mean it. You've done as much as you can possibly do. If you stay here, chances are you'll spend the day doing meaningless little tasks and you'll end up more depressed than you already are. Bob Lee's office is familiar and nonthreatening. It'd be good for you."

"I don't think so—"

"Besides, you could talk to Bob." He was an old and dear friend as well as her employer. "He's sympathetic. And he might even come up with some things that we haven't thought of."

"I suppose he might."

"Please."

"And what will you do?"

"I don't know," I admitted. "I'm running short on fresh ideas myself. Maybe if I have some time to focus on it. . . ."

"I'm no use at all, am I?"

She looked at me bitterly, and with a trace of hostility I'd never seen before. It was important that we get away from each other, at least for the day. I walked around behind her and put my arms around her neck. I kissed the top of her head.

"Don't," I said.

She just sat there.

"Please, Patricia," I said, "will you do it?"

She thought about it for a long time, staring off at some bleak scene of her mind. Finally, she sighed deeply. She got up and mechanically disengaged herself from my arms.

"I guess," she said as she headed for the bedroom.

When she reappeared she had on a conservative gray business suit. She looked much better. The act of dressing for work had probably been beneficial in itself. It was a familiar ritual, through which she could establish some contact with a more normal existence.

We kissed and there was a hint of warmth in it. But only a hint.

"Call me," she said, "if . . . if anything."

"Of course," I said.

She left, and I sat down at the table for coffee and whatever thinking I could manage.

I hadn't thought of anything at nine-thirty, when Ridley Campbell called.

"Any word from Patrick?" he asked.

"None. You haven't spotted the van yet." It wasn't a question. I knew he hadn't.

"Nope. I did get the tax returns. Fella brought 'em by first thing this morning. Surprised the hell out of me, feds moving as fast as that. 'Course it was a pretty big favor I called in."

"And?"

"Well, there ain't much here that I can see, Swift. Maybe you ought to take a look at them, find something escapes me."

"When I have the time, Sheriff. Can't you hit the high-lights?"

"I tell you, it looks clean," he said. "He lists his primary occupation as auto mechanic, just like he says. There's a lot of income reported from self-employment. Then there's some salary stuff. Like from so-and-so yacht club or such-and-such marina. A couple of boat sales places, too. The only strange one is the last two years he was there, there's a fair amount of money paid to him by something called Diversified Invest-ments, Inc."

"Interesting. Sounds like a laundry to me."

"Washing drug money, you reckon?"

"Could be."

"Yeah, I wanted to know who they was myself. So I phoned back down to my man in Miami. He said he'd try to get back to me today, that he had to get the information from Tallahassee. It takes time to figure out a corporation, I sup-pose. He got pretty interested when I told him we think there might be drugs involved. A big bust can make your name down there. I told him go ahead and call me at home tonight if he had to."

"Don't expect much," I said. "There may be corporations within corporations. Half of them may be dummies. Or they may all be legitimate businesses. You probably won't be able to tell a thing."

"Worth a try, though."

"Yeah. Well, keep me posted."

"I will. Hope something breaks for you soon, too. The boys are still looking."

"Thanks."

The next call came five minutes later. It was brief.

"Mr. Swift?" the voice asked.

"Yeah. Who's this?"

"Mr. Johnson will see you this evening. Be in front of the downtown library at seven o'clock. You'll be picked up there."

The man rang off.

162

It was a break, but I didn't know how much of one. Nickel Johnson would have the information I wanted. The problem was, how to get it out of him. I settled the question into the back of my mind, where it would turn over and over during the day. Then I went out into the hot, muggy streets again.

Around three, I found the service station. It was on U.S. 29, north of the city limits. The evening attendant had just come on.

He remembered the van, all right. It had stopped in Wednesday night at nine-thirty. The guy hadn't realized Patrick was paraplegic, since it was dark and no one had gotten out of the van.

No *one?*

Yeah, neither he nor his companion. They were very quiet. The attendant had only recalled them when I showed him Patrick's photo.

Could he describe the companion?

Dark.

Was that all?

Dark hair, dark complexion. He didn't make a habit of studying customers' faces. I should feel lucky he remembered as much as he did. If it hadn't of been a nice-looking van, he probably wouldn't have even been able to identify Patrick.

Had they made any small talk?

Nope.

Which way were they headed?

He didn't bother to notice.

How much gas had they bought?

Five bucks' worth.

Had they wanted the oil and water checked?

Nope.

Had he noticed anything at all unusual about the two of them?

Well, now that I mentioned it, maybe he had. After he'd pumped the gas, he'd mentioned to Patrick that that much wouldn't take him very far. Patrick had started to say something like, "we don't have far—" then stopped in the middle of the sentence. As if something had suddenly shut him up, though what it might have been the attendant couldn't guess. Then Patrick had stared at the attendant like he wanted to say something else but had gotten his tongue tied. Then he'd paid quickly and left. It was a little odd, but the attendant had forgotten about it almost immediately. The memory had only come back when I asked my last question.

Was he sure Patrick had said "we" and not "I"?

Pretty sure.

I thanked the attendant and walked to the station's pay phone.

So Patrick hadn't been alone. That meant that he wasn't lying by himself in a van wreck in the woods, which was good. Otherwise, the news was probably very bad. Yeah, it could have been a friend, but I didn't believe it, especially considering his behavior. Much more likely was that Patrick had taken his unknown passenger somewhere and hadn't come back. And who was the other guy? It looked like he'd been someone who was there intentionally, not some escaped loonie Patrick had picked up hitchhiking. Patrick had referred to the two of them as if they had a common destination. Plus he was acting like he already knew he was in trouble. The facts pointed hard toward a conclusion I'd rather not have come to: whoever the other guy was, he was responsible for Patrick's disappearance.

An ugly thought. I pushed it aside and concentrated on what I'd learned.

I found that I could make a few inferences. U.S. 29 is a divided highway, running north and south. The service station is on the east side. The logical conclusion was that they'd been headed north, away from town, else they'd have had to cross the median strip to get to it. They wouldn't have done that. They'd have picked one that was convenient to the direction they were going.

Now, why had they stopped? It's not a silly question. If something sinister was going on, then Patrick's "companion" would undoubtedly have preferred getting away from the city, away from places where they might be recognized, before stopping. Therefore, the gas gauge must have been about on "E". Knowing Patrick, that was no surprise. But they'd only bought five bucks' worth. As the attendant had pointed out, that doesn't get you far, though it doesn't take much time or necessitate making change. And they hadn't had the oil or water checked. Assumption: one of them was nervous or in a hurry or both. Second assumption: "they" really didn't have far to go. That was the one that worried me.

I called Campbell and laid the new information on him. He agreed things were looking worse.

"Okay," he said. "I'll have the boys in the northern part of the county start asking questions. Somewhere there'll be someone who's seen the van. And I'll alert the sheriffs of the other counties in that direction as to what's going on."

"Rid," I said, "time's getting short. I know you've got a lot on your mind, but if the kid doesn't have his insulin, he's in deep trouble about now."

"I'll mobilize as many men as I can, Swift, as fast as I can. It's all I can do."

"Thanks. Look, I've been thinking. I'm worried Patrick may have accidentally gotten mixed up with the people behind Beavans. Because of me or something."

"I hope not," he said.

"Give it some thought, will you? Maybe you'll see something I've missed."

"Okay."

Almost as an afterthought, I said, "You heard anything from Florida?"

"Not yet."

I hung up and called the city cops. I repeated my story for them. They were polite and promised to continue looking into the matter.

Then I tried to decide what to do next. Drive the back roads north of the city, looking for an abandoned van? That was absurd. Ridley's men would do a better job of searching than I ever could. The nasty truth was that every time I learned something new it didn't really lead me anywhere.

I got into Clementine and sat there as the August sun turned my car into a very efficient solar collector. My gun pressed into the base of my spine. A drop of sweat ran down my face and hung from the tip of my nose. I ignored it. Patrick's passenger, I thought, who was he? Equally important, where in hell had he come from?

As I pondered what I'd heard over the past few days, I began to get uneasy with the sequence of events Wednesday night. Things were just slightly off. Maybe. It might mean nothing. Still, I went back over to the station attendant. I waited while he filled a tank, then asked him again what time the van pulled in.

He looked at me with annoyance as he repeated himself. Nine-thirty.

That's what I thought he'd said. He'd been specific. How could he be sure of the time?

That was easy. He'd been watching a favorite show on a small TV in the station. It ran from nine to ten. He hadn't missed any of the program when he gassed the van, because the whole transaction had taken place during the cluster of ads at the show's midpoint. Nine-thirty. Like he'd said.

I thanked him again and returned to my car. I sorted through what I had.

The jogger had seen the van leaving after dark, "around nine." Scott had told me he returned to his office at "eight-thirty or possibly nine." Yet the attendant was positive the van hadn't gotten to the service station until nine-thirty. It didn't take a half hour to get from Rose Hill Drive to the station. Fifteen minutes, if there was traffic and you missed all the lights. Another stop? Possible, but highly unlikely. No time.

It was a very small discrepancy, but it began to loom very large in my mind. I assumed that the jogger and service station attendant were telling their stories to the best of their recollections. There was no reason to believe otherwise. That left Scott's statement. It was made casually, but he was a precise sort of man. If he'd meant "between eight-thirty and nine-*fifteen*," that's what he'd have said. So maybe he was mistaken. Or else . . .

Despite the summer heat, I felt a chill. I remembered my conversation with Scott after the disappearance, and how he'd inadvertently referred to Patrick in the past tense.

Or else *Patrick had still been there* when he returned to the office, and he'd deliberately lied to me.

Some ugly questions began surfacing, and the man with the answers was Howard B. Scott. I drove over to Pan-Caribbean Imports.

I sat across the big desk from Howard B. Scott once again. He looked like nothing more than a prosperous businessman. The photos on the walls glowed with their suggestion of the good life.

And yet, there was a difference from my previous visits. I was suspicious of him. Whether he picked that up, I don't know. I was careful, I did my best to conceal it, but he was sharp. And very difficult to read. Was the air between us very subtly charged? I couldn't tell.

"No progress, I take it," he said.

"Some. I know now that Patrick wasn't alone when he left here."

"Not *alone?* What do you mean?"

His surprise seemed so genuine that I began to waver. Maybe I was just creating phantoms in the shadows. Compensation for my inability to get anywhere in reality.

"I mean there was someone in the van with him," I said.

"How do you know?"

"I found someone who saw them. A neighbor of yours."

"Good Lord," he said, sitting back, "who could it have been?"

"That's what I'm trying to find out next. All I know is that it was a man and he had dark hair. Any ideas?"

"No, none. Do you think they met here at the office?"

"Looks that way."

"Damn! I must have just missed them."

"Yeah, you must have. What time did you say you got back here? I've forgotten."

I asked it casually, but I thought the question stiffened him just the tiniest bit. What did he know? I wondered. More important, how could I find out what he knew?

"I'm not certain," he said. "It was around nine, as I recall. Why do you ask?"

I shrugged. "I'm trying to reconstruct Wednesday night," I said. "As precisely as I can. It isn't easy. If I can pinpoint some times, I'll be that much closer to the answer."

"I don't follow you."

"Just thinking out loud. Look, I'd better get going. I only wanted to check in with you, see if this new information would get us anywhere."

"I'm sorry. It doesn't look like it has."

"Well, thanks anyway."

He ushered me into the outer office. As we shook hands, I looked around. Nothing had changed. The computer work station seemed to be awaiting Patrick's return. I stared at it, and suddenly a small light bulb went on in my head.

"The diskettes," I said, "the ones Patrick was using for Pan-Caribbean Imports. Where are they?"

"I don't know," Scott said. "I imagine that he took them with him. All he left was the command diskette on that shelf."

I went over and picked up the floppy.

"May I borrow it?" I asked.

"Certainly."

I started to leave, then stopped. I turned and stared at the microcomputer one more time. What was it? What was I trying to see?

Then I saw it.

"That thing," I said, "it's a hard disk, isn't it?"

"Why, yes. You can't run a serious accounting system without one."

I thanked Patrick. His efforts on my behalf hadn't been totally wasted.

"I'll need to borrow that, too," I said.

I walked over and disconnected the hard disk from the CPU. Out of the corner of my eye, I watched Scott. His face was impassive, but I sensed that he wasn't pleased. If he *was* hiding something, the chance of the disk containing incriminating information was remote at best. But he couldn't be sure.

"I don't know," he said. "There may be private company data on there." It was the right thing to say, whether he was concerned with the business or something else.

"Mr. Scott, I am not interested in Pan-Caribbean's financial secrets. But there may be some indication on that disk as to what Patrick was doing just before he disappeared. We're talking about possible vital evidence. We *need* to take a look. Now don't worry, I'll return it as soon as I can. We really should have thought of this long ago."

"I'd rather it not leave the office. Couldn't you have someone come here to read it?"

Sure, I thought. And in the meantime you accidentally walk by it with a big magnet in your hand.

"Sorry," I said. "Time's short."

His look was as cold and calculating as a campaign promise. I had him. He couldn't show excessive concern about something that was probably valueless. That'd just intensify my suspicions. Plus I had the hard disk tucked safely under my arm. I was going to walk out of the office with it unless I was physically prevented. If he could read me, which he likely could, then he would realize that.

He stretched the silence out, so I'd feel the full strength of his disapproval. I felt it, but it didn't change my mind.

"Very well," he said finally. I think he did not like me anymore.

I drove back to Patricia's.

She got home at five. She was gloomy and withdrawn. I sat down and told her everything. The news seemed to energize her. She immediately got Paul on the phone, and he agreed to come over after dinner to see what he could find on the hard disk.

"So," Patricia said, "you think Scott might know more than he's letting on?"

"It's still just a feeling," I said, "even if it is a strong one."

"Is there anything we can do?"

"Not until we have something more concrete."

"What about Ridley? Can't he . . ."

"Ridley's no help. Even if we had something to move on, Scott lives in the city. Out of Campbell's jurisdiction."

"And the city police?"

"Same problem," I said. "No hard evidence of a crime. Plus there's no one on the city force that I know well enough to trust. Whenever there's cocaine money involved, you can't be sure that one or more of the locals isn't on the take. With our luck, we'd go straight to the wrong person.

"There's something else, too. If Scott's in on this, we don't want to spook him. That could be disastrous for Patrick."

"You're right. We can't afford to take chances. But what do we do, then?"

"Patricia, something's about to snap. I can feel it. You work with Paul, I'll keep my date with Nickel Johnson. Then we'll get with Rid and see what we can put together."

As I said it, I realized that I'd better be right. If Patricia's hopes were raised only to be dashed again, she'd likely kill me.

"Okay," she said.

The unspoken question lay between us like a stone: What if Patrick was *already* beyond help?

At seven I was standing in front of the downtown library. Paul had arrived just as I was leaving. He and Patricia would now be at work on the disk and the one floppy from Pan-Caribbean Imports. I'd checked with Ridley but he didn't have anything new. I hadn't told him what I was up to. He doesn't like it when I nudge the line between what's legal and what isn't.

A black Cadillac stopped at the curb and the rear door opened. I got in. We pulled out into the traffic on Market Street. I was the only one in the car except for the driver, a black man in his early thirties who was dressed in a conservative blue suit. He drove for a couple of blocks, glancing at me a couple of times in the rearview mirror, before he spoke.

"You're Venable's friend, ain't you," he said.

"Yeah," I said. Delmos Venable was the basketball star I'd been involved with the previous winter.

He chewed on that for a while, then said, "I'm Jerome."

"My pleasure," I said.

They were the only words we exchanged. Jerome drove out Route 250, the same way Ann Luden had gone to meet her lover Gentry about two centuries earlier. We didn't get as far as the motel where they'd played in-out, though. We stopped at the Phoenix, a night club on the outskirts of town that catered to a primarily black clientele.

I followed Jerome inside. The place was a cavern, with two bandstands and a bar like command central in the War Room. In a few hours, the club would be wall-to-wall people. But just now there was only the hardcore, those who wanted to get a few drinks up on the crowd.

Nickel Johnson was alone at a table in one corner of the room. I went over and sat down with him. Jerome stood slightly off to the side.

Johnson was a fat, sweaty man of about my own age. His head was shaved and bare. He wore a pair of beltless black slacks with knife creases and a billowy mauve silk shirt. The shirt was unbuttoned halfway down the front. There was a gold chain around his neck. Real gold, I guessed, about half a pound of it. It nestled comfortably in his chest hair.

"Swift," he said, "you know I'm seeing you only account of Venable."

I nodded.

"Speak your mind, then."

I'd thought it over on the ride out. What I'd decided was to tell the truth, at least as much of it as Johnson needed to know, and take my chances. I didn't really have anything to bargain with. All I could hope was that he would respond to me as one person to another.

"Mr. Johnson," I said, "a very good friend of mine is in some serious trouble. He's accidentally gotten mixed up with some of the heavies in this town. It wasn't his fault. Now I have reason to believe that they want him hurt, or worse. I want to find him before it's too late. I don't know where he is, and I'm sure you don't, either. But I think you could tell me the name of the person who does know. Just a name is all I'm after. The name of the man . . . ," I paused, "who controls the cocaine traffic in this area."

He looked at me impassively. I waited.

"Why should I trust you?" he said.

"You can't for certain," I admitted. "But I give you my word that I'll never use the information against you personally. My only interest is helping my friend."

"You out of your league, Swift."

"Probably. But he's that kind of friend."

Johnson was silent for what seemed like several minutes. I sat and sweated. When he finally spoke, it wasn't to me.

"Jerome," he said, "see the man gets home now."

I deflated like an old balloon. I'd lost. I'd given it my best shot and come up empty. There was no point in pursuing the subject. Johnson had made up his mind, and nothing I said was going to change it.

We didn't say anything on the way back into town. I'd banked heavily on being able to convince Nickel Johnson to cooperate. Now it seemed foolish of me. We had other leads, sure. But the best one was blown.

I forced myself to repeat in my mind, over and over: we will find him, we *will* find him.

Jerome dropped me where he'd picked me up. I let myself out of the Cadillac. I stood on the sidewalk, staring stupidly at the stone facade of the library.

Behind me, I heard the sound of a window being electrically rolled down. I turned around. At that moment there was no traffic on the street. I could hear the Cadillac's engine turning over and the soft ticking of its air conditioner.

Jerome looked me in the eye and said, "Landon Gentry."

I was speechless.

When I didn't say anything, he added, "Delmos Venable is my cousin."

Then the window slid back up. By the time I started to

thank him, the Caddy had already pulled away from the curb. My check had just been cashed, in full.

I raced to my car and hurried back to Patricia's. When she heard me come in, she rushed out of Patrick's bedroom.

"I got it," I said.

"We've got something," she said at the same moment.

We paused, then both started simultaneously again. We stopped. It was like an old-time comedy routine. Finally, she just grabbed my hand and pulled me into the bedroom.

Paul was sitting in front of one of the monitors.

"Mr. Swift," he said, "we may have something here. I checked out that diskette, but there was nothing on there except the operating system and some purchased software. Then I looked into the hard disk. It had a lot of files on it, as you might suppose. One of them intrigued me. It's called "Worklog," and when I tried to call it up I found out it was password protected. You know what that means, right?"

"You can't see the file unless you type in the proper password," I said.

"Exactly. An eight-character word or less. It could be anything. If you had no idea what it was, you'd never be able to access the file. Fortunately, I know Patrick's habit. We have a number of passwords that we use in common that'd be safe from someone who didn't know us. I've started trying them."

The cursor was blinking in the middle of the screen. To its left was PASSWORD?

Paul typed DUNGEONS and hit the "Return" key. The word disappeared and the cursor went back to its original spot.

"Wrong again," he said.

He typed DRAGONS. Same result. He tried RIPKEN, DOSXX, PRETNDRS AND OVERSEXD. Still nothing doing. Then he typed SUPRSTAR. There was a pause. The disk drives buzzed a couple of times. And the file unrolled on the screen.

"Bingo," Paul said.

The file was headed WORKLOG FOR THE PAN-CARIBBEAN IMPORTS PROJECT.

"We keep one of these for each project," Paul explained.

173

"It's a log of tasks scheduled and completed, and problems encountered. When we finish, we print it out and go over it. It serves as a record of what's just been done and helps us make future plans."

The log was divided into three columns. In the first was the date, in the second time required, and in the third detail information. Patrick's documentation was extensive. In the lower right corner of the screen the cursor blinked next to the word MORE.

"If there's anything here, it's probably at the end of the file," Paul said. He held down the "Control" key and hit the "Q" and the "C" simultaneously. In a moment we were looking at the entries for Wednesday. I began to get a bad crawly feeling.

"What's that?" I said, pointing to a series of numbers and letters. They were the final entry in the detail column and consisted of five groups of ten and one group of four. The sequence looked like this:

1422151E1B
0F1A0A2219
230E0D101B
0C140C1E1B
0F1422191B
1521

Paul stared at the screen. "It's hex," he said.

"Huh?" I said.

"Hexadecimal representation of numbers and the letters of the alphabet. Computer code, so to speak. Each cluster of two equals a letter or number, starting with "01" for "1". "0A" is "A", "10" is "G" and on up to "23" for "Z"." He began to transcribe groups of letters. "It wouldn't confuse anyone with a math head for ten seconds. But he may have been in a hurry."

I watched with no comprehension as Paul wrote:

KYLUR
FQAYP
ZEDGR

CKCUR
FKYPR
LX

"That's nothing," I said.

"No," Paul said, "he'd offset them. Make the letters higher or lower than the value of the ones he meant. If he was doing it in his head, he wouldn't offset by much. Let's try up one." He rewrote the groups of letters. It was still gibberish. "Down one," he said. Gibberish. "Down two."

And there it was. Paul saw it first, then I did.

He had written:

MANWT
HSCAR
BGFIT
EMEWT
HMART
NZ

Grouped into shorthand words it came out: MAN WTH SCAR BG FITE ME WTH MARTNZ. A "man with a scar," a "big fight," and "me with Martinez." Bad news.

"What does it mean?" Patricia said a little hysterically.

"John Doe," I said softly.

"Who?" they both said.

"The man with the scar. The one they fished out of the reservoir."

"Oh, my God," Patricia said.

"He must have come into the office," I said, "and had a big fight with someone. Then Martinez came in and got Patrick. He has to be the one in the van."

"We need to go to the police," Paul said.

"No!" I snapped. "Not yet. Patricia, I need to talk to you. Excuse us."

I steered her through the connecting bathroom into her bedroom and closed the door. She was wild with anxiety about Patrick and angry at me.

"Loren, what are you *doing?* Paul's *right!* They'll *listen* to us now!"

"Patricia, trust me. The cops will only slow us up right now. We need to find out where Patrick is before we go to them."

"God damn you! We don't *know* where Patrick is!"

"I realize that, but I know who does know."

Whatever she was going to say froze in her throat. She just gaped at me.

"Please, I need you to be calm," I said. "Someone has to stay here and make sure Paul doesn't do anything rash."

She sat down on the edge of the bed.

"Stay here?" she croaked. "While . . . what?"

"While I find out where Patrick is. Then we grab Ridley Campbell and go and get him."

If he's still alive, I thought, but I didn't say it.

Then I told Patricia what I'd learned from Jerome.

"So," I said, "Gentry's the key. He's also the weak link. He's the one I have to go after. And I have to go alone. We don't have the time to wait on proper police procedure. That'll just shut Gentry up after he screams for his lawyer. I don't need to obey the rules. If I have to beat it out of him, I won't hesitate, I promise you. We'll know where Patrick is tonight."

"You're right," she said. She was pulling it together. "It's our best chance. But for God's sake, hurry."

The phone rang.

"Keep hold of Paul," I said. I went to answer it as she returned to Patrick's bedroom.

"Swift," Campbell said, "I heard from Florida, and you ain't gonna believe this. They broke down Diversified Investments, and it's a umbrella for about eight companies, one of which is—"

"Pan-Caribbean Imports, Incorporated," I said. It had to be. That was the final connection, the one that tied Beavans into the whole thing.

"How'd you know that?" Campbell's voice was ice.

"A hunch," I said. I filled him in on what we'd found in the computer. I didn't tell him about Gentry, or that I was about to intimidate the star witness.

"Patrick's in danger," I said softly, so I wouldn't be overheard in the bedroom. "If he's alive. If he is, we can't go at Scott directly, or they'll kill him before we can get to him. We need a plan, and it had better be a good one. Can you come over to Patricia's right away?"

"I'm on my way."

"Bring a couple of men you trust."

"You got it."

We hung up. I called Patricia out and told her what was happening.

"Now," I said, "I've got to get moving before Campbell gets here. He's going to be furious. Do you think you can stall him?"

"Maybe for a little while."

"Good, that's all I need. A half hour, forty-five minutes. No more. Just keep him off my trail until then."

"I will. And . . . be careful, will you?"

"Not to worry."

10

Sometimes it happens like that. You stumble around in a daze, knowing nothing. Then, suddenly, you know everything.

I should have known all along, I told myself. Especially about Gentry. I *knew* the symptoms of cocaine abuse. God knows I'd seen them enough times. The runny nose. The paranoia. Jonesy had even alerted me that Gentry hadn't always been like that. Of course, I hadn't been looking for evidence of drugs at the time. But still.

No point, I told myself. The only thing of any importance was what had happened to Patrick. Obviously, he'd seen the man who ended up in the reservoir. And he could tie him to Howard Scott.

That made the chances of Patrick still being alive very slim. Scott would eventually have to kill him. There was no reason to think he hadn't already done so. All there was was a tiny hope, and I clung stubbornly to it.

Everything hinged on the last remaining unanswered question: Where had Patrick's abductor been taking him on Wednesday night? Somewhere north of the city, that's all I knew. I assumed the other man in the van wasn't Scott and that he and Patrick weren't headed for Scott's house in the city. Either of those things would have been risks too high for the big man to take.

That left two alternatives. One, of course, was that Patrick had been taken into the woods, killed, and buried. If that was the case, there was nothing to be done about it now.

So I had to suppose the second alternative. That Patrick had been taken somewhere and was being held until such time as it was convenient to dispose of him. If so, they'd most likely be holding him someplace owned or rented by Howard Scott or one of his intermediaries. And it was a near certainty that Landon Gentry, the realtor, would know where it was.

I worked my anxiety into a cold determination to do whatever was necessary to get him to talk.

Gentry lived in an exclusive development over by the reservoir, just outside the city limits. It was one of those subdivisions where every home is custom built on its own heavily wooded two-acre lot. The kind where the last thing its inhabitants want to see are their neighbors, in case it's like looking in the mirror.

I'd called ahead to see if Gentry was in. As soon as I recognized the voice, I mumbled wrong number, hung up, and took off for his house.

He answered the door himself. How convenient.

"Gentry," I said, "I need to talk to you."

"I'm sorry, I don't think I know—" He looked closer. "Oh, you. I don't have anything to say to you."

"Look, it's important. Let's go inside, okay?"

"What is this about?" He'd stiffened quite a bit.

"I'll tell you in private."

"I don't believe I need to—" He was beginning to close the door.

"Ann Luden," I said.

He stopped. "What?" he said.

"Ann Luden, Ann Luden. Getting your ashes hauled at lunchtime. If you want, I'll start screaming it so your wife can hear."

"No," he said quickly.

"Do you have a place we can talk?"

He hesitated.

"C'mon, Gentry," I said.

"All right," he said, "come in."

I followed him into the foyer. A TV was blaring somewhere off to our right.

"Who is it, dear?" a woman's voice called.

"It's nothing, dear," he called back. "County business."

That apparently satisfied her. We turned left, into a private office. The door closed automatically behind us. He started to turn around.

"Now, what in the hell—" he began.

I planted my foot in his back and shoved, hard. He stumbled and went down. He came up spluttering.

"What is the meaning of this—"

When his face got within reach, I slapped it. I cupped my palm, to make sure it hurt. He went down, but he bobbed back up again. I'd gotten him angry. Darn.

"How dare you—"

I hit him again. This time once with the palm, once with the back of the hand. Quick blows. I hadn't said a word. I looked at him coldly, as if I might kill him any second. He was a skinny bastard, and he was beginning to get very afraid. The tic under his left eye was firing like crazy.

"What, what do you want?" he gasped. He'd raised his hands defensively. He was worried that I might decide to hit him for real. A small amount of blood was trickling down his chin.

I switched roles quickly.

"Mr. Gentry," I said. "Please get up. Let's act like civilized people."

He was badly confused. He got up, tentatively, still shying away from me. There were a couple of leather chairs along one wall. I gestured to them and we sat down.

"I should call the cops," he said.

"Be my guest," I said. "With what's happening in your life, I bet you don't want to be within five miles of the cops."

He dabbed at his split lip with a monogrammed hankie. The man had class.

"Who are you working for?" he said.

"Skip the questions, Gentry," I said. "You're through. You've got a cocaine habit that won't quit. Too bad. Shouldn't use the product yourself, y'know. Hurts you as a dealer. I know where you get the stuff and I know where it goes. Anything else I need to know, or is that enough to ruin your life?"

He was disintegrating before my eyes.

"What . . . do you want?" he said.

"Luckily for you," I said, "I only want one thing, scumbag. The answer to a very simple question. But before I ask you, let me tell you something. If you don't give me a straight answer, here's what I will do. I will personally break one of your kneecaps so badly that you will walk with a cane for the rest of your life. After that, I will tell your wife all the details of your extracurricular sex life. So much for your marriage. Then I will call the county sheriff, who is a good friend of mine, and tell him to come here with a search warrant, specifically for controlled substances, and I will stay with you to make sure you don't visit the toilet while we're waiting for him. That about cover it?"

He tried to say something, but only a strangled croak came out.

"If you cooperate," I said, "I won't say anything to your wife, and maybe, just maybe, you can hold your family together through it all. Because any way you slice it, the roof is about to fall in on you. You may need their support. I will also not fetch the sheriff right away. You'll have time to at least clean up the premises.

"Now, here is what you are going to tell me. I know that you bought a property for Howard Scott in northern Albemarle County, or maybe Greene. You are going to tell me where it is. Tell me now."

I didn't know that Gentry had actually brokered the deal, but it was a reasonable shot. His face was a jumble of conflicting emotions. Here was his whole world unravelling and he didn't have any idea which end to grab.

"I can't. . . ." he said. "He . . ."

"Listen to me, cokehead," I said. "You don't have any *choice*. Your little turn around the funhouse is over. Now I can dig up everything I need at the Registry of Deeds tomorrow. But I don't want it tomorrow. I want it *now*. Tell me and do your knees a favor."

"I don't . . ."

I jumped up and slapped him hard. He cowered from me. I balled my fist.

"Tell me!"

"Don't hit me anymore," he said. "Don't. I'll . . . I'll tell you."

He'd slumped back in his chair. His eyes were on me, but they weren't seeing me. They were watching scenes from a clean, shiny world that was gone forever. Mechanically, he told me about Scott's place. It was two hundred acres in a secluded section of northwestern Albemarle County, near Brown's Cove. He gave me directions. The deal had been a private one, made two years earlier. Scott had paid in cash.

"That's when it all began," he said. "At first, I thought he was just an ordinary businessman—"

"Who went around buying two hundred acre properties for cash," I said. "Tell it to the judge. I'm not interested."

But he kept pouring it out. He didn't really need an audience. His nose was running from the last snort of cocaine he'd had. He didn't bother to wipe it.

"Now listen to me," I said. "There's one more thing. If Scott finds out what you've told me, I'm coming straight back here and I'm going to hurt you very, very badly. You understand me?"

He nodded dumbly.

"Call your lawyer, Gentry," I said as I left.

Then I got careless.

Probably what I should have done was call Ridley from Gentry's house and tell him everything. But I didn't. I was in a hurry. I wanted to get back, to tell Patricia there was hope, to sit down with her and Campbell and carefully plan what to do next, to go out to Brown's Cove and get Patrick. He'd suddenly come very alive to me. In the heat of the moment, all I wanted was to *do* something after the long days of frustration and not knowing.

But no excuses. I got careless, and it was just not a time to get careless.

If I hadn't been in such a rush, I would have checked automatically, and I would have seen him. As it was, I'd slid into the driver's seat and closed the door before I sensed the presence of the man in the back. By that time, it was way too late. He was already thumbing back the pistol's hammer. That little click is one of the loudest sounds in the world. Especially when the barrel of the gun is a couple of inches from your ear.

My first thought was: no, not now. Not when we're so close. But I quickly realized that the man had no intention of killing me here. Later, maybe. Later, probably. Not now, else I'd already be dead.

I thought about escape. If we'd been in a more heavily populated area, I could have tried to bluff him. But here the houses were so far apart there was a good chance the shot wouldn't be heard. Even if it was, it wasn't the sort of place where people are apt to go to the aid of their neighbor. He didn't *want* to shoot me here, but that didn't mean that he *wouldn't*.

As far as my own gun was concerned, I was virtually sitting on it. There was no way I could get it out and into a useful firing position before half my head went missing.

The fellow in the back seat held all the good cards. There was no alternative but to do whatever he wanted.

He smiled briefly. The gold tooth caught a streetlight and glinted for a second in the rearview mirror. I was very glad that I hadn't tried anything foolish. Not with this guy.

"Put both hands on the steering wheel and leave them there," he said.

"Martinez," I said. "Long time no see. I guess I should have been expecting you." Not only that, I should have spotted him. He'd probably been tailing me since shortly after I walked out of Scott's office with the hard disk. He would know that I'd been to see Nickel Johnson and that I'd wound up at Gentry's. He would have to assume that I knew about the cocaine and that I could tie it to Scott. My only hope was that he'd think I had needed to talk to Gentry before I could put all the pieces together, and that I had therefore not talked to the cops yet.

"You know Swift," he said, "you have been making a very big pain out of yourself. If it was my choice you would have been dead last week. I hope you've enjoyed the time in between."

"What happened to the kid?"

"Oh, he's alright."

There wouldn't be any reason for Martinez to lie now that I was under his gun. So Patrick was alive! There was still hope.

"What do we do next?" I said.

"Drive," he said.

I did. I told him I already knew the way. He said fine, and that he'd correct me if I made any mistakes. He reminded me that he was a professional, in case I had any funny ideas. I told him that I knew who he was and that I hadn't had a funny idea in over three years.

I drove cautiously, keeping my hands on the wheel, moving very deliberately when I shifted. The gun was no longer right in my ear, but it was back there, pointed at me.

We headed west until we got to Whitehall. On a sunny day, it's a very pleasant drive. Countryside like that around Connie Brock's place, which we passed a few miles south of. Pleasant —that is, if you're not riding with a hired killer.

At Whitehall we turned north, drove about halfway to Brown's Cove, then turned west again, toward Pasture Fence Mountain. Another three miles and we were there. I was keeping close track of the mileage. Habit.

Martinez told me where to turn off. There was a short stretch of dirt road, then a chain link fence with a gate in it. There was barbed wire on top. My guess was that it would be electrified as well, with alarm sensors built in, the latest technology. Martinez opened the gate electronically and I drove in. The gate closed securely behind us.

The driveway wound through dense woods for a quarter of a mile. Then the land opened out. A hundred yards ahead and off to the right was a large white farmhouse. It stood on a slight rise. Nearby was a good-sized barn and several smaller outbuildings. As best I could see, the forest encircled the cluster of buildings and rose upward from the cleared area on all sides but the way we'd come in.

"Drive into the barn," Martinez said.

The place was well-lighted. There wasn't any hay inside, but there was a number of vehicles: some cars, a four-wheel-drive Jeep, a large tractor, and the famous brown pickup truck. One section of the barn was a modern service garage with repair bays, hydraulic lifts, racks of tools and whatnot. There were two gas pumps. Leaded and unleaded. Patrick's van wasn't anywhere to be seen. I didn't like that.

I stopped and turned off the ignition. "Fill it with regular," I said.

"Keep your hands on the wheel," Martinez said. No sense of humor in the man.

He flipped the lever that tilted the passenger's seat forward and opened the door. This was the moment to go for him, as he was squeezing out. I glanced over at him. His gun hand was dead steady and he had that look that said go ahead, make my day. I decided against it.

He was very careful. The pistol remained trained on me. He had me crawl over the passenger's seat and out that door, keeping my hands in front of me at all times. Then he spread-eagled and searched me. The Walther went into his pocket, leaving a strange empty sensation where it had been.

"That's better," he said. "Now let's take a little walk."

Martinez guided me to the side of the white farmhouse. We went through a screen door. Straight ahead was a long hall with a large open room at the end. To the left was an open door and a stairwell. I started ahead but Martinez prodded me the other way. Down.

I was expecting maybe the second circle of hell, but the basement was much like the first floor. There was a long hall running underneath the one above, with several closed doors along it. There was an open room at the far end. The area was

not at all like a cellar. It was cool and carpeted and illumi-
nated with soft lighting, no mustiness to it. A lower-level
living area. There were no other people about.

Martinez took me about halfway down the corridor. Then
we stopped and he turned me so that I was facing back the
way we'd come. He did not take any unnecessary chances.
Behind me, I heard him get some keys out and unlock one of
the doors.

He turned me again and said, "Inside."

I opened the door and went in. Martinez closed and locked
it behind me.

It was a small, windowless room. The walls were sheetrock,
and they didn't have any pictures hanging on them. There was
a cot along one wall. Next to it, a night table with a shaded
lamp. Along the other wall was a desk littered with continuous
computer paper, pencils, books, and so on.

Ahead of me, in his chair, with a lopsided smile on his face,
was Patrick Ryan.

For a moment, I didn't know whether to be happy that he
was all right or depressed that all my worst fears were con-
firmed. Then I went over and hugged him.

"How you doing, kid?" I said.

He shrugged. "The food's okay," he said. "But the enter-
tainment's lousy. Is that what you're here for?"

"Yeah, I do a terrific Michael Jackson these days."

"I can hardly wait."

"You need insulin?"

He shook his head. "I didn't tell them about that. I had, I
don't know, some crazy idea that if I started to get sick they'd
take me to the hospital or something. But after I'd been here
a couple of days a guy showed up with insulin and needles,
the whole bit. They don't let me shoot myself up. No sharp
objects, y'know." He lolled his tongue out the side of his
mouth as if he were insane.

I remembered my talk with Scott on Friday, when I'd mentioned Patrick's diabetes. Small favors.

There were a couple of straight-back chairs in the room. I

pulled one of them over, turned it so I could rest my forearms on the back, and sat down.

"Okay, kid," I said, "let's have it from the top."

"Well," he said, "I guess you know whose place this is."

"Our mutual friend, Howard B. Scott."

"Right. I appear to have been, ah, a tad mistaken about him. Perhaps you can tell *me* a few things."

"Later. Just go over what happened Wednesday. As much as you can remember."

"Well," he said, "I went to the office—Pan-Caribbean Imports—about nine in the morning. Scott wasn't there, but he'd had a key made for me and I let myself in. I worked for about three hours before he arrived. I was working hard. The project was moving along fast and I wanted to finish up as soon as possible, so I could start on something new. You know me.

"Scott arrived around noon. We had a few words about the project, and then he went in his office and shut the door. I went out and got some lunch. When I got back, he was still in there. I didn't see him again until close to five. Then he came into the outer office and we talked for an hour or so. About the project and about general stuff, too. My future plans, that sort of thing. He seemed to be in very good spirits, like he'd just worked out a major deal of some kind. He was getting ready to go to dinner when a guy came by. Someone I'd never seen before, a Mexican-looking guy with this big scar down his face."

"I know. We found the note on the hard disk."

"Detective Swift. Who was he, do you know?"

"Later. Go on," I said.

"Well, when the guy with the scar arrived, Scott's good mood vanished. He tightened up. I hadn't really seen him like that before. The two of them went into the inner office and the guy came out five minutes later. He was steaming. Scott was angry, too. I thought the two of them were going to have it out right there, but they didn't. The guy with the scar stormed out.

187

"I just kept on working. It wasn't any of my business. Scott stood there fuming for a few minutes, then he gave me a very strange look and asked me what my plans were. I told him: to work until eight or nine, then go to a friend's house to play with some new software. He nodded and went back into his office without another word.

"A little later, Martinez arrived and Scott went out. Martinez stayed in the room with me the whole time Scott was gone. He didn't say anything, didn't do anything except lounge on the couch, drink coffee, and look through magazines. It was odd, but I didn't think about it. I was busy. Martinez was a familiar face. At one point, I used Scott's phone to confirm plans with Paul and let Patricia know what I was doing.

"Scott returned about eight. He and Martinez talked in the inner office. When they came out, Scott said he had to leave and asked me if I was close to finishing up. I said yes. Then he asked me if I could stop by his house when I was done, to go over some stuff he had there. The way the two of them were acting I was beginning to wonder what was going on, but I still said okay. I guess I'm too trusting."

You sure are, I thought. If I can figure a way to get my hands around the throats of these people, I will do them some damage.

"After Scott left," Patrick continued, "I kept working, with Martinez still hanging around. I ran into some problems. About nine Martinez began to get nasty. He asked me if I was finished yet. I told him no, but he could go and I'd let myself out. He said I was taking him to Scott's house with me and that we needed to get moving. That's when I suspected there was something wrong with this whole setup. So I quickly put that message into hex code. Martinez was watching, but I'm sure it just looked like computer nonsense to him. I loaded it into the worklog file and signed the machine off.

"Then I told Martinez that I'd changed my mind and wouldn't be able to go to Scott's after all. He said we were going whether I wanted to or not. When I asked him why, he showed me his gun. That was enough. We went out and got in the van. He told me that we weren't going to Scott's, naturally, and that I should follow his directions. The only thing was that I didn't have any gas in the van, as usual. We had to stop. Martinez had his gun stuck in my side the whole time. When I was turned away from him, I tried to give the attendant a very pained expression. Communicate with him telepathically. I guess it didn't work."

"I found him," I said. "Talked to him. He thought you acted a little strangely, but not enough that he thought it was worth telling anyone."

"I guess they see all types in a day. What do they care?"

"Uh huh."

"After we bought the gas, we drove here. I've been here ever since."

"What happened to the van?" I asked.

"I don't know. Isn't it here?"

"I didn't see it. How many people live here?"

"Live, I don't know. I've seen five different men so far. Scott and Martinez and three others. One of them's black and the other two are Hispanics. They carry automatic rifles slung over their shoulders sometimes. The kind that have those banana-shaped cartridge cases, you know?"

Yeah, I knew about automatic weapons. I'd humped an M-16 in my day. A sudden memory of the stinking jungle stabbed at me. For an instant, I was there again, trapped in the perpetual twilight of the rain forest. I fought myself back to the present. I didn't like what the news of the rifles said about our chances of getting out of here alive.

"What's Scott got you doing now?"

He gestured at the desk. "Working," he said, "what else? You probably realize that Scott's not just an importer of Caribbean handicrafts."

"I figured that out all by myself."

He snapped his fingers. "That's right, you're a former private eye. So you know that he's running drugs and maybe a few other things as well."

"I know," I said. "Where do you come in?"

"Well, our Mr. Scott's a modern businessman. He wants to computerize so he can keep track of his operation, just like anyone else. He started with some basic packages for Pan-Caribbean Imports. I suppose he thought they'd be easy to modify for his other enterprises, once he had them down. He's like any intelligent but computer-naive person. Thinks you can just sit down and start doing this stuff. He quickly found out that it's not so simple. I guess when he realized how good I am, he just kidnapped me in order to put me to work directly for his primary occupation."

"There's more to it than that," I said. "Unfortunately. The angry man you saw in the office on Wednesday was found floating in the reservoir the next morning. With a bullet in his heart and his nose missing."

"What does that—" Then he knew. "Oh, shit," he said.

"Yeah. I'm afraid you became expendable, Patrick. I'm sorry."

"I don't think he wants to kill me yet, though. My combination of hard- and software expertise is very rare. He's savvy enough to see that. And I'm doing some things for him that he really wants. I'm stalling them, of course."

"What kind of things?"

"Basically," he said, "it looks like he wants to use this place as a drug distribution point, don't ask me why. He's setting up a computerized assembly line for the stuff. Testing, sorting, packaging, everything. I don't yet know the full scope of it, but he's got a lot of fancy equipment, all of which will eventually be computer controlled. You should see. It's in another part of the cellar. Used to be a bomb shelter. I'm still in the preliminary stages of the master programs. I'll be stuck there as long as I can."

The cutting edge of technology, I thought. Replace people with machines whenever possible. An especially good move in the drug business; the fewer tongues, the better. Maybe Scott could get it down to where one person was running the whole show. If so, there were more expendable people around than just me and Patrick.

"I agree," I said. "I think you're safe for the time being. Now, what else do I need to know?"

"They feed me at eight, one, and six. I'm expected to work

when I'm not eating or sleeping or in the can." He looked at his watch. "You've kept me up past my bedtime."

"Sorry."

"No problem. Now, how about telling *me* a few things."

"All right. This is what it looks like," I said. "Scott grew up around here, then migrated to Florida, where he prospered in the drug trade and whatever else. After a number of years at it, he decided, for reasons still unknown, to move his operations back up here. Maybe he just got homesick.

"At about that time, he met Lester Beavans, if he hadn't known him before. Lester's also from Albermarle County. He's a bad boy. He was down in Florida and he was on the make. Scott decided he could be useful, because if you're going to be a successful drug smuggler, the first thing you need to do is buy the cops. Light bulb time: Why not run Lester for sheriff of Albemarle County? Scott had the money to bankroll a major campaign. And, as it turned out, they had an issue to be on the other side of from Ridley Campbell. Conversion to a county police department. Beavans moved back here in time to establish residency and things fell into place. They were off and running.

"Scott needed some land, too. Isolated, but near enough so he could oversee things. He found the spot with the help of a realtor named Landon Gentry, who also just happened to be on the Board of Supervisors. Once he brokered the deal, probably in a phony name, Gentry knew more than was good for him. But he was a popular local politician, therefore more useful alive than dead, as long as he stayed in office. If he could be bought, that is. Which he could. Scott got him strung out on coke, then got him dealing it, or maybe vice versa. He threw in a mistress as well, and Gentry was in the bag.

"What Scott's plans are from here we can only guess. It may be that he's going for political control of the whole county, like the old-time bosses. You can finance a lot of wheeling and dealing with cocaine profits."

"Whew," Patrick said. "And it was our great good luck to land in the middle of it."

"More or less. If it hadn't been for Ridley Campbell's cop

191

instincts, I wouldn't be here. You wouldn't have gotten involved if not for that stupid newspaper story."

"God does throw dice, eh?"

"Huh?"

"Nothing. It's just that Einstein said that God didn't play at dice with the universe. I think Einstein was wrong."

"Very wrong," I said.

"Why do you think they grabbed you tonight?" Patrick asked.

"Scott knew I was getting close. I dropped in on him this afternoon and I think he picked up that I was suspicious of him. In any case, he put Martinez on my tail. Martinez is good; I never spotted him. I probably should have, but . . . Anyway, he followed me to a meeting I had tonight with Nickel Johnson, who's a middle-level drug dealer. Then I went to Gentry's house. At that point, Martinez realized that I was *too* close. Maybe he picked me up on his own, or maybe he called the boss when he found out where I was headed. Somehow the decision was made to get me off the streets immediately."

"Well, what do we do now, Swift?" Patrick said after a short pause.

"We get the hell out of here."

Patrick laughed again. "They give you a key to the door? You grow some bulletproof skin?"

"Wiseass kid," I grumbled, but he was right. The only way out was through the door, and they weren't letting me use it whenever I wanted. Then, too, we had to be careful not to talk specifics. The fact that they'd thrown us both in the same room suggested the possibility that it was wired.

"Seriously," Patrick said, "we got any chance at all?"

"Yeah," I said, "there's always a chance. Maybe they'll decide we're swell company and want to keep us around like pets."

In my mind, though, I didn't think much of our chances. I went over what would be happening back in Charlottesville. By now, Patricia would have realized something had happened and told Campbell everything. He'd be on his way to see Gentry. After he found out where the property was (and made the assumption that I'd be there, too), he'd have to get some people together. He might need to go to the state boys or the feds. When he got to Brown's Cove depended on how long all that took. But he'd be here, you could rely on it. Before dawn, I'd guess. All I needed to do was keep our hides intact until then.

Of course, there was the question of what would happen when help *did* arrive. It didn't seem likely that our hosts would just surrender. Even if they did, they might well kill us first. More probable was that they'd use us as hostages.

Any way you peeled it, it looked bad. I didn't mention any of this to Patrick, but I motioned him over to me. I cupped my hand and whispered right into his ear.

"They may be listening," I said. "Help is on the way, if we can hold it together for a few hours, but it would be nice if we could get out of this house. Start thinking. See if there's anything that you've noticed about their routines that might give us an edge."

An hour and a half passed. We thought up a storm, but nothing useful came of it.

There was the sound of the door being unlocked. It opened, and Martinez was standing there. He'd exchanged his pistol for the nasty beast that was slung over his shoulder. An Ingram M-10, complete with the MAC suppressor. A two-hundred round banana clip was fitted under it. Nothing but the best equipment, I thought. With that thing you could empty the entire clip in under twenty seconds. Each round would make about as much noise as a healthy spit.

It wasn't the sort of weapon you wanted to go up against without a very, very good plan.

"Swift," Martinez said and motioned with the weapon.

I shrugged. "See you later, kid," I said to Patrick. "Hold the welcoming committee until I get back." It was the tiniest seed of an idea. I stared at Patrick to see if I could implant it in his head through ESP.

"Move it," Martinez said.

I moved it. He made me stand several paces down the

corridor while he relocked the door. He was truly good; he'd be a difficult man to take. But not impossible. No one was.

Just before we got to the end of the hall, Martinez gestured to a door on the left. I opened it and went in. It was a small, windowless room like the one they had Patrick in. This one had photos on the walls. Those tropical beach scenes and such. There was a desk and behind the desk there was Howard B. Scott.

"Mr. Swift," he said, getting up. He nodded to Martinez, and the Nicaraguan left us alone.

I didn't wait. As soon as the door closed, I jumped Scott. A moment later, I was sitting on the floor, gasping for breath. I hadn't even seen him move.

"You're out of your class, Swift," he said. "At that angle and velocity, that blow knocks the wind out of you. Adjust it slightly and it kills. Do we need to discuss this any further?"

I shook my head.

"Good. And I'm sure you know enough not to run. Virgilio is just outside the door, of course."

I nodded.

"How about having a seat?" he suggested.

I pulled myself up and sat where he indicated.

"Now, you've been a terrible problem to me, Swift," he continued, "though I've really done my best to politely discourage you. I guess you appreciate how much of a problem. Else you wouldn't be here now. You know, you're an intelligent man. It's unfortunate that we appear to be on . . . opposite sides. I could use someone like you."

"With the emphasis on the 'use'," I said. My breathing was getting back to normal, though my diaphragm was going to hurt for some time, I judged.

"Pity you have that attitude," he said. "You've lived a poor life and soon you're going to die like a dog."

"As opposed to the shining example you've set."

"See? You're so bitter about your failure, it shows in everything you do. The real tragedy is that you're a cut above the ordinary man. He wanders through life in a daze, wondering what it is he's supposed to do next. Nothing to guide him but his most basic appetites, which makes people like myself easily rich. But you, you're a man of some principles. Misdirected, to be sure, but principles all the same."

"We belong to the Brotherhood of Principled Men, you and I?" I said.

"Exactly."

"And what are yours, may I ask? Profit, manipulation, and murder?"

"Those aren't principles, they're means. Superior people use what means they have to, in order to achieve their ends. What happens to the others is, in the long run, irrelevant. It's the superior man who writes history. The founders of this country knew that. They built the nation on a foundation of lies, theft, and wholesale slaughter. But that's not important because it *had* to be done. The important thing is that the goal was achieved. The greatest nation in the history of the world emerged from nothing."

"You're a sick man, Scott," I said.

"*Am* I? Then who *is* healthy? Our corporate executives who allow defective products to be dumped in foreign countries? The weapons brokers who are arming the world to the teeth? The politicians who encourage all this to happen? Who, Swift? Tell me."

I've never been very good in debates. I suspected that he'd always been the opposite. He was quick-punching me with some very tricky questions and I wasn't swift enough to find the fallacy in them right off. But I wanted to prolong our conversation. The longer I held his interest, the better my chance of not dying like a dog before Campbell arrived. When it came to goals, that was mine. To keep us talking.

"You're still a drug dealer," I said weakly.

"So are most of the doctors in this country. Along with a fair percentage of our students, our lawyers, our politicians, and our cops. But you've missed the point. Drugs is not the issue. You're still confusing means and end."

"You choose your means, don't you?"

195

"Of course," he said, "and I do it willingly. Risk capitalism is the most exciting thing in the world. And the cocaine business is the leading edge of risk capitalism in America. Millions can be made overnight, Swift. And as easily lost. The competition is intense. It's exactly like it was in the Texas oil fields sixty years ago and it will end in exactly the same way. The superior man will consolidate his fortune and the rest will fall by the wayside. Eventually, the government will replace prohibition with regulation. By that time, those of us at the top will have long since moved on."

His eyes shone with a fervor that I normally associate with evangelists. In a way, I guess he wasn't too different from them. There'll always be those who do the plucking and those who are only too happy to be plucked.

"You sound like any boring old greedhead to me," I said.

"Swift, you disappoint me," he said. "You refuse to step out of your preconceptions for a moment."

"Look, Scott, you sell coke to people at exorbitant prices that most of them can't afford. I don't see any high-falutin' principles in that."

"The people who pay all that money for a transitory pleasure, they're fools. They don't count."

"And what *does* count?" God, he was wearisome.

"Our way of life, Swift. The United States. Free enterprise."

"Behold the patriot."

"I am. And I'm proud of it. Don't you realize that the world is full of people who would love to take all this away from us?"

"Oh yes," I said. "Our godless enemies. The teeming people of color, waiting out there to overrun us. I remember them. I even fought them once upon a time. You see, I'm a patriot, too. Funny thing, though. The only ones ever made it to American soil were the ones we bused in ourselves. The others never even tried."

"Swift, your politics are positively prehistoric."

"What about yours? Your idea of democracy to buy up all the local pols, is it?"

"If that's what it takes," he said. "Most people are not capable of making important decisions on their own. They must be helped."

"And what about Patrick, you bastard? You helping him along?"

"Ah, Patrick. A brilliant boy. Brilliant. I wish I could keep him with me forever."

"For Christ's sake, Scott! What's he *doing* here? He never did you any *harm!*"

"True." He shook his head sadly. "But he saw something he shouldn't have. I'll greatly regret it when he's gone."

"You could've buried that guy in the woods out here and no one would ever have known. There was no need to involve Patrick."

"I'm afraid it's not quite that simple," he said. "I had to make an example of the person in question. That's the way this business is. Sometimes you have to make examples, so that things go more smoothly in the future. If you show weakness, they eat you alive. Unfortunately for the boy, an example is ineffective if it's not made publicly."

"You sacrifice an innocent kid to the passing need to send somebody a message."

"I said it was unfortunate, but that's the way it works out sometimes. Besides, he has the opportunity to do some excellent work, too. Be part of the greater plan."

"You really are evil, Scott." God, I wished I had a weapon. Anything. "All your values aren't worth the ten cents' worth of shit it took to grow them. If I had a gun right now—" I stopped myself. Whatever the cost, I was going to have to put the lid on my anger. I couldn't afford to have him lose interest in talking.

"Yes," he said.

"It doesn't matter," I said with a sigh. "Does the condemned man get to ask a few questions before he goes?"

"If you wish. I do enjoy your company, as I've said."

He said it as though we'd never had a moment's disagreement. I was sitting across from the most evil man I'd ever personally known and there wasn't a single outward sign of derangement. He was as calm, as well-mannered, as civilized as anyone. I felt my equilibrium slipping.

"What are you doing here?" I asked quickly.

"It's a perfect spot, isn't it?"

"No, I mean here, in Albemarle County, Virginia. What are you doing here?"

"Ah, the return of the prodigal, you mean. Why shouldn't I be here? It's my home."

"Competition a little too tough in Florida?"

He looked at me with amusement, and something that appeared to be pity.

"You have no idea," he said finally. "No one who hasn't lived it does. It's a jungle down there. You've got the Colombian gangs and the Cuban gangs and the Anglo gangs. You've got the Coast Guard and AWACS planes and DEA cowboys in cigarette boats. Who needs it? All the intelligent people are moving their operations north. Our boats are just passing Florida by. Bring it on up and turn into the Chesapeake and you've got hundreds of secluded spots to offload. The local law is . . . undermobilized."

"Neat," I said. "Then you truck it here by road and do your distribution under the protective wing of Sheriff Beavans."

"Very good, Swift. Of course, as soon as Lester is elected, we'll have to get him a quick drug bust. That way he'll establish credibility with the federals right away. You need that, or they'll run their operations outside of you. I'm sure we'll be able to find someone to throw them at that point."

"Another unfortunate sacrifice?"

"You just refuse to see the larger picture, don't you? Drugs are nothing, Swift. The people who deal in them are nothing. With certain exceptions. It's politics. Politics is everything. It's history. Political control is now within my means. It's within anyone's who has vision and works hard enough for it. And with political control, you write history. You create your own form of immortality."

"Thank God for a system that makes a man like you possible."

"Yes, as a matter of fact. And while you're at it, thank the founders, who weren't afraid to do what they had to do."

He got that look again, as if he were peering into the future as authored by Howard B. Scott.

"The question now is," he said, "what are we going to do with you? You've been awfully inconvenient, you know. First bothering Lester, then poking around my business affairs. Virgilio wanted to get you off the streets long before this. He finally did it on his own initiative. It was the right decision, don't you think?"

"Not for me."

"No, of course not for you. But you were close, weren't you? Did Gentry talk a great deal?"

"Enough to tell me about this place. I threatened his kneecaps."

"Yes, I'll bet you did. And then what did you expect to do, ride out here on your orange horse and rescue the boy?"

"Something like that. I didn't really have it figured out."

"So the net result would have been the same. And we're still left with the central problem. What to do with you. Your disappearance is going to cause me some difficulties no matter what. Do you have a preferred way to go?"

"Yeah, one where there's no death in it," I said.

He chuckled. "You're an amusing fellow, Swift. I especially like a man who jokes in the face of the unknown. So many of them lose their sense of humor at the end. It's a pity that I haven't been able to . . . educate you."

He got up.

"Actually, I'm a pretty quick learner most of the time," I tried.

"I'm sorry, Swift," he said. "But it's late and I need some time to think about this. You may see Patrick again before . . . whatever, if you like."

"Just a couple more questions—"

It was no use. He opened the door. Martinez was waiting in the hall with his automatic rifle. If Campbell worked fast, he'd be here any minute. If . . .

"Virgilio," he said, "put Swift back in with the boy. I'm going downstairs to attend to a couple of things while I think this through. Meet me back here in a half hour and I'll tell you what I've decided."

Martinez grunted. I think he would've preferred to do it then and there.

"Goodbye, Swift," Scott said. "I've enjoyed our brief acquaintance."

Martinez prodded me back up the hall, keeping me a couple of paces ahead of him. Scott disappeared in the opposite direction.

The quiet was eerie. Our footsteps were swallowed up by the thick carpeting. No noise came from the other parts of the house. The only sounds were those made by the clothes against our bodies.

I walked past the room and kept my back to Martinez. I knew the routine by now.

He unlocked the door.

"Inside," he said.

"You're a chatty fellow, Virgilio," I said, turning around. He didn't say anything. There are people like that.

I pushed the door inward, with Martinez just behind me.

Patrick was in his chair, straight ahead, and his timing was perfect. He was coming at us, cranking as much speed as he could in the small room. I jumped to the side, without thinking. He missed me by maybe two inches and hit Martinez head on. It wasn't exactly what I'd had in mind, but it was damn close.

The Nicaraguan's feet went out from under him. As he pitched forward, Patrick hit him in the stomach with a short left hand punch. It was enough to take the breath out of him before he had a chance to cry out.

The two of them fell to the floor in a jumble of arms and legs and steel. The gun skittered out of Martinez's hands. He lunged for it, but by that time I was involved. I brought my heel down on his hand, hard, turning my ankle slightly at the end. Bones broke. His face contorted with pain, but he made no sound. He couldn't. Desperately, he sucked at the air, trying to get enough in to be able to call for help.

He never made it. Patrick had gotten himself sufficiently untangled to get one arm under him and the other one free. He hit Martinez on the side of the neck. Patrick has a well-muscled upper body. Despite the lack of leverage, it was a tremendous blow, and it knocked Martinez senseless. For good measure, Patrick hit him again. Over the ear. Martinez lay still.

I snatched up the Ingram and looped it over my head, so it would dangle at my side without slipping off. I made sure the safety wasn't on.

Then I turned to Patrick. The whole thing had taken maybe twenty seconds, and I didn't think we'd made enough noise to attract attention. Of course, if the room was wired, and if someone was listening . . .

"Let's get the hell out of here," Patrick said. He was grinning. Unbelievable.

Somehow, between us, we got him up on my shoulders. He was heavy, but manageable. The main problem was weight distribution, since he had so little below the waist. We fiddled around and finally got it right. I was staggering some but I could move. The house was deathly silent.

Down the hall we went. Up the stairs.

Halfway to the top, all hell broke loose.

An alarm siren started screaming in a high-low, high-low wail. The lights dimmed and brightened, dimmed and brightened in synch with the alarm. I froze momentarily with fear.

"C'mon, Swift," Patrick said in my ear.

That got me moving again. That and what I heard behind me. It was Scott's voice. It was yelling and getting louder. Moving our way.

"Virgilio! Someone's breached the fence! Virgilio! *Virgilio! What*—"

I scrambled up the rest of the stairs. At the top, we crashed through the screen door and I started running for the tree line. I was so pumped up that it was almost like Patrick wasn't holding me back at all. The ground flowed under my feet. Before me, I could see headlights coming up the drive and fanning out at the far end of the field. A bunch of them.

Spotlights came on behind me. I felt like I was running on the face of the full moon.

"Shoot him!" I heard Scott yell insanely. *"Shoot him!"*

I whirled and fired a long burst from the hip, toward the house, as a couple of soundless bullets exploded the dust next to me. There were three men. They ducked back inside. I thought the blocky one might have staggered. Scott.

I turned and ran another thirty feet. But I knew I'd never make the tree line before Scott's thugs found cover and cut the two of us in half.

"Ridley!" I screamed. "It's *Swift!* And Patrick! We're *safe!* Shoot, Ridley. *Shoot!"*

Then I threw Patrick forward and fell on top of him. As I was going down, someone kicked me hard in the back of the leg.

Gunfire erupted from the tree line. Unsilenced gunfire. Rifles, shotguns, the thump of tear-gas canisters being launched, I couldn't tell what else there might be. The roar was deafening. . . .

Deafening . . .

Gunfire and light . . .

The NVA regulars were coming across the field when the flares turned the night into noon. I raised my head. The sergeant was lying underneath me. How . . . ? He grabbed my shirt front and yanked.

"Stay down, you idiot!" he yelled.

I pulled away from him.

"I've got to help them!" I yelled back. "They're still out there!"

"Help *who?* Swift, it's *me*, goddamn it! What are you *do*ing?!"

"Leave me alone, sergeant! I'm going to get them!"

I tore free of his grip and pushed myself up. It wasn't right that he should be trying to stop me. My leg buckled under me and I howled with pain.

"The bastards!" I yelled. "The bastards've *shot* me!"

I got myself up on hands and knees again. It was agony but I had to help. The men were pinned down and the NVA were coming across the field.

From somewhere below, the sergeant got a hand on my shirt. He was stronger than I was. It wasn't right.

"Let me *go,* you sonofabitch!" I screamed.

I saw him ball his fist and I saw the punch coming, but I couldn't get out of the way of it. The sound of the gunfire hammered on my ears.

Then the flares went out.

11

PATRICIA RYAN AND I WERE IN BED. MY PLACE.

They'd only kept me in the hospital a couple of days. The bullet had passed through my thigh without hitting bone or severing any major blood vessels. So they only needed me in there long enough to clean out the wound, sew me up, replace the lost blood, and warn me to stay off the leg for a while.

I'd been turned loose in Patricia's care. I was a hero, though I couldn't quite fathom why. All I'd done was run away from some killers. But the newspapers had played the story at max volume. There'd been national coverage. Once I got back on my feet, I'd be certain to have more business than I could handle. And Jonesy was talking about doing a quick book and splitting the profits.

The shootout in Brown's Cove had left one of the bad guys dead and two wounded, neither seriously. The fight was on among the survivors to see who'd get the chance to turn state's evidence. No one in Ridley's posse had been hurt. Scott himself had been nicked by one of my bullets and was in custody. No bail. He was finished. His buddy Beavans had skipped town. Campbell had flushed the turncoats from the sheriff's office and was cruising toward reelection. As for me, I hadn't had to kill anyone, and that pleased me. I'd seen plenty of bodies during the war. I never again wanted to be personally responsible for one.

Patricia had been radiant ever since Patrick returned home unharmed. Our relationship had never looked more solid. The two people I most loved were safe. I was happy, bum leg and all.

"Did you hear about Gentry?" she asked me.

"No, what?"

"He hanged himself this afternoon."

"I guess that's not much of a surprise."

"No. There's the kids, though. It's sad. What a waste, and just because of a little money."

"Don't forget sex and drugs," I added.

"Those, too. It's still not worth it."

"Not to you, anyway. For which I'm grateful."

She was quiet for a while, then said, "You know something, Loren. I've learned a lot about you because of all this."

"You didn't know me before?"

"I guess I knew. But I didn't really *know*. I'm not happy it happened, of course. But I've been able to see why it is that you do what you do."

"Light bulb," I said.

"Don't make fun of me, please."

"Sorry."

"It may all be obvious to you, Loren, because you're seeing it within the context of your life, where everything makes some kind of sense. But it's been almost entirely out*side* of my experience. Until now. It's been enlightening. I now see not only *why* you do it, but I see the *value* of it, as well. Obviously. Without you, I would have lost Patrick forever."

"Hey, you helped too, don't forget."

"I know that," she said. "For better or worse, I now see what the attraction is."

I laughed. "You going into the P.I. business?" I asked.

"No. But I'm going to get my license."

"Huh?"

"In the fall. The community college has a course. I can be licensed by December."

"You're kidding."

"No, I'm not. Right now, I'm a legal secretary for Bob Lee. I like my work and I like my employer, and I have no desire to leave my job. But with an investigator's license, I could be that much more valuable to him."

"You're trying to steal my business," I whined.

She laughed. "I have the feeling you're not going to be hurting for business. And speaking of not hurting . . ."

She bent over and began kissing me here and there.

"Uh, Patricia," I said, "do you think a man in my condition . . ."

"I don't see anything wrong with your condition," she said. And she was right. There wasn't.

Patricia was asleep. I'd been dozing off and on. It was hard to get comfortable because of the leg. But it wasn't the leg that had awakened me. My internal alarm system had gone off. It had sensed someone in the room with us. I switched the bedside light on.

I blinked in the sudden glare, then I saw him. He was probably the last thing on earth I wanted to see.

Lester Beavans, leaning against the door jamb.

Patricia stirred, came awake muttering sleep words, then fell silent when she saw what I saw. She started to tremble. I wasn't too steady myself.

"Swift," he said. "I don't like you. I reckon I've *never* liked you."

He pulled something from his belt. It was a stainless steel rod about a foot long. He flicked his wrist and the rod telescoped out to three times its original length. There were two clicks as the sections locked into place. It was a nasty weapon. With it, a man could slowly beat you to death and not get his hands dirty.

I lunged for the bedside drawer. The Walther was still in there. I was quick, but Beavans, despite his bulk, was quicker.

206

He came across the room fast and brought the steel rod down on my wrist. There was intense pain and the shattering of bone. The Walther dropped back into the drawer. He picked it up and stuck it in his pocket. My eyes were watering, but I wasn't going to give him the satisfaction of crying out.

While Beavans was occupied with me, Patricia leapt out of bed and made a run for it. It was a bad mistake. Beavans's stride covered twice the distance hers did. He caught her before she reached the door and hit her in the back of the head. There was a sickening sound as metal struck bone. Patricia crumpled to the floor and lay very still.

I threw myself at him, trying to land a punch with my good hand. It would have been ludicrous even if the leg hadn't slowed me. He sidestepped me with ease and clubbed the point of my right shoulder. The whole arm went numb. I went down.

Slowly, painfully, I dragged myself into the living room. Lester followed, striking out at me whenever he felt like it. I gritted my teeth against the pain and pretended to cower from him, twisting this way and that. I took blows anywhere in order to protect my left arm. It was all I had.

Lester was chuckling. This was the part he liked. He'd make it last as long as he could.

I crawled, weighed down by my useless arm and leg.

Beavans hit me hard below the shoulder and I pitched forward on the rug. Dust and lint went up my nose. I sneezed, sending shooting pains through my ribcage. He thought that was particularly amusing.

It seemed to take days, but at last I reached the corner of the room. I turned to face Beavans, jamming my back against the wall.

He came for me at a leisurely pace, flicking the steel rod, smiling broadly, savoring the moment. Good ole boy to the finish.

I reached behind the sofa with my left hand, tore the Police Positive loose and pointed it at him. The hand was shaking, and it's not strong to begin with, but there was no way I could use my right. I drew up my knee and rested the gun on it. I thumbed back the hammer. The gun wavered. I forced every available ounce of energy into the hand, steadying it.

"No closer," I said.

Beavans continued to smile. Maybe he thought I'd never be able to shoot straight. Or maybe he actually thought I wouldn't do it, not point blank. He was wrong. On both counts.

He lashed out at the pistol and I fired. The bullet hit him in the shoulder and knocked him backward. The rod dropped to the floor. He snarled and rushed at me barehanded. I shot him in the chest. Twice. He staggered but he kept coming, throwing himself onto me.

His weight was suffocating. They had to have been heart shots, or close to it, yet there was enough life left in him that his hands were groping for my throat. His blind instinct to kill was terrifying. Tiny whimpering sounds trickled out of my mouth. I squirmed frantically beneath his bulk.

He got the choke hold on me. Almost immediately, my consciousness began to fade. But my own survival instincts were strong, too. I gave a wild, half-strangled yell to energize myself, pushing up my left shoulder with the last of my ebbing strength. I twisted my gun hand around. There was no longer any way to tell for sure exactly where the thing was pointing, but there was no alternative. I fired again.

The bullet burst from the middle of his back in a spray of blood. His hands fell away from my throat and his head flopped forward. He lay still, his face inches from mine. The eye closest to me was open. It looked no more empty in death than it had in life. A mixture of blood and spittle leaked from the corner of his mouth.

I gagged, felt the contents of my stomach beginning to rise. I fought to keep them down. The nausea ebbed.

And Mrs. Detweiler arrived. Just walked right in as if there were no possible danger to her.

My landlady was hard of hearing, but not so hard that she didn't pick up the sound of a .38 calibre pistol being fired four times underneath her feet. She looked around. I was lying on the floor with a huge dead man on top of me, the air was thick with the stench of blood and cordite and Beavans's final evacuation of himself, but it didn't faze her. She'd seen it all before. She was a beautiful old lady.

"Mrs. D.," I croaked, "Rescue Squad . . . Patricia . . ."

But she was already headed for the phone. She knew the number by heart. She called the Rescue Squad, telling them only what they needed to know to be prepared for Patricia, then she came over to help me out. Between us, we managed to get the corpse of Lester Beavans off me.

I crawled over to Patricia and held my hand under her nose. She was still breathing. Shallowly. I didn't dare move her, for fear of complicating her injuries. I hugged my knees with my good arm and rocked back and forth, waiting for the ambulance to arrive.

They were there in just over five minutes. Carefully, they hoisted her onto a stretcher and loaded her into the wagon. Only then did Mrs. Detweiler call the cops. She knew without asking that I couldn't stick around to answer dumb cop questions. She'd handle the law, bless her.

I rode to the hospital in the back of the ambulance, watching them work on Patricia.

Along the way, I mumbled the words over and over, as if they themselves might carry the gift of life.

"Don't die, please, don't die . . ."